BLOW ME AWAY

A Mile High Matched Novel

CHRISTINA HOVLAND

For rights information, please contact:
Prospect Agency
551 Valley Road, PMB 377
Upper Montclair, NJ 07043
(718) 788-3217

Holly Ingraham, Development Editor
Michelle Hope, Copy Editor
Shasta Schafer, Proofreader

First Edition February 2019

For my mom.
Who taught me how to read.
How to write.
And how to love.

Praise for Christina Hovland

Going Down on One Knee

"An **utterly charming** opposites-attract-story. Hovland perfectly balances simmering sexual tension with a surprising amount of emotion, and the stomach-flip-causing ending is the perfect example of **why I read and love romance**."
- *New York Times Bestselling Author, Lauren Layne*

"I wasn't expecting to **laugh** as much as I did. ... Anyone looking for a **light, funny story** will find it here in Christina Hovland's *Going Down on One Knee.*" - *Romantically Inclined Reviews*

"If you are a fan of **opposites attract stories** that make you laugh one minute, and swoon the next, you'll not go wrong with one of her books. Well done, Christina Hovland! Very, very well done." - *The Reading Cafe Reviews*

"A delightful blend of **witty humor and romance**!" - *Jenn (YeahOrNeighReviews)*

"Brek and Velma. He exudes tranquility. She exudes tension. The chemistry between them is **palpable without being forced**." - *Avidez Literary*

"This is **so much more than a romance novel**. It literally describes how life is. You have to let go to find yourself. " - *Reckless Readers*

The Honeymoon Trap

"*The Honeymoon Trap* is adorable, clever, funny—in short, completely charming." - Serena Bell, *USA Today* bestselling author of *Do Over*

Chapter One
THE BEGINNING

Jase Dvornakov's abs made Heather Reese seriously reconsider swearing off men.

Almost.

Gawking at the smokin'-hot florist while he had his own private dance party for one wasn't Heather's thing. She was a woman in control of her own destiny. That's what she tried to tell herself, anyway. Still, she stared through his storefront window in the posh Cherry Creek neighborhood of Denver, Colorado. Her feet remained cemented on the sidewalk, a burst of her breath fogged against his window, and she memorized every move shirtless Jase made—instead of opening the stupid door to step inside.

His hips thrust, shoulders rolled, and...who was she kidding? She couldn't look away. If he was going to put it all out there, she might as well appreciate the view. The man had moves. She'd give him that.

It was like watching one of her favorite game shows: Which door was she going to pick?

Shops along their street were barely starting to open; it was too early for a dance party at her friendly neighborhood flower shop. Apparently, Jase—her neighbor—didn't agree.

She shook the foamy haze from her brain.

Sweet Goddess of Gold's Gym, this man distracted her. She opened door number one and stepped through, stumbling over her feet only a little.

"Hey, Jase." As soon as the words slipped past her lips, she knew they couldn't be heard over the music blaring through the shop.

She cleared her throat and shifted in her pink *Heather's Cookie & Co.* embroidered polo shirt, hopeful the man dancing across the concrete floor would pause long enough to toss a glance her way.

Not because she wanted him to *glance her way* but because she needed his attention. So she could give him his poster.

Advertising the senior "senior" prom for the nursing home where she volunteered.

Nothing more.

He didn't. Instead, he continued gyrating his hips and stuffing lilies into a wreath with a gold banner that read, *In Loving Memory, Phyllis.*

"Jase?" she called, raising her voice over the music.

Okay, that got his attention. He finally glanced her way, paused mid–posy thrust, and a wicked smile crept across his lips. "Heather. Hey."

Her blood heated from his gaze, tingling as it swished through her veins.

Oh, for pity's sake. Her body begged her to grin back, say *hey* to him, and get her out of the drought that had become her dating life.

She told her body to hush. She had spent months detoxing from men and their unkept promises. Men and their unwillingness to fit her into their lives.

Okay, maybe not all men, just the ones she'd dated.

There was absolutely no need to jump back in and take another hit just because Jase said, "Heather. Hey." All sexy-like.

Two quick strides brought Jase to the cash register. He flicked a switch and the music zipped to a stop.

Heather gripped the stack of posters in her hands. Her brainchild. A prom for the senior citizens at a nearby retirement home. Something to get them up and moving and having a good time. Also, another distraction to prevent her from breaking her no-men rule. "Sorry. I can come back later, if you'd rather."

She inhaled a long breath of floral-scented air and tacked on a smile.

"Don't be sorry." He scrawled something on a notepad. "Now's good. I just lost track of time. Didn't hear you come in."

"That would explain the dancing, and the lack of clothing." She gestured to his bare pecs and quickly glanced away to the assortment of potted cactus plants dotted along the windowsill.

"Oh, ah, right. I got distracted. I work best when I'm in the zone." He yanked a thin white T-shirt from under the counter and tugged it over his head.

There, much better. Sort of.

"So…" She set the stack of posters on the countertop and tapped her fingertip against the top one. "I brought you a poster for your window."

He studied her handiwork and flicked the end of a pen against his palm in time with the beat of the now turned-off music.

"Prom, huh? Fun." He dropped the pen, rubbed his hands together, and locked his gaze to hers in a way that made her insides purr in anticipation.

What are "things you shouldn't do" for five hundred, Alex.

No men for you, Heather. Eye on the…well, the poster, in this instance.

"This is at the retirement home up the street?" he asked.

"You know it?" Of course he knew it, it's not like their street was that big.

"Yeah, I know it." He lifted a corner of his lips, just the one corner. Damn, that was sexy. Elvis sexy.

"I volunteer there, and they've lost a lot of residents lately. Some passed away. Some moved. So I had this idea to help drum up new business. A way to showcase the place for new seniors." Okay, she should get to the other reason she'd stopped by. "I was…ah…also hoping you might be willing to help out with flowers? It'll be a fun opportunity for us to get to know each other better."

He stilled when she mentioned getting to know each other better.

"I mean, not like that. You know. For everyone to get to know each other better. You as a business owner to get to know some of the residents. And they can get to know each other. Not for…" *Us*, she finished in her head.

"Dean said you're single." Jase squinted his espresso-colored eyes in that way guys tended to do right before they dropped a mammoth pickup-line bomb. He'd never looked at her like that before, but she'd witnessed his pick-up line game before. It was strong. "You and your guy broke up."

Dean was her friend Claire's husband. Jase was friends with the significant others of her two best friends. Which meant they ran in the same circle, saw each other regularly. She'd chatted with him. Danced with him at their friends' weddings. All that time, she'd been seeing Logan, so she had ignored any of the chemistry between her and Jase.

Logan. Ugh. They had broken up. But that had nothing to do with anything.

The lies she told herself were sometimes mammoth.

She'd been 100 percent into Logan. Certain that they were heading to a chapel with a white dress and forever bells. She'd been epically wrong.

"Logan and I broke up a while ago, actually. Why?"

"You look hungry," Jase announced.

"Don't do it, Jase." She shook her head.

Oh, he acted so innocent, but she knew better. Knew what was coming.

"Do what?" he asked.

"Give me whatever line you were about to throw at me."

His eyes danced. "What line?"

"You know what line."

"Fine. Your loss." He didn't wink. He didn't have to. He paused a beat. "You want to hear it, don't you?"

She tilted toward him, just a touch. "I already ate. I'm not hungry."

An English-muffin-sandwich thing about twenty minutes ago.

He leaned forward, elbows on the counter, and flashed another grin. "I'm thinking you look hungry because you're the girl I'm about to ask to dinner tonight."

A sigh escaped her lungs. Cue the horrible pickup line. She'd called that one. Still, this was new. Jase had never asked her out before. He was a flirt, but he was an equal-opportunity flirt. She'd never read more into it.

"In that case, you look like the guy I'm about to turn down." She bit her tongue to prevent it from turning that no into a yes and toyed with the edge of the stack of posters.

The flash of teeth against his lips nearly undid her. Nearly. "I've been waiting for you to ditch your boyfriend."

Well, she wasn't the one who'd done the ditching, but he didn't need to know that.

He straightened, standing at his full height. She hadn't noticed quite how tall he was before. Tall and built and… nope. That assessment about summed him up.

Heather didn't date cocky guys. Not anymore.

She had dated her fair share of players in the past. Mark, Ben, Craig…they all had a great time with her until they were ready to move on. She was nothing but a good-time-girl to them. Then she had started seeing Logan. Who she thought wasn't a player. She'd gotten in too deep, and it had turned out he was the king of players. He'd played *her*, anyway. She had been certain they were in the kind of relationship that lasted. But what she'd thought was a relationship with potential was tossed aside after the newness wore off. He'd gone off to find his next conquest.

It ended. She swore off men.

And opened a cookie shop. As one does.

"Heather?" Jase stuck tape on the corners of the top poster.

"Hmm?" Her eyes met his again, because she refused to show weakness.

"You catching that?" he asked, his focus returning to the poster and the tape.

"Catching what?"

Poster in hand, he moved to the front window and pressed it against the glass, smoothing it before turning back to her. "Catching the little buzz we have going on between us."

"A little… The thing is…" *C'mon, Heather, be strong. You are the cookie lady now. You don't date. You are all you need.* That's what the podcast she'd been listening to said to her over and over again. Mantra in hand, she slapped on her I'm-in-charge-here-buddy mask. "It would never work between us."

The edges of his lips ticked up ever so slightly. "You can't know that."

Oh, she knew.

He sauntered toward her.

Unwilling to back down, she stepped toward him. Expression firm, she said, "I can already see exactly how this whole thing would play out if we let it. You'd start with a horrible pickup line."

"Guilty." His hands fell to the belt loops of his jeans.

Her palm itched to press against the front of his tee, but she refrained. "Then I'd counter with a witty response. This time, my reply would be even better. Funny, intelligent…everything."

"Now, that I'd like to hear." Nothing but a foot of crackling air sizzled between them.

"Trust me, *if* I had said it, it would have been epic. You can't repeat something like that. It has to happen in the moment." She shook her head, the sleek ponytail she'd carefully arranged earlier brushing against the collar of her jacket.

"That right there is why we wouldn't have worked out. I mean, you couldn't even come up with a snappier reply." He crossed his arms, the little veins of his muscled forearms flexing with the motion.

"Oh, I would've. It would've been the best response in the history of pickup line replies."

"I don't believe you." The glimmer in his eyes lit up his entire face.

He was enjoying this exchange entirely too much.

Control. She needed the power back. "Trust would've always been one of your issues in our relationship."

"Maybe you just couldn't be honest with me about how you felt. That's probably why we would have always argued." He raised his eyebrows in a clear ultimatum.

Challenge accepted.

She stepped the tiniest bit closer to him. "Let's say you threw out that awful line again. The one about taking me out."

"I'm with you so far." He glanced down to the floor in clear acknowledgment of her movement forward, but he held his ground.

"We'd banter for a good bit—"

His face sparked with humor. "Sounds about right."

"Both of us would get that tingly feeling of attraction. You know the one." So maybe she made her voice a little breathier than usual. Sue her.

His mouth parted, the exaggerated fullness of his lower lip apparent. "You have a tingly feeling?"

She shook her head and raised a hand. Not touching his chest like she desperately wanted to, but getting within millimeters. "That's not the important part. Eventually, you would convince me to go on a date."

"I'd take you to this great taco stand. I love tacos."

"Despite that, I'd probably let you take me out again. And again," she said, not willing to acknowledge the way she wanted to nip at his lip with her teeth.

He nodded. "I'm digging this relationship so far."

"Eventually, you'd ask me to move in. I'd say no. You'd pressure me, even though I wouldn't be ready."

"What can I say? I wouldn't want to spend a night away from you. No use paying for two apartments."

She shrugged, dropping her hand. "I'd cave, and we'd finally move in together—"

"Do we get to hook up first? Don't skip that part." This time he moved forward, just a smidge.

She stayed put. She refused to back up first. "Of course. It would be awful. Sorry Speed Racer, but I need more than three minutes of go time."

"That's not what you'd say after you screamed my name." He leaned forward, the whisper of his words brushing against her ear.

God, there wasn't but a breath of space between them. She was all turned-on Heather, ready to throw her why-have-a-man-when-you-can-have-cookies resolve away.

His breath smelled of cinnamon candy and coffee, turning her knees effectively to melted butter.

No, she stopped herself. Back to the fictional breakup at hand.

Cookies were just fine for her. Better, even.

"Then we would be horribly irresponsible one night and, surprise, it's a boy!" She waved her hands and grinned.

He frowned. "I'd never be that irresponsible."

"It would happen. And then you'd insist we get married in a huge production I'd totally resent." Now, she stepped to the counter to grab the rest of the posters.

"C'mon, baby. I'd tell you we could keep it small."

She held the posters against her front like weak card-stock armor. "It wouldn't matter, you'd be all kinds of grumpy when you stopped getting your full three minutes on top. Before you could say 'honeymoon,' we'd hate each other. The divorce would be sweet relief for everyone involved, and we'd never speak again." She flashed him a goodbye smile. "Aren't you glad we aren't doing that?"

He followed her to the door, opening it for her. "That's tragic. But we could still have an affair every once in a while, right? Let's move straight to that. Avoid all the other stuff."

Every alarm bell in her head rang out. *He's a player. He's not a cookie. He's a player. He's not a cookie.*

She patted the anchor tattoo inked on his bicep. "Sorry, sweetie. I think it's best we let the breakup stick. I'll see you—"

"Jase, thank goodness you're here," a female voice called from behind her. "I have a ribbon emergency."

Jase tore his gaze from Heather's, stripping nerves she hadn't realized he'd exposed.

A perky cheerleader-type with a button nose breezed past Heather into the shop holding a floor-length formal gown. "Cassidy changed her mind about prom. She's wearing green, so we need to match the ribbon to this dress instead of the purple one I brought in before."

Time to go. Heather moved out the door but glanced over her shoulder at Jase. "So, you'll help out with the prom thing?"

The dark intensity of his gaze held her in place. "Absolutely."

Perfect.

"And, Heather?" He flashed a grin, and the fuzzy Jase-induced haze filtered over her vision again. "Sorry I broke your heart."

Crap.

"You've got that wrong, bud. I did the breaking up."

"See, that's why it never worked. You always have to be right. Even when you're wrong."

Heather opened her mouth, but the now wide-eyed, green-dress-wielding customer caught her attention.

"Should I come back?" the woman asked.

"Nope. He's all yours." Heather hustled outside into the cool morning air before either of them could say anything more.

Chapter Two
SENIOR "SENIOR" PROM COUNTDOWN:
35 DAYS

They'd been trying to come up with a solution for over an hour. Over an hour of ribbons and lace and a persistent head cheerleading coach—Becca. Some days Jase missed his old life. The wife, the white picket fence, his job with the Navy defusing roadside bombs. He'd get all warm inside and sentimental. Then he'd remember that had all gone to shit and now he did the safe thing—swapping overseas operations for the single life and the safety of running one of his family's flower shops.

When he'd left his job as an Explosive Ordnance Disposal Tech in the Navy and decided to get back in the family business, he'd done it because flowers were safe. Flowers didn't blow up. When he'd divorced his wife? Well, he'd done that because she had insisted. She'd also found another husband. That had a lot to do with his decision.

Jase held another spool of wired ribbon up to the prom dress Becca had brought in for one of her students. The color was nearly spot on.

Becca shook her head. "That's got too much aqua. What else do you have?"

Most days he loved his job. Today? Not so much. The

crazies that came out during high school prom season could be just as unstable as a grenade with a half-pulled pin. Case in point: Becca.

He dug through his box of ribbon remnants, sending a silent prayer to whoever might be listening that he would find the right shade of green.

"What about a contrast?" he asked. "We could do black."

"For a corsage?"

"Just the ribbon. Red roses, black ribbon, green dress."

"No. That won't work. It'll look like gothic Christmas." She tossed a spool into the bin. "This whole thing is giving me a migraine."

He could relate. He held up yet another swatch of ribbon that was nowhere near the right shade.

Becca shook her head.

The thin fabric of the dress she'd brought along gave no inspiration. Nothing.

"Any luck?" he hollered to his assistant, Elizabeth, who was digging through boxes in the back. She'd arrived to work halfway through his search for the perfect ribbon.

He didn't need to wait for her answer when he already knew the result—they'd been through every ribbon in the shop.

"Not yet," she called back.

They'd even called his sister's shop in Castle Rock to see if she had anything that might work. Negative. Maybe the answer wasn't ribbon. Perhaps it was something totally different.

"What if I use leaves instead of ribbon—an orchid in the center and some kind of peacock feather where the bow would go? It'll be one of a kind."

"That would work," she said on a breath. "I love it."

"Great. I'll write up the order, and it'll be ready for Cassidy next Saturday," he said with all the enthusiasm he could muster.

"Elizabeth, we've got it." He raised his voice so she could hear as he scribbled the details on his order book and handed a copy to Becca.

He nodded to Elizabeth as she emerged from the back room. "Elizabeth will check you out."

He had a funeral wreath to finish and a day of deliveries to prepare ahead of him. The front door opened, and his grandmother shuffled into the shop. Unable to help himself, he groaned. Babushka was on a mission, along with his mother and sister, to find him a replacement wife. They brought women through daily, most of them had been promised he would be interested in far more than just a good time. Most of their prospects already had an engagement ring picked out and the wedding dress on layaway.

The thought made his balls shrivel, just a little.

His family had gone a bit insane about the whole deal, no matter his attempts at neutralizing the situation.

"Hey, Babushka. You're early," he said.

She generally didn't arrive until after noon.

"Never too early for vork," she replied in her thick Russian accent.

If you could call what she did for the flower shop work. Mostly, she sat around gossiping with the other employees. Sometimes she went out with the delivery driver while he made his rounds. Back in the days when his grandfather had operated the shop, she'd done just the same.

Babushka grabbed a handful of roses and went about wrecking the symmetry of the wreath he'd been working on. Her slight frame seemed almost fragile, but he knew better. She was built from solid steel and, even as she'd aged, her fashion sense never changed. Her family ran flower shops. She wore all floral prints, all the time. Even if the prints clashed. Today was bright orange and neon green with a red silk scarf printed with roses. On anyone else it would just seem loud. On Babushka? Her style announced her presence.

"Thanks for your help." Becca lifted the obnoxious green prom gown and sashayed to the register.

"She vas pretty. Strong hips. She vill make good babies," Babushka said, a bit too loud.

"For another man, yes, I'm sure she will." He snatched the coffee mug he'd set aside earlier and took a long pull. His gaze trailed across the street to Heather's cookie shop.

Heather, with her long brown hair held back tight in a ponytail, her shirt falling perfectly against her chest, her precise makeup. Not too much, just enough to amplify her big brown eyes and draw his attention to her lips. He wouldn't mind running his palms over her waist, down her hips—

"I vill be dead soon." Babushka cut straight through his daydream.

He slid his gaze from the yellow-and-pink shop across the street to his grandmother. "You're not dying."

Despite her continual insistence, his grandmother's health was not an issue. Her eyesight, yes. She struggled with vision these days.

"Every breath, I come closer to death. Every breath, he passes me over. But soon I vill be gone and you vill be alone. You break my heart, Jason. I vill see you married."

"I had a wife. Don't need another." Nope. Been there. Done that.

"Your vife, she vas no good. You need good vife." Babushka nodded along with herself.

Whenever she brought up his love life, it never boded well. In fact, it usually meant a parade of women would soon slink through the door to try and convince him Babushka was right. Which meant: deflect and get the hell out of there.

"Actually, I met someone new." Truth was in the eye of the beholder, and he *had* met someone new. Heather. Granted, he'd officially "met" her over a year ago. Details. Details.

"You did this? Ven?" Babushka paused wrecking his flowers to focus her attention on him.

"Things got serious so fast. It didn't work out. I need some time to deal with it." Truer words had never been spoken. Sort of. "My heart's a little raw."

"Who did this thing?" Babushka's eyes narrowed.

"The lady who owns the cookie shop across the street. It's over. Done. I'm going to lick my wounds for a while." And that was how it was done. He'd bought himself a few solid weeks of heartbreak.

Babushka smacked his shoulder. "You did not tell me of this voman."

He rubbed the spot where her palm had met his shirt. "Some things don't need to be shared."

"Your heart is broken?" Shit. She didn't look like she bought it. "You vill swear this on the image of your *dedushka*?" She rummaged through the oversized purse she dragged everywhere.

"I'm not swearing anything." He crossed his arms, ready to stand firm against his overbearing grandmother.

"Jason Mikhail Dvornakov." She yanked the eight-by-ten photo of her late husband from her purse. Holding it out faceup so Dedushka glowered at him.

She wasn't going to let this go.

He glanced to the image of his dead grandfather.

Fuck.

"Hand on Dedushka's face." Her eyes turned serious, her expression firm—as it should've been when pimping the image of her dead husband to manipulate innocent grandchildren.

"My heart's broken, there's no need to swear anything." No need to involve dead relatives.

"You vill swear on your grandfather's image vhat you say is true. Lies vill haunt you for your days. Vhen I die, I vill haunt you for your days. You vill be haunted."

He had a suspicion that, whether he swore or not, Babushka would haunt him. Still, one did not swear on a dead person's image without being totally honest.

Babushka picked up his hand and set it on the glass.

A chill ran through him. It was not the first time he'd been forced to swear on his grandfather's picture. The last time he'd been eighteen and had to swear he hadn't stolen a bottle of vodka for a party at Brek's house. He hadn't. His sister, Anna, had.

"I swear I am not ready for a relationship. My heart can't take it." There, that worked. Not a lie.

"Because of the woman across the street," Babushka said, nudging him to say it.

He lifted his hand from the glass just enough so he wouldn't be haunted on a technicality. "Yeah, because of the woman across the street."

Babushka gave him a soft look he knew to be total bull-shit. "Time is precious. I have so little."

"Speaking of, any birthday requests or should I just wing it?" The family always threw a big shindig for her birthday.

She harrumphed. "I vill be dead by then."

"So no card?" he asked. She'd been saying she was dying for years. She couldn't see for shit, but otherwise, she was healthier than the rest of them.

"For my birthday I vish you vould find a voman to make you happy."

He gave her his sincerest look. The one he'd practiced to perfection in front a mirror at fifteen years old. The one he saved for important occasions. The one he used for getting his way. "A little time and then I'll be ready to try again."

Now they were both liars. He slid his arm around her for a side hug, the frail bones of her shoulder a lie to the iron-plated woman who was his grandmother. Then he snagged the vase of hyacinths for the jewelry shop up the street and headed out to deliver it.

Successful deflection. Next: evacuation.

The mountain air was crisp like it always was right before summer. Spring would hold on for a few more weeks. This type of weather used to make him antsy, make him wonder what else the world had to offer. But he'd traveled. He'd seen the world. He'd had his skin sandblasted off in the heat of the desert and he'd strapped an oxygen tank to his back to defuse bombs in the Atlantic. The mountain air didn't make him antsy anymore; now, it made his muscles relax and his mind clear.

He tugged open the glass door to the jewelry store, and his heart stopped beating for a nanosecond.

Heather.

He was definitely a leg guy. She was blessed by the angels in that department. Her toned calves outlined by tight jeans curved up and up and up to her ass…assets.

The object of his intense observation cleared her throat. He jerked his gaze to Heather's.

She was looking over her shoulder, frowning like she'd sucked on sour cherry candy, clearly catching him checking her out.

He jerked his chin her way and gave his best you-know-we'd-be-good-in-the-sack smile.

She rolled her eyes.

Chandra glanced up from the posters. "Hello, Jason."

"Good to see you, Chandra." He grinned at his mother's best friend. "I brought your flowers."

Chandra skirted the edge of the jewelry case and plucked the vase from his fingertips. "Thanks." She arranged the vase on a mirrored table near the diamond engagement rings.

Her shop wasn't the typical jewelry shop with the clear cases and the soft carpets and the bright lights. Chandra's shop was silver and white and pops of gold. Subdued lighting everywhere but over the cases. For those, she'd added sparkling chandeliers. No matter which way you looked, shit sparkled—in the cases, on the ceiling, even the walls had tiny mirrors edged tight together to give the appearance of bling. It was enough to make a man shiver just walking inside.

He sauntered toward Heather. "What're we shopping for today?"

"Rings." Chandra scooted around the counter once more, removing two boxes with rings. "Heather was thinking traditional gold, but I think rose gold goes better with her coloring."

Heather slid her fingertip along the edge of the first small ring with little diamonds around the edge. "I like this one."

"You should try it on." Jase couldn't take his gaze from where the tip of her fingernail traced the trinket.

"My niece is in town this weekend." Chandra raised her I'm-in-cahoots-with-your-mother penciled eyebrows at Jase. "I told her all about you. She'd love to have a drink with you."

"I'm off the market for a while. You know how it is when you get your heart broken." In for a penny. In for a pound.

He lifted the little ring from the silk-lined box and held it out for Heather.

She took it, slipped it on her right hand. He couldn't care less about rose gold and regular gold and skin tone, but that ring belonged on Heather.

"You were seeing someone?" Chandra asked, apparently perturbed she wasn't in the loop.

"I was. Total whirlwind." He played the innocent card—dash of heartbreak, sad eyes, big sigh. "We broke up this morning. Very sudden."

He glanced to Heather. She looked up at him and rolled her eyes.

"You know what they say: when you fall off the horse it's best to get right back on." Chandra admired the ring on Heather's hand.

"What do you think?" he asked Heather, his question having nothing to do with jewelry.

"I think when you fall off the horse, you should evaluate why you fell, so it doesn't happen again. For example, did you say something to the horse that made it buck?" Heather fiddled with the ring, sliding it over her knuckle and back down.

"Maybe the horse is just sensitive with a bad temperament." He shrugged, doing his best to keep his face neutral.

"Maybe the horse expects to be treated a certain way." Heather pulled off the ring and ran her fingertip over the diamonds.

Chandra glanced between the two of them, eyes wide.

"Maybe the horse doesn't know a good thing when she sees it." He pressed his stance wider.

"Or maybe it has absolutely nothing to do with the horse." Heather smiled the confident smile of an executive on Wall Street and tucked the ring back in the box. "I'm going to think about it," she told Chandra.

"Sounds good." Chandra put the box back under the glass. "I need to go help this lady with her repair for a moment. Holler if you need me." She headed toward the other side of the room.

"Why'd you tell her we broke up?" Heather asked.

"Well, she's friends with my mom, and Mom is on a tear for me to get serious with someone. My family gets a little nutty about that stuff. I figure our pretend breakup will buy me about three weeks of peace." Four if he played it right.

She raised her eyebrows at him. "You know how crazy that sounds, right?"

He lifted a shoulder. "You clearly haven't met my family. How goes the poster delivery?"

"Chandra's going to help me with the dance. I think it'll be fun," Heather mused, eyeing the other rings. "You should join the committee."

That was a negative. "I'm in for all the flower donations you need, but I don't do committees." He supported with cash and donations, but when it came to committees, he was no good. Too much talk, not enough action. Committees were his mother's domain; she loved telling people what to do. Chairing a committee was the perfect pastime for her.

Jase leaned toward Heather, the scent of lavender and vanilla swirling in the air around them. "Second chance. Dinner. No tacos."

"Saturday?" Heather asked, her voice breathy.

"Works for me." *And that's how it's done.*

"I have plans." Heather's brown eyes sparkled.

"Fuck me," Jase said under his breath, low enough so only he could hear it.

Well, maybe Heather caught it, too.

Heather nudged his shoulder with her own. "What good is a breakup if you keep asking me out?"

He laid his hand on her arm, the warmth of it settling in his palm. "We can always try for round two."

"Nah. Why ruin a perfectly good breakup?" The laughter in her tone hit him straight in the gut. She'd won this round, but he'd make sure there was another.

____

Chapter Three

____

The delivery van pulled up right behind Jase's shop door in the alley behind his building. The alley was tight, only room for one vehicle at a time, and bordered by a metal chain separating it from the parking lot where the business owners parked so the street spots stayed open for customers.

He stepped up to the back of the van, opened the double doors, and did a quick check that everything was ready for the rest of the morning deliveries to be loaded.

Jase held a clipboard and scribbled the delivery instructions for the funeral flowers before passing it to his driver, Ethan. "Funeral starts early, so those need to be there before nine thirty. Hit the mortuary first."

"Sure thing." Ethan set the clipboard on the bumper of the delivery van, hopping inside to adjust arrangements so they wouldn't topple over.

Jase glanced across the parking lot. Along the opposite side, Heather had parked her hot-pink delivery van with a giant, plastic chocolate chip cookie perched on top. The thing was loud, obnoxious, and it made him crave cookies whenever he saw it. Her marketing worked, he'd give her that.

He focused on the van, just as his grandmother's black Buick crept across the lot. Slowly. Too slowly.

He squinted. She was driving.

His gut dropped to the floor of the alley. *What the hell?*

She couldn't fucking see well enough to drive. That's why the family had hired her a professional driver. That's why they'd taken her keys away. Last time she'd driven, she'd taken out three cars and one of those big blue mailboxes outside of the post office. They were lucky no one had gotten hurt. It'd taken some tricky legal work for the family attorney to get her off the hook with only a fine, restitution, and the loss of her license.

And now she was behind the wheel again.

Son of a bitch.

She edged toward Heather's cookie van like a slow-motion replay on Monday night football, with Al and Frank and Dan…

"No. No. No. No. No." Jase hit the side of his delivery van with the palm of his hand and sprinted toward his grandmother. He jumped over the cable chain midrun, skirting the cars in his beeline for the Buick.

"What?" he heard Ethan say behind him. Followed by a loud, "Shit."

The bumper of the Buick made contact with the side of the van. The soles of Jase's tennis shoes pushed against the asphalt, propelling him toward the accident.

Breaths came ragged, not because he was winded from the run but because his grandmother was going to hurt herself. And get her ass arrested.

He ran straight to the driver's side window of the Buick and banged against the glass. His grandmother ignored him, put the damn tank in reverse, and backed up.

His lungs released a huge gulp of oxygen.

Okay, this was all right. There was only a small scratch on

Heather's van. He could buff that right out. No one ever had to know.

His grandmother hit the gas, the bumper of her car crunching against the side of pink paint and vinyl cookie decals.

Shit.

The Buick? It was fine.

The van. Not so much.

The metal crumpled like it'd been hit with twenty pounds of bang.

That would not buff out.

"What the hell is she doing?" Ethan huffed as he jogged up beside him.

He had to yell, because Babushka hadn't let off the gas. The rubber of the Buick's tires burned against the asphalt as the wheels spun, the van skidded and tilted, and, holy fuck…

Jase's heart thudded, but he couldn't figure out what it was doing because it obviously wasn't pumping blood, given that his entire body had turned to ice. He couldn't get himself to move. "I think she's getting revenge."

"What the hell did the van do to her?" Ethan asked, dumbfounded.

Jase got his feet unstuck. He fell against his grandmother's window and pounded with his fists. She had a one-track mind, or she didn't hear him, because she didn't acknowledge he was there. Hands at ten and two, she stared straight ahead at the vinyl cookies attached to the crumpled metal of what had been Heather's delivery van.

"Should we call someone?" he heard Ethan ask.

Someone would be great right now. They should do that.

But a vortex of what-the-fuckage had sucked him in. He yanked on his grandmother's locked driver's side door as she put the car in reverse again. It moved back. Jase jumped away. He preferred his toes on his feet and not crushed under the rubber tires of his grandmother's cookie-van-destroying machine.

The Buick slammed against the already crumpled metal of the van, and the whole vehicle tilted. The giant plastic cookie on top of the van creaked, broke loose, and crashed to the pavement.

"*Stop,*" he shouted. His desperation wasn't lost on him. He threw his body against the side of the car, banging on the roof.

His grandmother finally glanced to him, his entire body plastered against the side of her door, his fingertips gripping into the roof of her tank-of-a-Buick.

The wheels stopped spinning. She tossed the car in park, grabbed her purse from the passenger seat, and pushed open the door.

Jase stumbled back, right into Ethan.

Babushka stepped from her tank as though nothing had happened. "I think I tapped it."

Jase pressed his hands against his temples as he took in the damage. "What were you doing?"

Babushka inspected the crumpled pink metal. "Moving my car. I probably should've vaited for my driver."

"Yeah, probably." If he had to guess, his eyes were likely bugging out right about now. "How the hell did you get the keys?"

"I asked for them." Babushka licked at her thumb and buffed at a scrape on her bumper. "My driver, he says okay."

And that driver was officially fired.

Jase blew a breath between his lips. "Why were you moving your car, anyway?"

"I didn't like the spot it vas in." Babushka shuffled around the damage. "This belongs to the horrible voman who broke your heart?"

He did some heavy nose breathing. "Yeah." And Heather was gonna kill him.

"It is… Vat do they say? Karma," Babushka grumped.

He never should've told her Heather broke his heart, but the damage was done and now he needed to keep his grandmother from getting arrested. She had no business driving anything.

"Someone should probably go notify Heather," Ethan piped up. "You want to go, or do you want me to?"

Jase took in the damage once again. This wasn't the kind of thing they could just leave a note about.

"I'll go get her. Can you keep an eye on Lead Foot here?" He gestured to his grandmother, who at the moment was inspecting the front of her bumper.

Ethan sighed. "Sure thing."

Jase started his walk of shame to the cookie shop. He punched his buddy Brek's number into his cell. Brek knew car repair. He'd know what to do about the van.

"You've got Brek."

"I need a favor." Jase's breath huffed against the mouthpiece. "Babushka just rammed Heather's delivery van with her Buick. Everyone's fine. Nobody's hurt. But the van doesn't look so good. I'm going to tell Heather right now, but I could use a second opinion on bodywork."

There was a long pause.

"The pink van?" Brek asked.

"Yeah." Would there be any other van?

"Shit," Brek replied. "That's her baby. She sold her car to buy that thing."

"Brek, what's going on?" Jase could hear Brek's wife, Velma, asking in the background. There were some muffled sounds while Brek relayed something to her.

Velma and Heather were tight. Once Velma knew, she'd call Heather. He picked up his pace to a jog.

"I'm on my way," Brek said before the line went dead.

Phone shoved in his pocket, Jase rounded the corner to Heather's shop. The outside was as pink as her van. She'd added cookie decals on the windows with polka dots all around. It looked like the happiest business on the block. At least, it would be until he told her what his grandmother had done. He pulled on the door, the jingle bells attached to a *Come In! We're Open & Awesome* sign bouncing against the polka dots on the glass.

"I need to talk to Heather," he said to the lady running the cash register.

"She's in the kitchen. Just one sec." Cash-register lady raised her just-one-sec finger and continued helping a customer.

No time for this. He practically jumped over the counter and pushed the swinging door to the kitchen open.

"Hey, you can't go in th—" Cash-register lady started to say, but he was already through the door.

He skidded to a halt.

There, laid out before him, were trays and trays and trays of cookies shaped liked penises and iced in bright colors. Fuchsia. Yellow. Teal. Neon green.

Hair-netted Heather glanced up from where she was icing the tip on a batch of blue-balled man rods.

He had thought the day was weird before. It wasn't.

"That is a lot of dick," he said to no one in particular.

Two of her staff were boxing them up, and one was arranging several dicks-on-sticks into an arrangement in a vase. The symmetry was on point, and one truly had to look closely to see the phallic shapes of the cookies. They looked like an adorable assortment of cookie flowers. Until you did a double take and realized they were a handful of multicolored edible erections.

"Jase?" Heather asked. The tip of her icing bag leaked blue icing onto the table.

"Okay, so first..." He shook his head. "We'll get to that. Second"—he waved an arm toward the erectile bouquet— "what the hell are these?"

Heather raised her eyebrows. "You've never seen a penis before?"

"Of course I've seen one. Every day, in fact. But why are they in cookie form?" And what alternate reality had he been transported into that morning?

Heather dropped the bag to the table. "They're cockies. They sell like crazy. What was the first thing?" She moved a finished tray to the waiting rack.

Right. His grandmother's personal demolition derby. "There's been a little accident with your van. My grand-mother shouldn't have been driving, but she gets determined sometimes."

She turned back to him, the color lost from her cheeks. "What happened to my van? Is your grandmother okay?"

"She is fine. Totally fine." He kept his tone upbeat, despite the verdict he was about to render. "Her car is also fine. Your van, on the other hand…" He paused. Pinched his lips and did a little shake of his head.

"My van…" Apron and vinyl gloves still on, Heather pushed beside him and bolted toward the door.

"It's not so fine," he finished.

Turned out, Heather was a good sprinter. He hurried to keep up with her pace. She bolted across the street, pausing when the broken plastic chocolate chip cookie came into view.

"My cookie." Only two words, but they were laced with desperation. She rounded to the side of the damage, and then she did that thing a woman does when she's at her most dangerous. She got quiet. Real quiet. Peaceful, almost.

That's what happened right before a bomb went off. Most people didn't know that from firsthand experience, but he did. That moment of still right before shit got real.

"Are you okay?" she asked his grandmother.

"Of course; is just a scratch." Babushka gestured to the not-just-a-scratch damage on the van. The old woman raised her weathered brows. "We have not met. I am Nadzieja." The old woman gave Heather some serious stink eye. "Everyone I like calls me Babushka. You vill call me Nadzieja."

Heather paused a beat. "Okay." She looked back to the damage. Then to Jase. "Well, you can call me Heather, and we should call the police. Get a report started for insurance." Heather patted the pockets of her icing-splattered, yellow-polka-dot apron. "Damn. My phone's at the shop."

"You can use mine." Ethan began to hand over his cell.

Jase stepped between them. "What if we…didn't. You know, involve the police? Just handled this between neighbors?"

"Jase." Heather looked at him like he'd been the one icing dick cookies, still oh-so calm. "This is a lot of damage. We need to exchange insurance cards. Get a police report. And I've got to figure out how to make my deliveries today."

Velma's Prius crept behind Babushka's car, stopped, and Brek opened the driver's side door. His wife got out of the passenger side.

"Holy cow." Velma's eyes went wide.

"Yeah," Jase said under his breath.

"Is just a scratch." Babushka lifted a shoulder.

Jase slid his gaze to Heather. The calm was gonna blow any minute. She pinched her lips into a flat line.

Brek wasted no time in running a hand over the damage while Velma grabbed their kid out of the back seat. Normally, Jase would go all Uncle Jase on the baby and coo and cuddle, but today he had a cookie-van-disaster to sort.

Brek dropped to the gravel and scooted so he could see under the van.

Then he pushed himself up, dropping his elbows over his knees.

"Frame's bent." Brek dusted off the sleeves of his leather motorcycle jacket.

Son. Of. A. Bitch.

"Then we'll bend it back." Heather gestured to where Brek sat on the ground, like he should get on that.

Velma had moved beside Heather, her free arm around Heather's back. "I don't think that's how it works."

"It's gonna be scrap." Brek confirmed what Jase already suspected.

"Like I say, only a scrape. Nothing serious," Babushka chimed in.

"I don't understand." Heather glanced between Brek, Jase, Babushka, and Ethan.

"He means, it's not fixable," Jase confirmed. "I mean, it's fixable. Everything's fixable. But it'll be too expensive. A bent frame is going to total the van."

Brek nodded in agreement. "I have a guy who can take a look. But it's bent as all shit under there. There's no way this isn't totaled."

Heather's mouth dropped, her pretty raspberry lips turning pale.

Babushka sat against the bumper of her Buick and pulled a peppermint candy from her bag. She carefully unwrapped it, popped it in her mouth, and glared daggers at Heather. "Tell me, vill you break all the hearts in the neighborhood? Or just my grandson's?"

Heather seemed to choke on air. Jase didn't have a mirror, but he knew his eyes were definitely huge. Babushka could not seriously be bringing this up right now.

"He's really upset about it all," Babushka continued. "You vill fix things."

Heather stared at Babushka. "Jase is upset…because we broke up?" She was still doing that calm thing. The one that did not bode well for anyone within a five-foot radius. Namely, him.

"You and Jase?" Velma asked, clearly confused. "Really?"

Why would it be such a shock if they'd hooked up?

He slid his gaze to Brek.

Brek, who obviously wasn't buying any of it.

"Heather? Can I have a word?" Jase jerked his head toward Velma's Prius, and started in that direction.

Heather followed. Silent. Too silent.

Jase hadn't expected his grandmother to approach Heather. He hadn't expected her to get revenge by smashing her van. He'd expected she'd let it go. He'd expected her to mind her own goddamned business and let him live his life.

He should've known better.

They reached Velma's Prius.

Heather crossed her arms, leaned against the edge of the trunk, and waited. Her gaze bore into his.

He knew this game. First one to talk lost.

Fuck it. "I told Babushka you broke my heart so she'd lay off her insistence that I need to meet someone. I had no idea she'd go all Cruella de Vil on you."

"So, this is your fault?" Heather waved a hand toward the van. "This is what you meant when you said your family goes a 'little nutty' about your relationship status. You did this to me? You did this to my cookie?"

Here it came. Where was a goddamned bomb suit when he needed one?

"I don't even know what to say right now." Her voice was getting pitchy. Raising with each word. "I mean, this is outrageous. You've totaled my van via your grandmother. I didn't even know that was a thing." She paced away from him. Then back. "Oh my God. Oh. My. God. My van is trashed." Her finger pressed against his sternum. "I sold everything I own to open this shop. I sold my car to buy that van." And she was yelling. "Now, it's gone because you couldn't tell your grandmother you didn't want to date anyone?"

He nodded and pressed at the bridge of his nose. "I fucked up."

Three words a guy never wanted to say.

The fight deflated out of her. She just stared at him.

"I don't suppose at this point there is any way you'll play along with the breakup so they will, in fact, lay off?" he asked.

"Your grandmother just took out my van." Heather tossed her arm toward the totaled van in illustration. "And you want me to pretend we were together?"

Not quite. "I want you to pretend we broke up."

"Because you don't want a girlfriend?" She crossed, then uncrossed, her arms and propped them behind her on the side of the trunk. "And you're too scared to actually stand up to your grandmother."

"Yes." Had she not just witnessed the devastation his grandmother could wreak when she was on a mission?

And why did he feel like he'd been summoned to the principal's office? A sexy-as-hell principal in a hairnet, but still.

"Even after your grandmother tried to get revenge on me for breaking your tender heart." She smacked her mouth closed.

"Well, yeah. But I'll make sure she doesn't do anything else to you." He could definitely, probably, make sure of that.

Heather took a few deep breaths. She paced from one side of the car to the other. "I don't get it. Why do you want to have a pretend break up? You asked me out. Twice." She held up two fingers, for good measure.

"I don't want the kind of girlfriend they want me to have."

"What kind is that?"

He shifted. "Look, chicks can be demanding."

And that was the truth.

"I had no idea." The sympathy in her tone was anything but sympathetic.

He stepped closer to her.

"You're not that kind of chick." He got close. Not up in her space, but close enough he could smell the lavender in her shampoo.

The light behind her eyes flared. "So if I agree to lie to your grandmother about us, what about my van?"

"Here's what I'm thinking." Jase pointed to his delivery van in the alley. "We'll share my van today. Ethan can help out with your deliveries. We don't call the police. We don't involve insurance. I just…" Fuck it. What the hell. "Buy you a new van."

"What about tomorrow? And the day after that?" Heather's voice started to get pitchy, but she held herself tall.

"Ethan and I will help you out until we get you another van. We'll order it today." Jase's grandmother was going to owe him.

"A pink one," Heather confirmed. "With a cookie on the top."

"Right. Just like this one." But without the Buick indentation along the side. "Though, my delivery driver may quit when he realizes he has to deliver penis cookies."

"Oh please. We box them up so you can't see what they are," she said. "I can't exactly walk through town with a cockie bouquet without getting hate mail."

Then everything was fine. Win. Win. Win. "Perfect. All sorted."

Ethan never had to know what he was delivering.

Heather didn't move. "I want a year of satellite radio, leather seats, a premium stereo system, and a fresh tank of gas every week for a year."

He groaned internally.

"And I'm not taking the bus to the grocery store. You'll lend me your car whenever I need it." She shrugged. "Or we can do this thing the right way. The way that involves police and insurance."

He focused his gaze on his grandmother. She had no license. And this was not her first offense. Hell, she should be the one forking out the money. But this was his fault—at least partially. He'd suck it up, open his checkbook, and take responsibility.

She could wind up in jail. Or worse, house arrest. Somehow, she'd probably manage to make that happen at his apartment. "Fine. Done. Leather. Satellite. Stereo. Gas. Plastic Cookie. Personal chauffeur."

"And pink paint," she confirmed.

"And pink paint."

"Will there be tears?" she asked.

"Sorry?" What had she asked? He was busy doing the math of how much money he'd just dropped on a delivery van that he'd never use.

"You're pretending I broke your heart. Don't you think you'd be so upset that there'd be some crying on your part?"

Ha. No. "Not a chance."

Her chest heaved on her exhale. "I think you'd cry for me."

"No."

"Give me sad, longing looks?"

"No."

"Then I guess I'll make that call to police." Heather started to walk away.

He hesitated for an instant. "Longing looks, mostly sad." He held his hand to her.

She turned. "Fine. With one exception."

"What?" His hand still hung in the air between them. Unshook.

"I don't lie to my friends."

"Fair enough. Just my family." He gave a pointed glance to his still outstretched palm.

She shook it, latex gloves and all, a naughty smile touching her lips. "Nice doing business with you."

Shit. If she kept that up, he would be in tears. Or at least he'd wind up on his knees.

Then again, that could be fun, too. On his knees. In her bedroom. Or office. Or kitchen.

They headed back toward the scene of the crime.

"Why aren't we reporting the accident?" Velma asked, genuine confusion written across her face.

Okay, just so they were clear.

"Babushka doesn't have a license," Jase began. "It'd be a huge help to me, a personal favor, if we didn't involve the police." Police who very well might arrest his grandmother for driving without a license…again.

Velma stood tall. "And you're gonna replace Heather's van."

"I am. And make Heather's deliveries for her in the meantime."

Ethan would murder him if he found out he was delivering penis-cookie bouquets. But Jase would deal with that. And everything else. When the time came.

Chapter Four

"You want to talk about it yet?" Velma asked from where she sat across the worktable in Heather's commercial cookie kitchen.

Heather had figured out the layout herself. The ovens and the huge kitchen vent were on one side of the room, separated by a line of racks for cookie-cooling. The other half of the room—the one closest to the front of the store—was for decorating and boxing.

Velma had offered to stick around and help ice eyeballs on the snuggle-bird cookies Heather had to finish up. She was on maternity leave but hated being stuck at home. So she sometimes came to help Heather while baby Lily napped in Heather's office.

Meringue icing flooded a wing of one of the birds on Heather's tray. The cookies, heart-shaped with two iced birds snuggling inside, were a customer favorite. "There's absolutely nothing to talk about."

"Okay." Velma went back to piping the black pupils on the birds. "You're just doing Jase a pretty huge favor."

A favor that would net her leather seats and satellite radio.

Heather ignored the way her blood pressure knocked around her heart at the mention of Jase.

She'd have thought that him catching her looking at rings would've been embarrassment enough. Nope, that was just the icing on the tip of the dick. When Logan left, she'd promised herself she didn't need to find a guy to find any sort of fulfillment in life—even though that was what all her friends were doing. Of course, calling off the search didn't mean she didn't like bling. So, she'd promised herself she'd buy her own damn ring. Pick it out. One that was a gift to herself.

A promise ring of sorts.

"And he's not hard to look at," Velma said, not looking up from the tray of cookies.

Heather's stomach fluttered ridiculously at the memory of Jase's early-morning dance party.

"Not that I'm looking," Velma continued.

Velma wasn't looking. She'd found her guy. He was the exact opposite of anyone Heather would've ever paired with Velma. And they were brilliantly happy together. For a while, Heather had thought she and Logan were headed that way, too. To the blissful relationship stage of things. Then he'd started shutting her out. Just like all of her boyfriends before him. Heather was a lot of fun, she'd been told that often, but she wasn't the kind of girl men wanted to spend forever with. Love like that wasn't meant for everyone. She'd come to accept that.

Heather's little sister and head-cookie-baker, Candace— mostly known as Candy to everyone she knew—brought Heather another tray of sugar-cookie hearts ready for icing.

"That man has abs that go on for miles," Candy said as she popped the tray onto the table.

Miles and miles. Heather refused to think about his body or the way he smelled of cinnamon.

What she needed was a night in with a marathon of *Family Feud.*

"I bet he's amazing in bed. With a body like that?" Candy smacked her lips together.

"Candy?" Heather asked, not raising her eyes from where the tip of her piping bag touched the pastry.

"Yeah?"

"No."

Velma snort-laughed. Candy winked at her.

Heather swallowed any thoughts of Jase in bed.

"You know Mom and Dad would adore him," Candy continued.

"Mom and Dad like everyone." Their soft-spoken mother and father rarely raised their voices. That was the kind of people they were. So, no, Jase wouldn't have to do much to win their adoration.

Laying down the piping bag, Heather grabbed Velma's finished tray of cookies and pushed through the swinging doors to arrange them in the case.

The string of jingle bells on the door tinkled as two women jostled their way in—Jase's Russian Mafia granny and a woman about Heather's age.

Heather's internal monologue dropped some serious cuss words.

"Hi," she said with as much cheer as she could muster. They headed toward her. "What can I get you?"

"Um, I'm not sure." The younger woman had a funny expression on her face, like she was trying to place Heather.

"Take your time." Heather refused to shrink away from the blatant inspection.

"Let's get this over vith," Nadzieja said. "I came to apologize for your van. This is Anna. She came to be sure I did."

Anna…Jase's sister.

Heather splayed her hands on the counter. Well, that was

nice of them to stop by. Nice-ish. "Thank you. I'm so glad you're okay."

"Also, ve vant you to let Jason take you to dinner," Nadzieja continued.

Shit.

"We're supposed to be smooth," Anna said out of the corner of her mouth.

"Excuse me?" Heather recovered from her momentary inability to process oxygen.

"He's a great guy and he really likes you. Whatever happened between you, we're hoping you'll hear him out." Anna shifted the purse strap on her shoulder and dropped it to the counter.

"You're both here." Heather pointed at them. "To get me." She pointed to her chest. "To get back together with Jase?" She pointed toward the flower shop across the street.

They had to be kidding.

"After you took out my van because he'd told you we'd broken up," Heather said with a firm look at Jase's grandmother.

"I have apologized. You vill call me Babushka and I vill cook for you," Babushka announced. "When you have dinner vith him."

The younger woman nudged Babushka. "That'd be weird. They can go wherever. Even here."

"And that wouldn't be weird?" Heather asked.

"Wherever you're comfortable." Anna leaned forward and whispered as if she were selling government secrets to Russian spies. "Just, you know, communication is a good thing."

"No, I don't think so." Heather made a sound in her throat—half clearing, half breathing. "But thanks for stopping in. Would you like to buy a cookie?"

"For sure. We'll take a dozen of whatever," Anna replied.

Heather started filling a box with snuggle birds. She made the mistake of glancing up at Anna.

Anna, who was chewing at her bottom lip. "Jase could just use a break, that's all."

"Hey, Anna," Velma said as she pushed through the doors behind Heather.

"Oh, Velma, good, you're here, too," Anna said, relief in her tone. "We're trying to get Heather to give Jase another chance."

"Oh, I don't think—" Velma started.

"What. The. Hell," Jase said from the doorway. Red-faced, out-of-breath Jase.

Heather's jingle bells hadn't even jingled.

"Your family is trying to convince me to take you back." Heather held up the cookie tongs and pointed at his sister and grandmother with them.

"All the Dvornakovs out of the shop," he demanded.

"Hey, now. Not until they've got their cookies," Heather said. Hey, a sale was a sale.

"No cookies. Out you two." He pointed toward the door.

"They're customers. They're buying things. If you have a problem, address it with management. In writing." Heather went back to boxing cookies.

"You own this place," he said, biting out the words.

"Then perhaps you should mail me a letter." Heather squared her shoulders.

A muscle in Jase's forehead twitched, or maybe it was a blood vessel.

"You can't throw out my customers." Heather continued loading the box. "Especially when they're in the middle of buying things. Once the transaction is through, you can take your family wherever you'd like."

"Holy hell." Anna glanced between the two of them. "She's perfect."

The tension in the room notched higher; even the cashier stopped mid-button-punch to watch.

"You two should talk privately. I vill run the counter." Babushka shuffled around the pastry case. "I vill need an apron."

None of Heather's muscles worked as the old woman headed toward the sink and began to wash her gnarled hands.

"What is she doing?" Heather asked Anna, with a glance to Velma.

"I think she's preparing to work here," Velma replied.

"C'mon, Babushka, you work at the flower shop. Let's go back there." Jase was clearly doing his best to stay calm.

"I quit." Babushka began familiarizing herself with everything behind the counter.

Heather tossed Jase her best please-help-me look. Okay, so maybe she should've let Jase toss out his family when he'd tried. Hindsight and all that.

"What are you talking about?" Jase asked.

"I quit. I vill be vorking vith Heather now." Babushka had found the stash of aprons and tied one on.

"Um…no. I'm all staffed up. Don't have the funds to hire anyone else." Heather's heart was kicking in her chest. What was this day, anyway?

She'd left a nice-paying job selling corrugated cardboard designs to open the shop. Sold everything. Her town house. Her car. Even some of her clothes. Moved into the small apartment above the shop and refused anything but success.

"No charge." Babushka shuffled toward the register. "Favor because I wrecked your van." She shooed her grandson. "Jason, you may go, I vill check in."

"This is so not what I expected," Velma whispered.

Candy popped her head out from the back. "Heather, there's a problem with the deliveries. The Smith delivery only got two bouquets, not three."

Oh no. The Smith delivery was three cockie bouquets and

an extra four boxes filled with very inappropriately shaped cookies.

Heather glanced to Jase. "I think there's a missing bouquet of..." She did her best to telepathically say *erection cookies* while keeping her face as neutral as she could.

Jase clearly got the message with the speed he pulled out his phone and punched in some numbers. "Hey, Ethan...one of the bouquets didn't make it to the Smith delivery...can you check the back..." He shifted from foot to foot while he waited. "No, I'm sure...they called Heather...where did you—"

He had gone pale.

Where the hell had the cookies been delivered?

"Then go back to the funeral home and grab them," Jase continued.

Heather's stomach pitched. Oh, that wasn't good.

Jase shoved his phone back in his pocket and gave her a look. A look that wasn't good.

"Tell me you did not deliver my cockies to a funeral." Heather's knees went weak, and she actually felt the blood drain from her scalp.

Jase didn't move. She'd never seen anyone go so still.

"I think that means he did," Velma said from behind her.

Chapter Five

Heather's arms wrapped around Jase's waist, the wind in her hair, the rumble of his motor between her legs—yep, Heather was on Jase's Ducati zipping through Denver. Her thighs pressed against him. And, dammit all, she enjoyed it.

For a moment, she closed her eyes, pretended they weren't going to rescue her cockie bouquet from a funeral home. Instead, they were riding through the Italian hillside. Just the two of them, maybe a picnic on the side of a hill. She'd lay out a blanket, and they'd cuddle together and make out for a while. No expectations, just enjoying the feel of each other's lips. The taste of one another. Things would get heated, and they'd make lazy love on a picnic blanket in a foreign country. No cares. Just the two of them.

He pulled the bike into a space in the back of the one-story mortuary, right next to his delivery van.

Nothing killed a wet dream quite like a visit to the neighborhood funeral home. Heather peeked around Jase to where Ethan leaned against the bumper of the delivery van.

She scooted off the bike. Jase followed.

"What's the damage?" he asked, setting his helmet on the seat.

"Funeral started before I got here. The director can't grab the bouquet until it's done." Ethan kicked off from the bumper. "I'm sorry, man. I was in a hurry and I totally screwed this up."

"Did they actually put out the cockie bouquet?" Heather asked. Maybe they'd just put it in the kitchen or something. Surely, someone would've noticed.

Ethan nodded. "I looked in the chapel. It's right next to the casket."

At first glance, it was just a bouquet of cookies, but if anyone looked closer? Heather shivered. The funeral-going crowd was probably not her target audience.

Jase made a noise in the back of his throat. He was going to grind his teeth right out of his skull. "How many deliveries do you have left?"

"Still have a bunch," Ethan confirmed.

"Go ahead and get to it. I'll wait here." He turned to Heather. "You want to wait with me or do you want Ethan to drop you at your shop?"

"I came to rescue an erection bouquet. I'm going to see that through." Heather crossed her arms. No one could say she didn't finish things once she committed.

Ethan nodded to her and climbed back into the delivery van. "Really, sorry."

"Don't beat yourself up. It happens," Jase replied while his hand ran over his face.

"That's not entirely true." Heather brushed at her jeans.

"What's not?"

"Well, it's just that an inappropriate cookie bouquet being delivered to a funeral home because an old lady decided to go all *Grand Theft Auto* on a delivery van isn't really something that just 'happens.'"

"Well, when you put it like that..." Jase shook his head.

Ethan headed out of the lot, turning onto the street.

"Poor guy," Heather said.

It wasn't his fault the morning had gone how it had gone.

"Man, this day," Jase said to no one in particular.

"Things you never expected to do today for five hundred, Alex." Heather turned to Jase. "This is not how I anticipated spending my lunch break."

"No kidding." Jase flipped over a white bucket and gestured for her to sit. Then he repeated the process for himself.

"For a fake couple who fake broke up, we spend a lot of real time together." Heather picked at the cuticle of her fingernail.

Jase closed his eyes and leaned his head against the brick exterior of the building. "Times like this make me seriously reconsider my commitment to our breakup."

"Oh no, bud." Heather patted his knee. "I get my leather seats out of this shebang. Don't try to weasel out of it by telling the truth."

He peeled open one eye. "Grab lunch when we're done here?"

"You buying?" she asked.

"Sure, what the hell," he replied.

"Then absolutely. But to be clear, it's not a date. It's just the two of us celebrating the freeing of the cockies."

The cockies, which were in a vase. A pretty large vase.

"How are we going to get the cockies out of here and back to the shop?" she asked.

He ticked his head to the side. "I guess you can hold them between us?"

"You want me to hold a vase filled with penis cookies between us on your motorcycle?"

"You have a better idea?" he asked.

"I could call a car. From my phone," she pointed out. It'd be a much more comfortable way to get back.

"Then you won't get lunch with me."

Well, there was that. Not that she wanted to have lunch

with him, particularly. Just lunch in general. Also, free lunch was a good thing.

They sat in silence for a beat.

"You, me, and a bouquet of cookies might be the kinkiest thing I've ever done," she finally said.

He closed his eyes again. "Then you need to get out more."

That much was true. She really should start getting out more. She'd thrown herself into her business over the past months. And any spare time was spent volunteering at the retirement home. She loved the elderly. They said what they meant and meant what they said. So, she helped out there. Anything to prevent her from actually getting out with people under the age of seventy-five.

"Why penis cookies?" Jase asked, eyes still closed.

She shifted on her bucket. "What do you mean?"

He opened his eyes, sat up, leaned forward. "I mean, of all the shapes in all the world, why'd you pick those?"

"Can't a girl just appreciate a nice—"

"Absolutely. And she should. But that doesn't mean she should immortalize them in cookie dough."

She gave him her slyest smile. "Maybe you just don't know the right women."

He snorted. "Touché."

"Years ago, I made the cookies for a bachelorette party and they were a hit." Looked like they'd be waiting for a while. She might as well tell the story. "Friends started asking for them, so I baked on the side for a while. Got pretty good at it, and expanded into other shapes. Then I figured one can't sell corrugated cardboard forever, so I decided to make cookies. The cockies were an obvious choice. I mean, I'd already created an underground following with them. Might as well monetize that." She lifted a shoulder. "Never thought that choice would lead me right here with you, though."

"Pretty awesome that it did." Jase lifted his eyebrows at her.

"See, this is what I don't get. We're all fake broken up, and you keep flirting with me."

"And?"

"And what am I supposed to do with that?"

He chuckled and flashed a set of dimples she had no idea he had. "Flirt back?"

Seriously, where had he been hiding those dimples? "I don't think you could handle my flirting. I mean, it'd ruin the breakup you're so committed to."

"You think?"

"I know."

"Give it a try, let's see what happens."

"And then what?"

"And then we take your inappropriate cookie bouquet and go grab lunch."

"Not tacos," Heather replied.

"Tacos are the best."

"It's just that they played such a pivotal role in the pretend demise of our never-happened relationship. Maybe we should have something else instead."

Jase cocked an eyebrow. "Sandwiches, then?"

That totally depended. "Hot or cold?"

"Which do you like?" he asked.

"Depends on the sandwich. Hot sandwiches definitely pair well with cockies." Oh dear Lord, had she really just said that?

Jase grinned huge. "Yes, I guess they do. Hot sandwiches it is."

"It's still not a date. Just you and me and hot sandwiches while we eat cockies."

"I'm not eating those," he said. "I make it a point not to eat anything shaped as an appendage. Personal rule."

"Turn it over and pretend it's a rainbow." Heather did her best to dare him with only her eyes.

"Don't you have to get them to their rightful owner, anyway?" he asked. "We could, you know, not eat them and deliver them after."

"Candy ran a spare set over. These are all ours," Heather said proudly.

The heavy metal door creaked open, and a man in a suit stepped through with the bouquet of cockies. "You're here for the cookies?"

"That'd be us." Jase stood and snagged the outstretched vase. "We're very sorry for the mistake."

"I hope whoever these are for appreciates them." Mr. Funeral gave Jase a pointed glance before heading back inside.

"Heather?" Jase asked.

"Uh-huh," Heather replied, taking the cockies from him.

"I need a drink." Jase headed across the lot to the dive bar up the road. "You coming?"

Heather shrugged.

Why not?

THE SCENT OF BOTTOM-SHELF BOOZE, peanuts, and powdery wood particles tickled Jase's nose. So maybe this dive took the word "dive" to a whole new level.

He held the door open for Heather and her bouquet, tucked against her side.

She barely set foot through the windowless wooden door of the bar on Champa Street before turning on her heel. She ran straight into a solid wall of Jase. Not that he intentionally blocked the doorway.

It just happened that way.

He didn't dislike the way her chest pressed against his own

in that instant. As a matter of fact, he appreciated the contact on a carnal level. He'd always been attracted to Heather, even when she was off-limits. Ever since he found out she was single again, his body seemed to be on a mission to override his brain circuits. He shook the sawdust haze from his brain.

"Trying to run already?" he asked.

"Not even a little." She shifted the bouquet a bit.

Hands on her shoulders, he twirled her so she faced the long bar top where a handful of rough-looking guys in cowboy hats tossed back bottles of beer. He did a quick inventory of the bar. Four cowboys at the bar top, a guy playing pool with a brunette, and the bartender. Some things stayed the same when he got discharged, including inventorying the room whenever he walked in.

She stumbled along as they shuffled across the peanut-shell covered floor.

"I wasn't running. Just checking to see if you were behind me." She clearly did her best attempt at recovery, sauntering deeper into the room.

"Beer?" he asked.

"Sure. I generally wait until after noon to hit the hard liquor." She winked at him.

Flirted.

Well, looky there. Just a little wink, and she made him go all warm inside.

"I'll take whatever's on tap," she continued as though she hadn't just given him the one-eyed go-ahead to flirt back.

He hooked his thumbs in the belt loops of his jeans so he wouldn't be tempted to touch her and headed toward the bar top. The place was decked out in neon beer signs, a small, empty stage splattered with God-knew-what, and a mechanical bull. He should get a mechanical bull for the flower shop. Now that would be kickass.

On that thought, he snagged their beers and headed back.

She nudged her bouquet to the side of the table and

glanced around the room in an exaggerated motion. "So, this is our first not-a-date, huh?"

"What can I say? It's where relationships go to die." He took a pull of Bud.

A couple of the cowboys at the bar glanced in their direction.

She ran a fingertip around the rim of her mug. "Did you know, every morning when I wake up, I start a list of all the things I need to get done that day?"

"How's that going for you?" He took the stool across from her.

A flick of her ponytail, and she hit him square with her brown eyes. "Today's list said things like hand out posters, make cookies, balance my checkbook, touch base with my parents. It said nothing about pretty much anything that happened after I tried to hand out my first poster to you." She tossed him a look that should've sliced him into individual bite-size pieces.

"If it makes you feel better, when I wake up in the morning, I just roll with life. After today, I'm seriously thinking about making some lists." And drinking more beer.

She chuckled. "Maybe there's a lesson in here for both of us."

"You know what we should do?"

"I bet you're going to tell me."

"We should embrace the crazy of the day." 'Cause fighting it wasn't working out. "Play hooky."

"Or maybe we don't?" She sipped at her beer.

"Give me two good reasons you don't want to do it." His mother played this game when he was a kid and didn't want to do something. It had always worked in her favor.

"One, I need to get back to work and, two, something tells me you'd go all in, we'd end up skydiving or bungee jumping, and, frankly, I don't want to break my neck." She counted the two reasons on her fingertips.

Heather was, apparently, quicker at the game than he'd ever been.

"You're not going to break your neck."

"Work." She gestured to her *Heather's Cookie Co.* polo shirt.

"Just remember Jase-and-Heather-Land could be our special, fun escape place."

"Work," she replied.

"Fine." He didn't push because, well, he liked his family jewels where they were and not rearranged by her toes.

"I tell you what. We can do something fun today. If you do something for me."

"You're already getting leather seats and satellite radio." What else did a woman need?

She leaned forward, right into his space. "Help me with the senior 'senior' prom. I need warm bodies on the committee."

Negative. Committees. His muscles tensed. "That's not really my thing."

She batted her eyelashes dramatically in his direction. "Please?"

"Don't do committees. But I can see if Mom wants to boss people around for you?"

She let out a deep sigh. "Okay, fine, no committee for you. But if we're going to hang out in Jase-and-Heather-Land, you need to tell me something about yourself. Something no one else knows."

"That's a hard one. I'm an open book." He leaned back and opened his hands wide in illustration.

She pursed her lips, crossed her arms, and waited.

Okay, there was one thing he never shared with anyone. Even his ex-wife never knew how random images on the television would trigger flashbacks to his time in the military. Then again, they had never shared their deep, dark secrets with each other. Hence, the ending. All over. Time to go. "I think television is overrated. I don't watch it. Movies, either. Don't even own a television."

Sure, he'd tried when his friends were around. Made an attempt at video games with them. But it always triggered nightmares. So, he stopped.

Heather's mouth dropped open. "How can you even say something like that? What do you do when you're relaxing? Trying to veg?"

What any man would do. "I listen to music."

Nothing like a good hair band to relax the muscles.

"Just music?" she asked.

"Yup. Music. A good workout. Ten-mile run? I'm all in."

"Ten miles?" She gave him the look like he'd just said his favorite pastime was sticking his dick in a meat grinder.

"Twenty just seems excessive, you know?" he said.

"Right, twenty would be excessive." Heather flicked her ponytail. "I think you just haven't watched the right TV shows. A little *Jeopardy*, *Wheel of Fortune*, *Price is Right*? Easy escape."

"I don't get why people go nutty over it. All the binge-watching? Not my thing." He'd told his secret. It was her turn. "Your turn. Something no one else knows."

She paused. "I don't like getting flowers."

It was like she was throwing down the gauntlet. Running right into the kill zone.

He didn't even blink. He'd accept this particular challenge. Aside from defusing 155 artillery shells, making people love flowers was his skill set.

He studied her for a beat. Pink roses. She was a pink roses kind of girl. Not just any pink roses—raspberry carrousel roses, to be exact. Sissy-ass name, but a kickass flower. Rich cream on the bottom, like the color of her skin. Deep pink at the tips, like the shade of her lips. "Then you're just not getting the right flowers," he heard himself say aloud.

"Nah. That's not it. It's just not my preference for gifts.

Chocolate? Yes, please. Sweets? For sure. Flowers? Eh." She pulled a face like her beer had gone sour.

Time to engage his inner fucking Freud. "What's the first time anyone ever gave you flowers?"

She tilted her head from ear to shoulder, ear to shoulder, then took a pull from her Budweiser before finally answering. "Twelfth grade. Guy asked me to a dance and used a dozen roses."

"That doesn't sound so bad. I'd think you'd have liked that."

"Well, maybe I did when I first got them. But he ended up breaking it off and going with a junior instead."

Ass. Jase leaned forward, elbows on the table. "Who'd you go with?"

She laughed. "No one. I didn't go. My date dumped me and went with someone else."

Well, that sucked.

"Don't feel bad, though," she continued. "It didn't work out for them, either, and it's not like he was crowned home-coming king or anything. He was just a jerk who went for someone else. No big deal."

That didn't sit right with Jase.

"Second time someone bought you flowers?" he asked, digging deeper.

She rolled her eyes. "Pretty sure the next guy who bought me flowers was probably a boyfriend who did something wrong and wanted to make up for it. It's not a big deal why I don't like flowers. I just don't care for them." She rolled her eyes at nothing in particular. "Don't get me wrong, I like them when they're in the ground or on a bush. I just don't think murdering them for my personal enjoyment makes much sense."

Whiskey. Tango. Foxtrot. Hold up. "No one murders the flowers."

She pinched her lips to the side. "They're alive one

minute. Hacked off their life source. Dead and on your dining room table the next. Seems like murder to me."

He crossed his arms. She'd fall in love with flowers. He'd see to it.

The phone in her purse chimed. She checked it.

He couldn't rip his gaze from her. There was an invisible weight there, holding it in place.

"Damn," she said. "Jase-and-Heather-Land is about to be cut short. Candy says your grandmother is still convinced she's employed by me. She's now taken over the kitchen."

Shit.

"We should go fix that." Jase pushed off from his stool. Yes, his grandmother and her fuck-with-you games.

Heather didn't look up from the text she tapped out. She tucked her phone back in her purse, stood, and stumbled a little.

Jase caught her around the waist.

She gripped his shoulders for balance and they stayed like that. Her eyes locked with his, her lips parting, her eyelids falling heavy. Lavender and vanilla countered the smell of the cowboy bar, inflaming his senses, forcing his body to demand more. He didn't ache for a woman. Hadn't ached for a woman in forever. But, in that moment, his desire for *this* woman bordered on crazy.

"I want to kiss you," he said.

She closed the gap between them, her lips brushing his. He wanted more, but it was Heather who took things deeper, leaning into him, opening her mouth.

God, she tasted good. He couldn't even describe it. Just Heather.

She broke the kiss for an instant, a look of shock written on her features. "Screw it," she said and then went back in for more.

He did not object.

Heaven. Kissing Heather was like heaven. Her mouth met his with hungry demand.

His hips pressed to her, the evidence of his arousal apparent against the zipper of his jeans. She moaned, her neck arching to the side. He moved his mouth to the indentation at the edge of her throat, using his tongue and teeth and lips to show her all the things he'd rather do in private.

Private.

Shit. They were in a bar.

He dropped his hands from her waist and pulled back. He clocked the moment Heather came back to her senses. She pursed her lips and pressed the back of her hand against her mouth.

"We should go," she said with efficiency, turning toward the exit.

Jase was not a guy to dissect every kiss, every tumble in the sheets. His philosophy was to just let things be what they were going to be. Enjoy the moment, then move to the next. Watching Heather as she hustled away from him? That philosophy seemed like the stupidest shit he'd ever thought.

"Heather?" he asked her back.

That kiss was not a moment he wanted to move away from.

She didn't even turn around, just grabbed her bouquet and gave a wave with her hand. "Nope. Not doing this."

The fact was, they had.

And he didn't have any idea what to do about it.

Chapter Six

Heather had kissed Jase. And he'd kissed her. And she needed a huge volunteer project or something to shift her attention off him. There was only so much prom planning needed. Maybe she should look at opening a second shop, so she could burn the candle at both ends and avoid thoughts of Jase's tongue and the way he felt so good pressed against her. The way his deep voice, with just a touch of sandpaper, mesmerized her.

"What happened shouldn't have happened." She stopped just outside the door of her shop, turning to him to break the silence. She hadn't said anything since they'd left the cowboy bar. He hadn't tried again once they were outside.

They hopped on his bike and, penis cookies in her grip, he brought her back.

On the sidewalk outside her shop? He'd had the audacity to look hurt.

That wasn't fair. He couldn't look hurt. Looking hurt meant feelings, and they were not doing the feelings thing.

"I trust you are as committed to our fake breakup as I am," Heather continued. "We'll just keep moving forward, like two people who are pretending that nothing happened."

"Heather…"

Ugh. He kept saying her name.

She pushed open the door to the shop. He followed her inside. It was immensely hard to ignore whatever was going on between them when he was *right there*.

Candy met her right at the door. "Okay, hear me out. I know I've been texting you that she's still here and she won't leave, but"—she tossed her hands out wide—"I just tried her cookies and they are ahh-mazing. I think we should let her work here."

"Her cookies are pretty damn good," Jase concurred.

Heather made a low gurgling sound in the back of her throat. No. Absolutely not. Heather gave her sister her best no-way-in-hell look and hurried through the shop toward the kitchen.

Candy and Jase were right behind her. Not that she turned around to see that they followed, but she could hear Jase going on about his love for Babushka's tea cookies as they moved behind her.

Heather shoved open the swinging door to the kitchen.

And there she was. Babushka. Hairnet in place, apron tied around her neck, with what appeared to be a flour bomb detonated on the countertop in front of her.

"Good, you have arrived." With a final *thwack* to a lump of dough, Babushka brushed her hands together.

The flour particles in the air tickled Heather's lungs. What this day needed was hard alcohol and carbs. On that thought, she reached for a cookie from one of the baking sheets.

Babushka edged the tray away from Heather's grasp. "They are not ready. They must cool."

Heather rubbed the throb starting in the center of her forehead. *Chin up. Be strong.* "I really appreciate your offer to help me out here in the kitchen."

Deep breath.

"I have a plan, and it's already in place." She tracked

Babushka as the old woman shuffled around the counter to the cooling rack next to Heather and snagged a half-dollar-size cookie. "I really cannot take on another employ—"

Babushka shoved the cookie into Heather's open mouth.

"Is good, no?" The old woman's eyes shone with pride.

The powdered-sugary shortbread crumbled against Heather's tongue in the most delightful dance of nutty, buttery goodness. Dammit all. The cookie wasn't good. The thing was extraordinary.

That was *not* the point.

A bit of cookie fell from the side of Heather's lip, but it did not deter from the fact that she was the boss and this was her kitchen.

Although, the cookie was damn good. Better than her own recipe. And she was pretty committed to her ability to bake just about anything.

"I am sorry." Babushka went about working the dough in her hands. "About this morning. You are *nice* girl. I lend you my car until you have a vehicle, and I vill vork off my debt to you vith pastry. Ve vill have some fun, yes?"

There were not enough deep sighs in the world for this day.

Heather only needed to step aside and think this through. Treat Babushka like she would any other business challenge. Step back, evaluate, make the best decision for the company.

So, yes, her van had been creamed by a demented old woman. A demented old woman who'd thought she was defending the honor of her grandson. Heather could, on some really weird level, appreciate that kind of dedication. It was, in its own screwed-up way, sort of sweet.

Jase was buying her a new van and making that situation right. She didn't even have to pay a deductible.

And she could use Babushka's Buick. That would come in handy.

Babushka had apologized and made exceptional cookies.

Perhaps the time had come to start embracing all that was Babushka. This was a woman offering to bake for free. Heather had been thinking she needed to bring on another baker, anyway. This would essentially lower overhead. And boy, the woman could *bake*.

"What if we start this as a temporary experiment and see how it goes?" Candy suggested. "I'll supervise. You don't have to do anything."

Babushka nodded as though she had no doubt this was the decision that would be reached. "I vill come in early every morning."

"Oh, we don't do that," Candy replied. "We aren't that kind of bakery. We just do cookies, so we have a solid eight a.m. start."

"Vell, that vorks even better." Babushka nodded. "I vill be here again tomorrow. Eight a.m."

"Okay," Heather heard herself say, against her better judgement.

"You sure you want to do that?" Jase sounded as unconvinced as Heather felt.

"Of course she is sure." Babushka laid her weathered, floured hands on the table and nodded toward Heather. "I vill vork in your kitchen until I die. Vhich vill not be long. I vill leave you my recipes vhen I am gone."

"She's gonna leave the recipes." Candy squeezed Heather's arm. "Isn't that the best?"

The best? Heather might not take it quite that far.

"This is just a trial. We'll see how it goes. It's temporary," Heather confirmed.

And she almost believed it.

Chapter Seven

Jase was bringing Heather flowers. A bouquet of two dozen carrousel roses, to be exact. These were now his so-you-hate-flowers-I'm-going-to-make-you-love-them flowers. Officially, he was just calling them "Heather's flower" from here on out.

He had a system—a flower for every occasion. From sorry-your-ex-got-married-today to I'd-like-in-your-pants-please. For Heather? He was going all in. Sometimes a florist just knew the right type of flower for a person.

While he waited in the shop, he shifted from foot to foot like a teenage boy. This time he didn't barge into her kitchen. Today he waited out front for her cashier to go get her. Like a good little Jase.

Babushka pushed through the kitchen doors and headed for his bouquet. "Jason, you brought me flowers. You are good boy." She leaned a cheek up so he could kiss it.

Shit, he couldn't exactly give Heather flowers in front of his grandmother. The grandmother he had convinced of the breakup that never was.

Babushka smiled a wry smile and took the bouquet.

Heather emerged from the kitchen in her apron, a smudge of flour against her cheek. "Hey, Jase. Your grandmother was just teaching me to make kolaches. They're freaking awesome."

He focused on the way she said his name. He liked it. She could say his name all day long. Scream it, even. He didn't mind at all.

"He brought you flowers. He is good boy." Babushka handed them to Heather.

Well, he had, but Heather didn't need to know that. Not with his grandmother standing right there.

With an abundance of reluctance, Heather took the bouquet. "I thought we had an understanding about my feelings toward floristry."

"See, he brings you flowers." Babushka fussed with a few of the blooms on the bouquet. "Is not big deal. You make such fuss about seeing him."

"You made a fuss about seeing me?" Jase didn't have to fake his surprise.

"Absolutely, no—" Heather started.

"She says, 'I refuse to hear him out.' I say, 'You be kind to your neighbors.' You two make up and give me grandbabies before I move back in with your *dedushka*."

"I see you and Babushka are getting along great." He swung an arm around his grandmother.

"Hey, I have some deliveries. Ethan hasn't been by. Can you send him over?" Heather asked.

"He is late, this Ethan," Babushka said on a huff. "Ve have deliveries to be made."

Because of her vengeance. She forgot to add that part. Deliveries to be made, because of her vigilante justice gone wrong.

That's what Jase thought. What he said was: "I'll send him over."

"Good. And I have doctor's appointment this morning. I need transportation. Who vill drive me?" She brushed his arm off and pointed between the two of them.

"That's a negative for me. I've got a full afternoon. But I can call Anna." He was already pulling his phone from his back pocket.

Babushka waved him away. "She is busy today. I asked her."

"Then I'll call Mom."

"She is at luncheon this afternoon."

"Dad?" Jase scowled at his phone in an apparent attempt to dream up more family member names.

"Golfing."

"Zach?" Jase asked.

"He spends time with his girlfriend. I not bother him. They will be married, and I will have grandbabies."

Jase leaned his hands on the countertop, a scowl plastered on his face. "I'll ask Ethan."

"I can do it," Heather volunteered. "It's her car and I've got to go pick up the prom tickets, anyway. They're done at the printer."

"You want to take her to the doctor?" Jase confirmed. Heather clearly didn't know what she was stepping in.

"I don't mind. I can drop her off and pick her up."

"Well, then, thank you, Heather." He hugged his grandmother and headed for the door.

"What time is your appointment?" he heard Heather ask.

"Foot doctor is at ten, then heart doctor, then eye doctor."

Yup, stepped in it.

"Oh," Heather said in reply.

"After eye doctor, then late lunch. Best steaks in Denver. All you can eat for ten dollars."

On that, he glanced back.

His grandmother's cheeks folded into creases with her smile. "My treat."

HEATHER DRUMMED her fingers against the arm of a chair in the waiting room of Cherry Creek's most esteemed ophthalmologist.

"Ms. Reese?" One of the nurses, the one in the blue scrubs, opened the doorway leading to the back rooms. "Nadzieja had her eyes dilated, so she's having a harder time seeing than usual. She should be better by this evening."

"I'll make sure she's taken care of." Phone stuffed back in her pocket, Heather stood and gathered her purse.

"She insists she doesn't need a wheelchair." The nurse's expression turned sympathetic.

Of course. She was Babushka, master of her own independence.

"I'll help her to the car." Heather followed the woman to where Babushka sat, ankles crossed like a demure debutante instead of a feisty old woman. "They say you won't use a wheelchair."

"I am dying. I'm not dead." Babushka boosted herself to stand and grabbed on to Heather's arm. "I vill use vheelchair vhen I am dead."

"Nadzieja, you're not dying. We've been over this." The soft-spoken nurse was no match for Babushka. Even Heather could see that.

"Vat do you know?" Hand raised in goodbye, Babushka pulled Heather toward the exit. "She knows nothing."

"The cardiologist agreed with her," Heather pointed out.

"He knows nothing. Now, ve go to lunch." Babushka plowed ahead.

Heather had to do a tug-and-yank combination to keep her from toppling over an old man with a cane.

"Vatch vhere you go," Babushka admonished him. If she'd shaken her fist at the guy, Heather wouldn't have been surprised.

"Let's head back to the shop. I'll order in." Heather could keep things contained at the shop. Things meaning Babushka.

"No. It is eye doctor day. Ve go to steak. This is how it alvays is." Babushka nearly stepped into oncoming traffic.

Heather gripped her arm and pressed the walk button. "Hold tight. The crosswalk is still red."

"Cars vill stop. You go. They stop."

"Or we can wait for the light to change so we don't become one with the asphalt. Then we can get in your car, head back to the shop, and I'll order you lunch."

"Steaks." The one word said it all. Babushka was going to get her piece of a cow.

"Yum," Heather replied. Thumb shoved on the crosswalk button again, Heather contemplated becoming a vegetarian.

"WE CANNOT GO IN HERE." Heather slumped farther down into the beige leather seat of Babushka's Buick.

"Vhy not?" The black-sunglass-wearing old woman peered at the building.

The building with the sign that read *Pistol Polly's* and showcased a vintage-style pinup woman riding a pony in short-shorts and pigtails. The building everyone in Denver knew housed a strip joint—as in poles, VIP back rooms, and topless waitresses. The building Heather was absolutely not taking Babushka into.

"It's a gentlemen's club." Heather slid a side-eye to her… whatever the heck Babushka had become to her. Baker. Grandmother figure.

"Vomen are velcome, too. This is Morty's place. Best steak in Denver. I alvays come after eye doctor."

After she couldn't see anymore.

"Always?" Heather confirmed.

"Oh yes, this vas my driver's favorite."

Well, Heather just bet. Her old driver appeared deserving of his firing.

"Your old driver? He brought you here?" Heather confirmed.

"Yes." Babushka *harrumphed*. "He knows good steak. Bad driver. Alvays goes so fast, but good vith picking restaurants."

That point was debatable.

"He brought you here because you had your eyes dilated and you couldn't see that… *It. Is. A. Gentlemen's. Club.*" Not that there was anything wrong with that. A girl had to make a living. But Jase would likely murder Heather in her sleep if she took his presently blind grandmother to lunch at a place that also served up half-price lap dances between three and five p.m.

"This is no true. He also brings me to Le Peep for breakfast." With that, Babushka pushed open the car door and scooted outside, her orthotic-covered feet shuffling across the parking lot.

Heather didn't trust her in a parking lot. The woman could barely make it from the ophthalmologist's office to the car without getting swiped by a Chevy. Heather rushed after her.

"You vill love steaks here," Babushka assured with all the confidence of a mostly blind elderly woman entering a strip club.

It better be the best damn steak of her life, because Heather was pretty certain she'd have a front-row seat at her own funeral soon enough. Throat thick, she heaved open the metal door to follow Babushka straight past the vacant hostess station, through a darkened waiting area with leather-covered walls, and straight into the lion's den. Low blue and pink lighting, fog-covered stage, polished poles where two women in bedazzled G-strings gyrated their hips to Lady Gaga for a couple of suits in the front row.

"Where are we going?" Heather stumbled along with Babushka.

She pointed toward the bar area, away from the stage. "My table is in back."

Of course Babushka had her own table at the strip club. Because *that* made total sense.

"Nadzieja." An old man with a comb-over and a wide smile ambled toward them. "I was hoping you would come today." He folded Babushka in a hug that seemed to go on a few seconds too long.

"Morty, it's good to see you again." Babushka leaned in for a cheek kiss as Morty held on a few seconds more. "This is Heather. She is Jase's fiancée."

Hell-to-the-no.

"Hello, I'm Heather." She shook Morty's warm hand. "Definitely *not* Jase's fiancée."

Babushka climbed onto the barstool and gestured for Heather to join her. The thickness in Heather's throat turned to ash. She glanced to the stage, to Babushka, finally settling on the varnish of the table. Perhaps she could step outside. Call Jase and explain what had happened. That would absolve her of any guilt.

"They have lover's quarrel." Babushka held her large purse tight against her lap, leveraging it between her knees and the table. "Vill make up soon enough."

"Ah...my Nadzieja. Always taking care of her grandchildren." Morty's cheeky grin spread even wider. "When will you let me take you out and show you a good time?"

Was he...? Yes, he was hitting on the old battle-ax.

Babushka waved him aside. "I am here for lunch, not romance."

"Ah, but my sweet, we have time for both." He had the glimmer in his expression of a fox about to devour his victim. "Let me take you to my office. I'll show you the time of your life."

One, ew. And, two, now there was no way Heather could

leave. He'd have Babushka in a VIP room before Heather could count to ten.

Babushka ignored his advances. "I vill have the steak. Medium. Vith vodka. The good kind."

"She always turns me down. Someday I will get through." Morty winked at Heather. "For you, my dear?"

Heather's phone buzzed in her purse. She ignored it. The sooner they ordered their steaks, the quicker they could be out the door. "I'll have the same. But water. Please."

"Coming right up." Morty strode away, whistling along to Lady Gaga.

"You see? This is how you do it." Babushka sat taller.

"Do what?" Heather asked.

"Get a man."

Heather scratched at her ear, she couldn't have heard that right. "Sorry?"

"You play the hard to have."

"Hard to get?"

"Yes. This is how you do it. I have decided I am a tiger." The smack of Babushka's napkin against the table was an exclamation point to her announcement.

What on earth was the woman jabbering about now? "A what?"

"A tiger. You know, a cheetah. A leopard."

Maybe the stuff they used to dilate her eyes had seeped into her brain. "I'm not following."

"Older woman goes after younger man," Babushka explained.

"A cougar?" Heather asked.

"Yes. That is the one. I am cougar. Morty, he is ten years younger."

A waitress with two star-shaped pasties covering her nipples dropped their drinks in front of them. Babushka downed her vodka and slapped the empty glass on the table. Heather was seriously reconsidering her choice to have water.

"If you're so sure you're dying, why start a relationship? Doesn't that seem like a bad idea?"

"Oh, ve vill have an entrance romance." Babushka nodded briskly.

A what? No, Heather didn't want to know. But still… "Entrance?"

"You know. He sees other vomen. Ve don't get too close. Just physical." Babushka waggled her bushy eyebrows and…ew.

"An open relationship?"

"See, you know these things."

Heather swirled the ice in her red plastic tumbler. "You're really going to go after this guy?"

"No. He comes for me. This is how it is. Next time he asks, I vill say yes. This is vat you do vith Jason. You say no, make him work for it, but vhen time comes, you say yes."

Not flipping likely.

"Heather Reese," a male voice called.

"Yes?" She glanced up.

Shit. Jase.

Not happy-go-lucky, dancing Jase. Not the Jase who would be propositioning her for a tumble in a VIP room. Not with the way the blood vessel pulsed in his neck and the tips of his ears tinged red.

No, this was furious Jase.

Oh. Hell.

Chapter Eight

"Dial it back." Eli, Jase's buddy, tightened his hand on Jase's shoulder in the dusky strip club.

Eli could dial it back when it was *his* grandmother lounging at Pistol Polly's. With Heather Reese. In a fog-filled room with a woman in a G-string dancing on a stage.

He closed his eyes and did a few deep breaths. Counted to twenty. The smoke. The lights. The flashes. Memories of another place hit him hard.

But this wasn't there. This was here.

The blood that'd been thrashing in his vessels kicked even stronger. He might die of an aneurysm right there next to a poster of Kitty Wyn—the weekend headliner.

The root of each hair on his head throbbed in time with his heartbeat.

His friend forced him to stop plowing forward through the neon haze of the club. "Don't do something stupid."

Like take-his-grandmother-to-a-strip-joint stupid? That kind of stupid?

"Breathe, man," Eli said in a low voice.

Jase's vision tunneled, but he took a breath.

Things Jase could do? Take a breath. Defuse an underwater bomb. Fast-rope out of a MH-60S Seahawk. Arrange tulips into a goddamned masterpiece.

Things Jase could not do? Control any aspect of his life, currently.

"Babushka?" he asked as calm as he could.

"Jason! You have come to join us for lunch." Babushka slipped from her stool and wrapped him in a hug.

Heather looked like one of the guys up front getting caught by his wife while he stuffed dollar bills into a purple G-string. Her lips round, her eyes mirrored his own shock when he'd stopped in to chat with his grandmother and she wasn't at the cookie shop. So he checked Babushka's location on her cell tracker and found it to be at Pistol Polly's. Of course he hadn't *believed* it could be right, but he had to check it out. Make sure her phone hadn't been swiped. He hadn't expected to actually find her here.

Eli had come along…well, originally because they were stopping at Pistol Polly's to figure out what was wrong with Babushka's phone tracking app that said she was there. Now, apparently, he was trying to save Jase from strangling Heather.

"C'mon, we're going home." Jase wrapped a protective arm around his grandmother and guided her toward the door.

"Vat? No. Ve have steaks." She pushed him away. Hard. "All you can eat for ten dollars on Tuesday."

His arm held firmer to get her to the exit. To sanity. "You shouldn't be in here."

"Vat? It is Tuesday. I got my eyes checked. Ve have steaks." The way she said it made it sound totally logical. And yet…nope.

"She had her eyes dilated at the ophthalmologist," the traitor on the barstool chimed in. "She can't see anything."

That made this better?

"You've got to be fucking kidding me." He dropped his

arm from around his grandmother and stepped toward the table.

On the barstool, Heather was nearly eye to eye with him. Nearly. She met his stare and didn't blink.

Of course she didn't. She was a traitor.

"I trusted you to take care of her, not bring her here." He gestured to the bared breasts on the stage to make his point.

"Okay, whoa. First of all, *you* trusted me?" She stood, planted her feet, and stared up at him. "You were too busy today. She needed help. I offered to help *her*, not you."

"This is crazy. She's not working for you anymore." And he needed a goddamned beer. At home. Once he got his grandmother out of there.

"You think this was my idea?" Heather had the nerve to laugh at him. "Try again. She dragged *me* here. The driver *your family* hired for her brought her here when she couldn't see. She doesn't *know* any better. And we'll leave *after* we've had our steaks because it's important to her. I had to suck it up and deal with the atmosphere. You can, too."

He ran a palm over his hair. God, this woman infuriated him. "It's important for my *grandmother* to have steak so close to naked women?"

"They're not naked."

"What would you call it, then?"

"They're just not totally dressed."

"You see? They fight so they can make up," Babushka side-whispered to Eli. She smiled like a cat that robbed the dairy section of the Kwik E Mart.

Eli with the stupid, smug-ass grin sketched on his conspirator's face helped Babushka back on her barstool and pulled one up beside her. Then the bastard called over the waitress with the stars glued on her chest.

It took everything Jase had in him not to cover his grandmother's eyes.

"We aren't staying." He would hold his ground like the

goddamned soldier he was trained to be. He didn't give up when the desert sandblasted his face and the sun burned off the top layer of his skin. He sure as hell wouldn't give up now.

"Ve are eating a nice lunch, Jason. Now, apologize to Heather and sit." Babushka gestured to the chair across from her—the one with the view of the stage.

Now, normally, he could appreciate a good bump and grind. But for the love of all fucks, this was the most uncomfortable situation he'd been in since Afghanistan.

"*Hhhhrhmm.*" Heather cleared her throat and continued to stare at him.

"I think she's waiting for that apology." Eli took a sip of beer out of a Fat Tire bottle. The jack-wagon hadn't even ordered him one.

No way was Jase apologizing. He wasn't wrong.

He turned to his grandmother and got close enough so he knew she would hear. "It's inappropriate that you're here."

His grandmother patently ignored him.

"For the record, Mr. Barge in Here and Pretend You're a Hero, your grandmother can't see *anything* right now. So, she's not going to be tarnished by star-shaped pasties or a"— Heather glanced to the stage—"bedazzled lavender G-string."

He looked down at the finger she'd pressed between his pecs. She blushed and dropped her hand.

She was right, though. He wasn't a hero. Never had been. All the medals in the world and all the reassurance couldn't change the fact that he'd never been, and never would be, a hero. He swallowed against that regret.

"How long you think before they have kids?" Eli casually asked Babushka.

Babushka scooted toward Eli. "Vedding vill be a vhile. Jason must apologize for yelling before they go on."

Heather's cheeks blotched a pinker pink. If Jase wasn't

pissed as all hell at her right then, he'd probably find it cute. As it was…fine, it was still cute.

"You think I'm going to do *anything* with this…this…jerk?" Heather asked. Now her cheeks blazed red.

"Jerk?" Jase shoved his hands on his hips. "That's the best you can come up with?"

"If the name fits." She climbed up on her chair and adjusted her sleeves. "Now. Where's my damn steak?"

JASE TOOK out all of his pent-up Heather frustration on the patch of drywall he drilled into the studs. He'd bought the entire building that housed his flower shop and his apartment. Unfortunately, between all the remodel expenses and ordering Heather's new van, his savings were dwindling. He'd had to take over part of the construction himself, wrangling Brek, Dean, and Eli into helping so they'd stay on schedule and get everyone moved in on time.

The fact Jase was remodeling the entirety of the building housing his flower shop was practically Brek's fault. His wife's, anyway. She'd convinced Jase to invest in real estate, buy up the building, and convert it into a wedding mecca. Eli's catering kitchen would move in next to the flower shop, a bridal salon would go in on the corner, and Brek's sister's event planning office would be tucked in between. So far, all the brilliant plan had done was give him a backache from hanging drywall and a drained bank account from covering all the unexpected expenses.

"And that's the story of how we had kick-ass steaks in a strip club with Jase's grandmother and his sort-of ex-girl-friend," Eli said.

He could take his backstabbing grin and shove it.

Brek, who he would currently refer to as his *ex*-best friend because he found the whole situation hilarious, leaned against the finished wall Jase had just screwed in place.

"I still don't understand exactly why you told your family you and Heather broke up," Brek said.

"I think I can explain it," Eli paused, studying the drill in his hand. "Since he's been so pouty after his wife left, his family has been on his ass to meet someone. But he decided instead of just telling them he didn't want to date, he would fib and tell Babushka that Heather broke his heart—which she didn't. Babushka took out Heather's van in retribution. Then Jase convinced Heather to actually tell his family they broke up—when they hadn't—and now Babushka's working for Heather." He inhaled a long breath. "Then they went to the strip club."

That about summed it up.

"And he agreed to buy Heather a new van, which now means we all have to hang fucking drywall," Eli continued.

Yes, that summed it up. Jase had really screwed himself.

"You forgot to add that Babushka's not allowed to play with Heather anymore." Jase drilled the current screw about two seconds too long until it made a grinding sound. "Are you assholes gonna stand around or are you here to work?"

"You know what your problem is?" Brek kicked off from the wall and held up a new sheet of drywall.

"Bet you're gonna tell me." Jase wiped the line of sweat that'd dripped in his eyes.

Eli tagged the extra drill. "I bet I know what it is."

The sheetrock slipped, and the turning screw burned against the pad of Jase's thumb. "Shit."

"You have a case of the Heathers," Brek said.

Jase's stomach turned over on itself. He did not have a case of the anyones.

"That's what I was going to say, too." Their buddy Dean piped in.

Eli went to work on the other side of the panel. "You

should've seen them. He was ten seconds away from tearing off her clothes so he could practice his caveman routine right there."

He was not. Although, the thought of Heather without clothes didn't piss him off as much as it should. Fine, it didn't piss him off at all. It turned him all kinds of on.

"Why'd you two fake break up, anyway?" Eli asked.

The question was innocent, but it ticked Jase right the hell off. His breaths came uneven. The setup was fake, but the whole thing felt like a real breakup. "Sometimes shit doesn't work out."

And sometimes the chick shuts you down before you have the opportunity to explore each other.

Brek released his grip on the now attached drywall and took a swig from a plastic water bottle. "She didn't really have a choice with Babushka."

Still, she'd indulged his grandmother in an afternoon that nearly made him stroke out.

"You can't really blame her for taking Babushka for steaks." The last screw in place, Eli stepped back from the wall. "I mean, have you met your grandmother? If she wants steaks at Pistol Polly's, she'll find a way to make that happen."

"It won't happen again. I forbid it. She's coming back to work at the flower shop. She's not allowed to work for Heather anymore." And that would be the end of that.

Brek chuckled. "You let us know how that ultimatum works out."

"I'm serious." Jase kept his eyes fixed on the thin layer of dust on the concrete floor, unwilling to glance up.

"Again, have you met your grandmother? Remember that time she convinced us to take the Lucas twins to homecoming?" Eli said.

That'd been one of the worst nights of their lives. It'd involved the Golden Corral salad bar and pudding. Jase shivered and refused to think about it.

Eli had that look on his face, the one he always got right before he said something that would make things worse. "You should probably apologize to Heather for being such a jerk at lunch."

The pulse in his throat throbbed. "I wasn't a jerk."

"Eh." Eli shrugged. "You kinda were."

Jase glanced to Dean. "You think I was wrong?"

He held his hand up flat and made a yeah-kinda wobble.

Well, damn. Maybe he'd overreacted with Heather. Maybe he should've given her some benefit of the doubt when it came to the extent of his grandmother's manipulation.

"You should make up so you can get on to the fun stuff," Dean suggested.

"I bet Heather's great at the fun stuff." Eli crossed his arms. "But, you know, if you're not interested, I might be."

There weren't enough expletives in the world right then. "Don't fucking think about it."

"I suggest roses." Eli tossed a drill in the air so it spun, then caught it.

Roses.

Yeah, he'd already done that.

"Work on that apology, too." Brek had the nerve to flash a grin.

Jase opened his mouth to argue, but damn, he did owe her an apology. Even if it choked him.

JASE KNOCKED on the thick wooden door of Heather's apartment and waited.

Nothing.

His palms got sweatier with each moment that passed. Apologizing sucked.

He shifted the box of chocolate in his grip and knocked again. "Heather?"

Now, he was definitely more of a rose delivery man, but when it came to apologies, he figured he owed the girl what she wanted.

More nothing. He glanced around the little foyer with the rickety table. She'd set the roses he—well, Babushka—had given her on that table. He could leave the chocolates and write a note. If he'd brought paper. Which he hadn't.

The door swung open and Heather glared at him. "What?"

"Heather. Hey."

She blushed. "If you're here to yell at me again, you should probably go."

"Who is that?" Dean's wife Claire peeked from behind her. "Oh. Hi, Jase. You're interrupting girls' night. Heather was just about to convince us all to buy tickets to her senior citizens prom."

"You should go." Heather started to close the door. She pulled it open quickly. "Hand over the chocolate first."

Still pissed. Good to know.

"Oh, he brought chocolates. The plot thickens," Claire said with a dose of drama.

Jase shoved the chocolate toward Heather, sliding the box into her palm, his fingertips grazing hers for the slightest second. God, she felt good. "Why am I constantly feeling the need to apologize to you?" he asked, totally genuine.

"Do you need a list?" She ripped open the box of chocolates and shoved one into her mouth. "Just 'cause I'm eating this doesn't mean I'm not pissed. It's just bad luck to waste chocolate."

"Oh, it's gourmet. Hand it over." Claire snatched the box and scooted back inside the apartment.

Heather crossed her arms over a silk shirt. A silk shirt that slid over her breasts and made his dick seriously question why he'd been such a…well, a *dick* earlier. The tree trunk that'd sprouted in his pants wasn't helping his ability to apologize.

"I am sorry for everything I've done over the past few days, and everything I'll do to piss you off in the future." That ought to cover it. Being married for a few years had taught him a few things.

"So, this is an all-encompassing apology?" Heather confirmed.

"Yes."

"You need more chocolate." The door slammed in his face.

He let out a long breath and knocked again.

She opened the door and raised an eyebrow in that way women always did when he fucked up.

The expression effectively killed the trouser timber pressing against his zipper.

"Babushka has her own way of doing things, that's for sure," he said.

She did the eyebrow thing again.

"Look, she doesn't always remember things. The last few years have been harder on her than she'll admit. I worry about her."

"Or maybe it's hard for you to admit that she's stronger than the rest of us." Heather's hand rested on the edge of the door, clearly ready to slam it in his face when the time was right.

He stepped forward and got a whiff of her—a mix of lavender and Heather. No woman had ever smelled so good. Never made him want to nuzzle her neck and stay there all night. Never made him lose his mind like he was doing now.

"Is that all?" Heather asked.

He shook away the lingering effects of being around her. "What?"

"You said that already. Apology accepted. You're absolved." She did a little hand wave that was adorable. "For what it's worth, I'm sorry, too. I should've tried harder to keep Babushka out of there. I should've kept driving when I saw where we were going."

"She would've convinced you to turn around." Now that his mind was clear, he was sure of it.

"You're probably right," Heather conceded.

"You gonna invite me in for chocolate?" He jerked his chin toward her apartment. "I can do girls' night with the best of them."

She let out a heavy sigh. "Do I have a choice?"

"There's always a choice."

"Are you going to buy a ticket to prom?"

Now it was his turn to heavy sigh. "Absolutely."

She paused, thinking a little too hard. "Claire, Velma, Jase wants to come in," she hollered behind her.

"Does he have more chocolate?" Velma called back.

Heather gave him a questioning look.

"Nope, but I have a Visa and the desire for a Beau Jo's pizza delivery," he replied.

"No more chocolate. No more funsies," Claire shouted. "And we can't talk about him when he's here. So, move along, Mr. Florist."

"I guess not." Heather's forehead crinkled.

"Listen, I'd really like to help you out with the prom thing. I know you've been wanting help, and I've been thinking. I have some ideas." His sneakers squeaked against the polished floor when he stepped toward her.

She gave him a look that was not a vote of confidence. Vulnerability passed over her expression. Fleeting, but it was there.

"Why?" she finally asked.

"Why what?"

"Why do you want to help me? You made it clear today you don't even like me."

Oh, he liked her. That was the problem. "You're doing a good thing. I can appreciate that."

Also, he'd get to spend more time with her. And for some damn reason, that's exactly what he wanted.

They stood there studying each other. He wanted to wrap her up and hold her tight.

Also, he'd like to discuss getting in her pants. But he'd save that for later. "What're you doing tomorrow night? I'll bring you dinner and we'll talk strategy."

"Just strategy?" she asked.

"Totally professional." Mostly. "We'll call it an official committee meeting." Except, this time he'd be damn sure someone showed up. Namely, him.

"Then dinner would be great." She stepped back into her apartment.

"Tomorrow," he confirmed.

"Tomorrow." She nodded to her apartment. "I should get back. Thanks for the chocolate." She didn't smile, but it was close.

In any case, he caught it. "Here? Or my shop? Tomorrow."

"Here." Now she did smile.

She wanted home field advantage. He could work with that.

"Seven?" he asked.

"Seven." She nodded and made a move to go inside but stopped and caught his gaze. "No steaks."

With that, the door clicked closed.

Chapter Nine
SENIOR "SENIOR" PROM COUNTDOWN:
31 DAYS

She shouldn't have told Jase to meet her at her apartment.

This was a bad idea.

"Not a date. Not a date." Heather repeated the mantra over and over while she paced her living room. She'd put on lip gloss for this not-a-date. And, fine, she'd even picked out a pair of underwear that matched her bra. That wasn't for him. Maybe she just didn't like mismatched lingerie?

"You look amazing," Candy said. "Stop fussing with your hair."

Heather hadn't even realized she was running her fingers through it. That's why she usually wore a ponytail—it was just easier.

She dropped her hand. "This is just a committee meeting."

That's what she'd told herself the entire time she was dressing, blow-drying, curling, and lipsticking.

"Uh-huh." Candy gave her a look that said she didn't buy it.

"What does that mean?"

Candy sighed. "It means you're wearing your sexy jeans,

and your hair is down, and that tells me this is not just a committee meeting."

Candy wasn't wrong. Heather had picked out designer jeans that did amazing things for her legs, a loose tank top that exposed a peekaboo red bra strap, and her hair *was* down. None of that meant this was anything more than a totally platonic night of prom planning.

"I've got to go meet up with Mom." Candy grabbed her purse and headed for the door. "We are hitting JoAnn Fabric so I can help make her a dress for that thing she's got with Dad's office. Unless you want me to stay? I can join the decorating committee." She sang the last part.

"You already told me no, twice." Heather flicked on the television and let Pat Sajak talk about the spinning wheel to distract her from Jase, jeans, and hair.

"That was before Jase joined the fun." Candy rifled through her purse, grabbing her keys. "I'm out. I expect a call later detailing how this goes."

The knock at the door signaled the start of a totally platonic evening of brainstorming.

That's all this evening's...*event*...was.

She switched off the television she'd just turned on and swung open the door. Jase grinned his patented I'm-here-now-you-can-get-naked smile. At least that's what she called it in her head. Likely, it was his everyday charisma. In any case—

"Can I come in?" Oversized picnic basket in hand, he nodded toward her living room.

"Yes," she said, only slightly awkward. She stepped back and let him through.

"Hey, Jase." Candy pulled her cross-body bag across her chest. "I was just on my way out. Have fun." Candy blew a kiss at Heather and headed out, the door clicking softly behind her.

Jase turned and studied Heather for longer than an instant. He gave her a solid once-over that she felt right down to the marrow in her bones. She shivered, and her nipples pebbled. *Only the air conditioning. Nothing more.* "I can honestly say, *that* has never happened to me with a member of my family."

"What's never happened?" Heather asked.

He glanced to where Candy had closed the door. "They've never willingly left. Usually they have to be shoe-horned out the door."

That was not her family. They were there when she needed them, sure, but they also had a solid grasp on personal space. "Yeah? No. My family isn't clingy."

"You mean your grandmother doesn't try to set you up with random nurses from her eye doctor's office? Your parents don't insist you check in every few days, and your brothers and sister don't make it a point to quiz your potential dates about dietary fiber and overall dental hygiene?" he asked, his tone totally serious.

He had to be exaggerating.

"Come on, your siblings haven't done that." She held out her hand for the basket.

"I'd call them so they can confirm it for you, but then they'd know where I am. Then they'd know how often you brush, floss, and eat salads. It's better for everyone if they can't find me." He passed the basket over to her still extended hand. "No comments on the basket. Not my idea."

Cumin and chili powder drifted from the blue cloth covering the top. Her taste buds did a happy dance at the scent. "What'd you bring?"

"Tacos," he said, deadpan.

Tacos. Like their imaginary first date. Her heart gave an extra beat at the memory.

"You didn't think I'd forget?" Oh, the way his voice went husky. It did funny things to her stomach, making her question her resolve that this was not a date.

What could she say to that? It was…sweet. Sweet in a non-date kind of way.

"There's a pitcher of margaritas in there, too." He pulled the covering off the basket and snatched the pitcher with the screw-top lid and the plastic margarita glasses, shaking, then pouring the tequila-spiked nectar.

Heather laid out the spread of a make-your-own taco bar. It'd been packaged in plastic containers with options for chicken, seasoned ground beef, four kinds of cheeses, and three kinds of salsa.

"You did all this?" she asked.

"Eli made it." Jase shook his head. "He's a master in the kitchen. Went a little crazy with the whole picnic thing, though. I told him a box would've been fine. That's what happens when a guy spends too much time in the kitchen and not enough in the outside world. He sticks his tacos in a basket." Jase handed a clear plastic plate to her and began to load up his own.

"This is really nice. Thank you." She meant it.

"Eh." He shrugged.

Just dinner. Not-a-date. Except "just dinner" didn't feel like *just dinner*.

"I figure it's kind of like our first date, so it should be special." His gaze caught hers, the flecks of bronze in his eyes branding the words in her mind.

"This isn't a date," Heather replied firm. Firm-ish. "This is just an opportunity for us to work together to make this prom perfect, while drinking tequila-infused beverages. I figured I'd put you on the decorating subcommittee."

The look on his face said he wasn't super thrilled about that idea. "Who else is on this subcommittee?"

"Right now?" she asked. "Just you."

He nodded. "Figured. How many people are on the other committees?"

She sighed. "That'd be me. I tried to recruit help, but

everyone bailed. It's fine, though, I mean, I don't mind doing it all. Most of it is done already—posters, invitations, all that. What's left is decorating and food. I figured punch and cookies for the food and…you can help with the decorations."

Plate in hand, it didn't slip past her that he moved to each point of entry—front door, windows—before he sauntered to the print of the red ballet slippers on a bright-pink background that hung over the fireplace. Heather had fallen in love with the print at an art show.

"I was thinking for the official theme, we'd do 'Jungle Safari.' Don't you think that'd be fun?" She added salsa to her plate.

"That could work." He moved to the table and set his plate there. "We can do lots of greenery, vines, that kind of thing. What kind of budget are we looking at?"

"Well…" She sat across from him. "How much can you donate?"

"We have no budget, do we?"

"Nope. We are one hundred percent reliant on donations for this shindig." She took a bite of taco. Now, Heather had said she wouldn't be impressed by tacos, but she was totally into his… tacos. "So I guess the question is, how much can you donate?"

"Here's the thing. I have a wedding the weekend before. If we switch the theme to garden party, then we can just reuse those decorations. It won't cost anything."

Damn. She'd really wanted the jungle theme. And it had nothing to do with the fact that it had been the theme for the prom she should've gone to when she was in high school. It was just an awesome theme, that was all.

"I guess that would work." She did her best to tamp down the disappointment. She couldn't exactly push him to donate more, if he already had a cheaper option.

Jase stared at her for a long beat.

She started to squirm under the examination. "What?"

"I don't get it," he finally announced.

"Get what?" she asked.

He gestured to the room at large. "Why you're single."

"What's there to get?" She tucked her bare feet up under her on the chair.

"Hey, I can appreciate the need to keep your business to yourself and not put everything out there. I'm a Dvornakov. We do guilt for information better than most families." He scooted closer to her.

"I just don't see the point of a relationship, you know? It's always such a disappointment."

"Then you have been with the wrong men."

And that's where they needed to get back to the topic of the evening. A senior citizen dance party as a distraction from the intensity of their discussion.

"Brek helped me book a band, and we're using the space at the nursing home." She grabbed a brown accordion file from the side of the table, dumping the contents between them.

Heather pulled out the legal pad with her notes and scanned them. Jase reached for her wild-crazy-ideas brainstorming notebook, flipping through the pages.

"Is this your diary?" he teased.

"No." It was not. "It's…brainstorming."

She glanced up as he flipped to the first page.

"They're just the big ideas I've had for the shop and this event and the future. Most of them aren't even viable. Just brainstorming, really."

"This is good stuff." He flipped through some of the pages. "Roses for all the ladies? I can help with that."

If Jase put on a suit and handed out roses to the ladies she worked with at the retirement home, they'd be over the moon. He must've caught the way she was eyeing him.

"What?" he asked.

"I was just thinking a guy handing out roses in a tuxedo would go over so well. The ladies would go bananas."

"Not a chance," he said.

"Oh, come on, I haven't even asked you."

"Yet." He flipped the page. "Add the 'yet,' because it's coming. My money says Dean and Eli are screwed, too. Good luck getting Brek in a tux, though. He didn't even wear one at his own wedding."

"Maybe we should focus on the simple stuff first." She ran her hand over the yellow legal notebook she'd been using to compile the things that had to be done.

Jase continued flipping through her brainstorming notebook. A slip of notepaper fell from the back.

Heather stilled. Her throat clogged. Damn. She'd forgotten that slip of paper was there.

She couldn't move. Couldn't make herself reach for it.

Finding that note ran on a replay in her mind. Most decent human beings broke up with their year-long girlfriend in person. Some jerks did it via text. Logan had done it with a note on her pillow.

That note.

It fluttered to the table, brushing softly on the polished surface. That piece of paper had hit her like a thousand-pound boulder, so it seemed to be laughing at her the way it floated through the air and landed on the tabletop so gentle. She just stared at it as a bit of splattered salsa seeped into the edge.

Still Heather couldn't get her body to respond to her brain's demand to grab the damn note.

Jase picked it up and read it. Of course he did. He didn't know what it would say.

He looked at her, and his expression was as soft as the way the note had fallen through the air.

And *that* hit her like another thousand-pound boulder.

He dropped the note. "I'm sorry."

They both stared at the breakup note.

A tear slipped from the corner of her eye. The slipknot looped tighter. Her breaths stalled in her lungs.

Jase ran his hands up her bare arms. When had he gotten so close? The motion was a balm to all that had been exposed. Without so much as a thought, she leaned into the comfort of his arms. She shouldn't do this. Heather Reese didn't need comforting. She handled things on her own. But, damn, his embrace felt nice.

She dropped her head forward so her cheek rested against his shoulder. The faint scent of cut flowers, cinnamon, and laundry soap calmed her.

He laid a hand over her hair.

She chanced a glance up at him.

He looked her over from top to bottom. "That guy is an idiot who lost a chance with an amazing person."

Her blood pulsed thick at his kind words.

Was it her or had he snuggled into her at that declaration? There was definite snuggling.

He stared at her with an intensity that actually made her curious about a man again.

Except, absolutely not. Not with him. Not with anyone. She ran a hand against his chest. Touching was bad. And yet, she touched him and didn't stop.

He snatched her hand, gently kissed the underside of her wrist, and rubbed small circles on her palm with the pad of his thumb—effectively pressing the pause button on her control. Each circle echoed lower, right between her legs. Had he scooted closer, or had she? She'd been too distracted with his fingers on her hand to notice.

"I'd like to kiss you now." It was not a request. No, it was a declaration.

"Okay." She raised her face to his, meeting him in the middle. *Wrong answer,* her inner voice of reason screamed.

His phone rang.

They both ignored it.

His hand moved from her palm to her jaw, his fingertips rubbing the soft spot underneath her earlobe before diving into her hair. Their mouths met, the warmth spreading from his hand in her hair to her stomach.

He made a noise in the back of his throat. A growl. An invitation to deepen the kiss. She flicked her tongue against his and then she was gone.

The slow burn turned hungry, and his lips pressed harder, his hands tilting her head exactly where he wanted it. He controlled everything—the pressure, the fire. And she let him. The relief of letting go of the control she'd been holding so tightly washed over her. She was simply along for the ride.

Jase closed the distance between them, running his hands over her shoulders and down her sides, leaning forward to rest them on her hips. He inhaled the scent of her and buried his nose in her hair. "What do you say, let's have some fun together?"

She melted against him. Her fingers crept up under his T-shirt to trace the ridges of his abs. Blood pooled in her core, and he caught her mouth with his.

"I think I've forgotten how to have fun," she said against his lips.

"Then I'll show you." His mouth pressed against hers, showing her just what a good teacher he could be.

He pulled away and lifted her chin so she had to look at him. "We're about to have a hell of a good time."

"I can be fun," she said. She used to be hella fun.

"Damn straight you can." He kneeled before her chair and held her thighs around his hips. His hands found the hem of her shirt and moved up under it to her bra. "Lace is my favorite."

Hers, too, right then.

He pulled down the cup on the right side, his palm

covering her nipple. She moaned. He worked her neck over with his mouth while he toyed with her breast.

She pulled him tighter with her thighs. "Should we go to the bed?"

He glanced to her bedroom door across the room. "Too far," he replied. "Here's good."

"The sofa?" Her voice was breathy.

"Negative," he replied.

"Jase?"

"Hmm?"

She stopped kissing him. "I don't think this location is going to work."

"Then you need to have more faith in me." He went back to business, and, damn, maybe he did know what he was doing.

She buried her face in his neck.

His phone rang again.

"You should get that." She tucked a stray piece of hair behind her ear.

"They'll call back," he said as his phone chimed with about a dozen messages all in a row.

She raised her eyebrows at him.

"Someone better be dead," he mumbled, and, resigned, he snagged his phone from his pocket.

His expression went chalky. He held the screen up to her, a text from his sister: *Babushka. Emergency. Now. Not a drill.*

Chapter Ten

"You called me here because Babushka's got a boyfriend?" Jase could've shaken his sister. Brother. Mother. Father.

He'd had sex in a lot of places, but he'd never done it on a kitchen chair before. It was official, he'd just been cock-blocked by his grandmother.

Didn't they know he had a life? Of course they didn't. This was how his family worked—they had to have a meeting of the minds over everyone else's business. He'd been the subject of plenty of these powwows. They'd wanted him to take his cousin Amanda to the prom in high school, and they had a family meeting to discuss it. They hadn't been thrilled when he enlisted, and they had a meeting to tell him so. The meeting after he told them he'd decided to be an EOD tech had been…explosive, to say the least. And after his divorce, they made it a point to have semiannual meetings to check in on his dating life.

Hell, he practically got hives every time he set foot in his mother's special sitting room. They only utilized the space for important guests and family meetings—their mother deemed the furniture too nice for everyday use. Especially when it came to her children who were "hellions on fine leather."

Though, apparently, fancy furniture was the perfect back-drop for dissecting everyone else's personal shit.

His brother Zach sat on the couch across from Babushka, arms dangling over his knees. "She's got a boyfriend and she gave him half a million dollars."

Every muscle in Jase's body tensed. "Say again?"

"You heard me." Zach shifted and sprawled across the sofa earning a stern look from their mother.

She never talked much at these meetings. Oh, she called them, but then she'd sit back and let everyone else hash out details. Mama was the kind of woman who bottled her feelings up and then let them explode all over an unsuspecting child later.

"Babushka, tell me you didn't do this." Jase sat next to his grandmother on the love seat.

She didn't respond.

She had dumped the contents of her purse on the coffee table and did her best to ignore everyone while she sorted her things into piles. This wasn't his first rodeo.

"I know you're listening, the jig is up," he whispered close to her ear.

"It vas loan," she huffed.

"Mamochka, you cannot hand out money this way." His father was in his let's-try-to-reason-this mode. That wouldn't last long. It never did when he wasn't getting his way. "This man, he only wants you for your bank account. He does not have feelings for you."

"Not true." Babushka continued sorting. "He vants me for things I do not discuss vith my son."

She didn't mean. No, she couldn't mean...

"Does she mean—?" Anna started to ask.

"Sex," the nearly one-hundred-year-old woman said as though it were her order at Olive Garden.

Jase's stomach flipped right over, threatening to empty on his mother's favorite Persian rug. His father paled.

Mama's cheeks burned pink and Anna snort-coughed into her hand.

Zach groaned and held a sofa pillow over his face. "Someone suffocate me."

"It vas *business* loan. Morty vill pay back. He promise me." Apparently, satisfied with her piles, Babushka scooped them back into the gigantic Louis Vuitton she hauled around.

The doorbell chimed a loud *brrrong*.

"I got it." Zach bounded off the couch, the bastard taking the escape the rest of them wished they could.

"Zat is my car." Already on her feet, Babushka slung her purse over her shoulder.

"You can't leave. We're in the middle of a family meeting." His father ran a hand over the back of his neck—a sure tell his temper was about to boil over if things didn't turn his way.

The reasonable portion of the evening was about to end. Jase had been on the receiving end of his father's temper more than once. He could see how the rest of the meeting would play out. His mother would say nothing. Anna and Zach would try to smooth things over. His father would say things he'd regret tomorrow. Jase would be the one left to figure out how to get half a million dollars back from some schmuck taking advantage of an old woman.

"I vill be staying vith friend who understand Morty is not bad man." Babushka nodded along with herself. "I vill get my bag."

"Jase, your ex-girlfriend is here," Zach announced from the hallway.

Jase turned as Heather sauntered into the room. Shit a brick. What was she doing in the middle of his family drama?

"Sorry to interrupt." Heather glanced around the room, uncertain.

She'd changed into a pair of yoga pants that fit her oh-so nice and a loose T-shirt that wasn't tight enough at all. Once his family shit was sorted, he'd take pleasure in removing it for her. She'd also ponytailed her hair. He'd make sure to remedy that so it fell around her shoulders.

"Heather." Jase scooted around the love seat to where she shifted on her feet. "What are you doing here?"

"Babushka texted me. She said she was ill and needed me to come by." She leaned closer so only he could hear. "After that other message you showed me, I was worried."

The last thing he needed was for Heather to see his dysfunctional family in action. By his calculations, they were only moments away from his father losing his shit all over everyone in the immediate vicinity.

Even worse, Jase didn't need the family meeting to swing in the direction of *his* personal business.

"This is the girl who broke your heart? You didn't mention she was hot. Heather, if you feel the desire to try out another Dvornakov, I'm available." Zach raised his hand.

Anna smacked him on the back of his head. "Shut up, idiot. You have a girlfriend."

Jase chose to ignore his siblings. "Babushka isn't sick. She's just lost her mind." With a hand on Heather's back, he led her out to the hallway by the door. "This is family stuff. Trust me, you don't want to be in the middle of it."

Heather's expression went blank. "She asked me to come. Can I at least see her? Make sure she's okay?"

Babushka rolled her suitcase toward them. "Heather, good, you are here. I vill stay vith you for a vhile."

Heather's eyes went wide, a confused expression aimed his way. She cleared her throat. Twice. "I'm—I'm sorry. I'm confused. You said you weren't feeling well?"

"I am fine. My family, not so much." Babushka waved to the sitting room. "I vill stay vith you until I am dead. It should not be long."

And…they were at the death declarations portion of the evening.

Heather cleared her throat again. Then she glanced between the two of them.

"She can't stay with you," Jase said. Enough was enough. "Babushka, stop being unreasonable and break up with your boyfriend."

"You finally agreed to go out with Morty?" Heather grinned wide. "That's fantastic."

"You know about this?" A heavy weight settled in Jase's gut, every alarm bell in his head ringing that this wasn't going to end well.

"Well, yeah. He owns…you know what? Never mind." Heather crossed her arms, stretching the T-shirt tight across her breasts.

He couldn't allow himself to be distracted by a nice rack.

"Did she also tell you she gave him five hundred thousand dollars?" Jase asked.

"Um. No." At least she had the decency to look concerned. She turned to Babushka. "Why would you do that?"

"Business investment. My business, no one else's." Babushka harrumphed and patted the suitcase she'd wheeled behind her.

"Did you at least look over his books first? Make sure he's legit?" Heather asked in total seriousness. Which was ridiculous because nothing Babushka could say would make this situation okay.

"Of course I did. I am not idiot."

"And you have a payment plan or something in writing?" Heather continued her line of questioning.

"Attorney draws up all papers."

"Then what's the problem?" Heather asked Jase.

"What's the problem?" he repeated. She couldn't be serious.

Heather stared at him, clearly not getting the *problem*.

"The problem is she's dating a man and dishing out a fortune to him."

"It sounds like the dating and the loan are totally separate. Is that right, Babushka?" Heather asked, dipping her toe straight into the idiocy of his family. She had no idea the undertow was about to drag her down.

"Yes. Of course. Sex has nothing to do vith money," Babushka confirmed.

Jase's body did that weird tensing thing again and his eye twitched.

His father chose that moment to check on things out in the hallway. "For the love of all things holy. Mamochka." His voice raised two ticks higher. "I forbid you to see this man again."

"You cannot tell me vat to do. You are son. I am mother." Babushka pressed her index finger at her chest.

"I said I forbid this nonsense." There it was, the red cheeks, his father's forbidding everything—they were at the final countdown for Mount Vesuvius to blow his top and take out the town of Pompeii.

"Forbid all you vant. I live life my vay." Babushka crossed her arms in defiance.

"This is my house. You live here? You break up with him." His father's tone rose steadily with the red in his face.

Jase could relate to how he was feeling at the moment.

"Zen I vill not live here." Babushka grabbed Heather's arm and tried to usher her toward the door. "That is settled. Ve vill go now."

"You may not go." His father's voice practically rattled the china.

Heather stood still, her face an expressionless wasteland. Welcome to the family. Pull up a chair and grab a tumbler of vodka.

"I vill go." Babushka raised her chin and tugged at Heather's arm. "Be a dear and get my bag."

Heather didn't move.

"I forbid it." His father kept the slightest tether on his anger. He'd raised his voice only slightly.

Jase was ready to sign on for another tour in the desert of Afghanistan just to get a vacation from this bullshit.

Babushka firmed her Russian backbone and stood tall. "You keep saying this thing. 'I forbid. I forbid.' It means nothing. You go forbid vat you vant and I vill do vat I vant. Everyone vill be happy."

His father cursed wildly under his breath in Russian before he turned and marched down the hallway.

"I vill vait in car," Babushka announced and yanked open the door, the wheels on her suitcase squeaking behind her.

"This. This right here is why you don't get involved in family shit." Jase turned to Heather.

"Are you mad because she has a boyfriend or because she made a business deal without asking first?" Heather asked.

"You don't get this. Of course you don't." He ran a hand over his hair. This was not how the evening was meant to go.

"What does that mean, 'of course I don't'?" She mimicked him, poorly.

"C'mon, Heather, it's not like you're in a place to discuss relationship dynamics." He scraped a hand over his face.

Her expression went slack, and her eyes flared.

"I'm sorry. That's not what I meant," he amended quickly. He meant she didn't understand *his* family's relationship dynamics. Fuck, *he* didn't understand *his* family. "Your family is all normal. My family is…well…" He tilted his head toward the room housing said family.

"No, I know what you meant." The column of her throat pulsed as she swallowed hard. "I should go. She shouldn't wait out there by herself."

"Heather, I didn't mean it like that. Really." He tried to extract his foot from his mouth.

Heather bit her lip. "Okay, but I should still…go."

"Right. Yeah." He nodded.

She hurried out the door, leaving him alone in the foyer.

His mother stood alone in the doorway to the family room and just shook her head.

Jase rubbed the headache that brewed beneath his skull. *This is why you don't get involved in family shit.* He repeated it to himself over and over.

Chapter Eleven
SENIOR "SENIOR" PROM COUNTDOWN:
20 DAYS

Originally, Heather was on the fence about letting Babushka stick around at her apartment. Turned out, Babushka was a pretty freaking awesome roommate.

Case in point? The laundry Babushka had washed, folded, and put away for Heather. Yes, she had rearranged all of Heather's drawers in the process, but it'd been a week and Heather hadn't had to touch the washing machine. It would take Heather a bit to grow accustomed to having her lingerie moved to the bottom drawer of her dresser, but she'd get used to it.

Not that she took advantage of the old woman. Babushka just always got to the laundry first. And the dishes. And the woman cooked like a dream. Heather slogged up the stairs after work every afternoon and Babushka had dinner ready for her.

Heather had told her repeatedly she didn't have to do it. But who was she to ruin the woman's happiness? If making Heather piroshki and potato pancakes was her thing, Heather could be totally on board.

And she'd shared her recipes with Candy and the other

bakers. Which meant, Heather was selling the hell out of some cookies.

To top it all off, Babushka also taken over personally hawking prom tickets to anyone over the age of fifty-five who came within a five-foot radius of the cookie shop.

A knock at the door and Heather stood from the table. "I've got it."

"No. No. You sit." Babushka shuffled past Heather to the front door. "You have vork. I vill answer."

Heather had spent the morning getting donations for her prom project. She went back to her notepad of patrons, marking who had agreed to donate what.

Babushka pulled open Heather's front door. Jase stood on the other side.

"Enough is enough, I've come to bring you home," he declared to his grandmother.

Oh. Hell no.

Heather moved to head off the swiping of the *babushka.* "Jase. Hello. Come in. Have some *golubzi.*"

He sucked in air. "Shit. She's turned you."

"Mouth." Babushka patted his cheek. "Cuss in Russian, like a good boy."

"*Gav-no,*" he replied, stepping into the apartment.

Babushka's smile would've been infectious if Jase weren't there to steal her back.

"What happened in here?" He glanced around the rearranged apartment.

"Your grandmother feng shui'd me." And Heather liked it.

"Babushka, we wanted to give you time to calm down, but it's time to come home."

"No." Babushka had set to work in the kitchen, making up a plate of the *golubzi* Heather assumed was for Jase. "I am happy here."

"Come home and be passive-aggressive with us like a true Dvornakov."

"She's happy here," Heather confirmed. She crossed her arms across her chest for good measure.

"She can't like sleeping on a sofa more than her bed at home."

"It's memory foam. She's perfectly comfortable." And it folded away during the day as a bonus. Everyone was happy.

Happy. Happy. Happy.

Except Jase, who was clearly unhappy with the continued setup.

"Heather, come on. Give me my grandmother back."

"She can go back whenever she wants." Which, Heather hoped, wouldn't be soon.

Jase squeezed his eyes shut. "Heather…"

She kept hers wide open. "Jase…"

"C'mon, help me out?" he asked.

"Your father, he is ready to apologize?" Babushka scooted a cabbage roll onto Jase's plate and shuffled to the table.

Jase followed her to the table. "Of course he's not. He's Papa. He doesn't apologize."

"And I don't move home," Babushka confirmed. "Now, come eat."

Jase glowered at Heather. "I'm only eating it because I haven't had lunch."

He didn't have to justify himself to Heather. Babushka was an amazing cook.

"Now, I vill go for a valk so you two can be alone." Babushka made a hasty, and rather loud, exit, the door snapping in place behind her.

Heather pulled a chair out beside Jase. A reasonable distance, given what had happened the last time they were alone in her dining nook. "Be glad she hasn't moved in with her boyfriend."

He stilled mid-chew. Swallowed. "Is that even under discussion?"

"She's mentioned it. I've convinced her that she should stay here." Heather fiddled with the edge of the plastic tablecloth Babushka had added to the table. "She's actually a really great roommate."

"She rearrange your cabinets yet?" Jase asked with a glance to Heather's small kitchen.

"Cabinets, furniture, closets. They've all been Babushka'd."

"You'll have a plastic cover on your sofa pretty soon." He ran a tongue over his teeth.

"Then we'll be able to wipe it off easily, won't we?"

"Fuck, she's really burrowed in good." He wiped his mouth with a paper napkin, tossing it on top of his now empty plate. "You coming to Brek's Bar tonight? Being around normal people might do you good. The cover band he's got coming in is supposed to be amazing."

"I was planning on it. Your grandmother has plans this weekend, so it'll be lonely around here."

"What kind of plans?" Jase asked, ominous.

Heather shifted in her seat. "She's going up to Blackhawk with Morty."

Jase stared at her. His mouth dropped open. "For fuck's sakes."

"She's a grown woman." Heather smoothed her palms over the tablecloth.

"And she's going gambling with the boyfriend who has already squeezed half a mil from her?" Jase confirmed.

Well, when he put it like that…

"You wanna go to Blackhawk and chaperone?" Heather asked. "We can go together."

He ran a hand over his face. "Fuck."

Yeah. That.

"What time are we leaving?" he asked.

Chapter Twelve

The thing about Blackhawk was it wasn't too far outside of Denver. Only an hour from town. Yet, it seemed like a million miles away with all the casinos built up against the side of the mountain, catering to the cottontops. It was a far cry from their urban neighborhood in Cherry Creek.

Babushka and Morty had insisted on driving alone in Morty's Cadillac. Jase had reluctantly agreed, following behind them with Heather in Babushka's Buick. Heather's large overnight bag wouldn't exactly fit on his Ducati, and her new van was still weeks away from being ready.

Now they were in the casino, and Heather trailed an incredibly grouchy Jase as he weaved through the blackjack tables. The lights on the machines flashed and the buzz of the blackjack tournament lingered.

Still, the vein in Jase's neck pulsed. And he was doing the deep-breathing thing she'd learned didn't take him to his happy place.

He glanced around the casino floor once more, the little lines between his eyebrows more prominent than usual.

They'd misplaced Babushka and Morty by the slot machines when Heather had insisted on grabbing a burger from the little café by the craps tables. Misplacing his grand-mother was her fault, but darn it all, she'd been starving.

"They just wanted some space, that's all." Heather ran her hand over his arm. Her phone dinged. She glanced to it.

At theater. Long movie. Enjoy your time with Jason.

Heather held the message up to Jase. "Your grandmother went to the movies."

"Thank fuck." He let out a long breath.

"Jase." Heather gripped the sides of his shoulders. "You need to relax, or this weekend will cause you to pop an aneurism." She had an idea. "C'mon. We're hitting the penny slots. My treat."

"You're taking me gambling?" He didn't look convinced that it was a good idea, but he didn't fight her on it.

She headed toward the cashier to fill out a gambling card. "Uh-huh. But we're doing the minimum bid. Let's make my five dollars last the whole night."

"It's like five thirty," he replied, following her.

She tugged a rugged-looking five-dollar-bill from her pocket. "Right, so let's make this Abraham Lincoln last until at least seven."

"Then what?" he asked, a sly smile starting to spread across his lips.

"Then I guess we'll see where the evening takes us next." She winked at him.

Dammit. She shouldn't do that.

He followed her to the cashier window, made the transac-tion, and headed for the penny slots.

"Okay. I have a system." She rubbed her hands together.

"Do tell."

"We walk around until I find a machine I'm feeling, then we take turns pulling the lever."

He jerked his chin toward one of the side rooms. "We should've headed to the poker room."

"Maybe." She trailed her fingertips along the top of a slot

machine. "But we're here now. Next round is on you in the poker room."

He grinned then. Full smile. "Deal."

Heather moved through the rows of slots, finally settling on one with a watercolor drawing of a buffalo on the top. "This is the one."

"Let's do it." Jase stood behind her while she settled into the chair. "Ladies first."

"Why thank you." Heather plopped onto the velvet chair while Jase flashed their five-dollar gambling card on the sensor.

She clicked minimum bid and pulled the handle.

Some people preferred to push the button, but she liked losing her money the old-school way.

Three cherries and a gold bar lined up. "Ha. I won."

"Four cents. Nice job." Jase dropped his hand to her shoulder, right near the curve of her neck.

The warmth of his fingers sparked the tiny nerve endings where his palm rested. She liked it. A lot.

His thumb started to rub a small line, back and forth, back and forth, over the sensitized skin.

She pulled the handle.

"I won again." Ten whole cents this time. She made a "whoop" sound and threw her hands in the air.

Jase dropped his hand from her shoulder at her movement.

Darn, she should've rethought that one—she'd liked the warmth of his hand there. If he could make her nerve endings fire with just a neck rub, imagine what he could do with her whole body.

She pulled the handle again.

A gold bar, a buffalo, a cherry, and a black bonus bar.

Blah. Nothing.

She went again.

More of the same nothing.

"You want a turn?" She angled so she could see Jase where he stood behind her.

"I'm good. You're doing great."

"I was, until you dropped your hand," she said under her breath.

"What?"

"Put it back, it's my good luck charm." She gave a pointed glance to where his hand rested at his side.

He raised his eyebrows and placed his hand back on her shoulder in as pointed a gesture as her glance.

There, much better.

Heather pulled the lever.

Nothing.

"Maybe I'm not doing it right," Jase suggested, this time putting both hands on her shoulders and kneading the muscles in a brilliant effort to win her some pennies.

That should work for sure. She pulled the handle. One buffalo. Two buffalos. Three buffalos.

She sat taller. Jase's hands stilled their massage.

Four buffalos.

She let out a huge "whoop," and the light on top of the row started flashing. The machine made the sound of a billion pennies crashing through the chute, and the number counter of her winnings whirred along. And along. And along.

It kept going.

And going.

"Oh my God, I hit the jackpot." She jumped from her seat and tossed herself at Jase.

He stepped back on one foot, catching her in his embrace.

The machine rolled to a stop. "How much did I win?" she asked, breathless.

He checked the meter. "Forty dollars."

She did an internal fist pump. "Hot damn."

Forty dollars and a neck rub.

"I'm not even going to tell you what you could've won if you'd done the max bet." He bit at his bottom lip. "Ready to go again?"

"Hell. No." She clicked the cash-out button and removed her card. "We are done at this casino. That's the problem with gambling, you get sucked in when you should stop. I mean, I've multiplied my five dollars eight times over. Time to call it a night."

"It's still only five thirty," he said, deadpan.

She gave him a not-gonna-gamble-my-winnings look. "Well…what do you want to do?"

He stepped close to her, right up in her space, reaching for her ponytail, pulling it over her shoulder and toying with the end of it. "I have an idea."

Oh. The ponytail-pulling kind of idea could be really fun. "That would make us the worst chaperones in the history of chaperoning."

"And?" He raised an eyebrow in her direction.

Well, his grandmother was occupied for a while and they had nothing to do.

"And I think it's a fantastic idea." She grabbed his hand and beelined for the elevators to their suite.

He'd insisted they get one of the three-bedroom variety with a sitting room. That way they could keep an eye on Babushka and Morty. Heather and Babushka bunked up in one room, Jase in another, and Morty in the third.

She paused at the jewelry store just outside the bank of elevators. "Oh. Look." She took an inventory at the glass, glancing over all of the glittering diamonds. "We should go in."

Just because she was going to have fun with Jase didn't mean she wasn't going to buy herself that promise ring. And she'd neglected shopping for it for way too many days.

Still scanning the rings in the window, Jase laid a hand at her waist. "Do you want to come with me, or stay here and stare at the pretty things?" he whispered against her ear.

His breath against her earlobe caused her blood to heat and her nerves to go haywire. "Come with you. Definitely come with you."

She could always look at the pretty things later.

The elevator doors slid open to let out an elderly couple. Jase moved to catch the doors before they closed. Heather hurried inside. They were like two kids being naughty with no parents around to supervise.

Thank God the car was empty, because when the doors slid closed, Jase laid a kiss on Heather that made her rethink her ability to have sex on a kitchen chair.

Her neck tingled where his fingers grazed the overly sensitive skin under her ear while the elevator moved to the top floor. His lips kissed the top of her ear and she leaned into him.

This was a bad idea.

A horrible plan.

The fact that this was a stupid idea wasn't going to stop her.

No, Jase wasn't what she wanted. He couldn't offer the promise of forever she'd once craved. But right then, it was just about the two of them. About letting loose.

Jase's mouth met hers again, and she practically climbed his leg like Humphrey the Humping Chihuahua. Without breaking the seal of their kiss, Jase pressed a button on the panel that made the whole elevator clunk to an abrupt stop.

They practically steamed up the entire elevator cab—mouth on mouth, hands in hair, her skirt shoved up around her thighs. Jase made some kind of grunting noise that sounded like both an encouragement and a promise. Wait. That could've been her making the noise. She couldn't really tell anymore.

He skimmed his hand over the edge of her panties on her

backside. Gripped the flesh there. Rubbed deep circles on her skin. All the while he moaned along with her as she wrapped her leg around his denim-covered thigh.

This was good. They did better when they didn't actually speak. Perhaps they could base a whole relationship on not talking to each other. They could just mount each other occasionally. But, no, that wouldn't work. That's precisely what she was avoiding.

Tomorrow. She'd go back to avoiding this type of thing. Tomorrow.

"Jase?"

"Hmmm?" He was doing something to her neck with his mouth that felt absolutely amazing.

"We're in an elevator," she pointed out.

"Mm-hmm."

"I think a bed would be more comfortable."

He used his tongue and teeth, finding a particularly sensitive spot that made her entire body tingle. "You keep saying that. I promise I don't need one."

His hand slipped between her legs, and he did some kind of maneuver with his fingers that—

Yeah. Thoughts weren't coming coherently. A bed would be nice, but alternatively, the floor of the elevator looked better and better.

He pulled his hand from under her skirt, skimming his fingers over the wet fabric between her legs on the way. She moaned. It wasn't like she could help it.

He tugged her skirt back in place, wrapped an arm around her waist, and pushed the button.

The elevator began to slide up again. She glanced at him. He ran the pad of his thumb over his swollen lips and stood as though nothing had happened between them. How the hell did he pull that off?

The elevator pinged at their floor. She stepped over the threshold into the foyer and paused—what was the photo of

Jase's grandfather doing on the table outside the door of their suite?

Jase stopped. "Is that?"

"Your grandmother really makes herself at home, doesn't she?" Heather waved her magnetic key card over the lock. Jase's hands came to just under her breasts as the door slid open. His mouth pressed heavy kisses along her shoulder.

A flick of the lights and—

Holy sweet mother of Jesus.

Naked skin. So much wrinkled skin and an image of the elderly having sex she'd never be able to scrub from her brain. Or that couch. Dear God, there wasn't enough Lysol and Clorox in the world to sanitize—

She slammed the light switch off and shoved Jase back into the hallway.

No. He couldn't have seen... Except, the way his face managed to be both pale and furious red meant he had...

The pulse over his temples thumped in time with the one in his neck. He was going to blow. "Jase—"

"My grandmother." He pointed a finger toward the now closed door.

"Yes."

"Not my grandfather." His voice cracked like a teenager in the midst of puberty.

Well, no, but she was pretty sure it wouldn't have mattered who had his grandmother naked on that sofa—that was an image neither of them would ever be able to forget.

"I'm going to rearrange his ass and his head," Jase declared and grabbed the key card from Heather's fingers.

Heather's heart stopped. The way Jase's hands shook, she was pretty sure he would throttle poor Morty.

"You'll have to open the door." She held his wrist so he wouldn't make the attempt without fully thinking it through.

"What?" He looked at her like she'd grown two heads.

"To rearrange his ass and...stuff. You'll have to open the

door. If you do that, you'll see…" He'd see more of what they'd just seen together.

The red drained to nothing, leaving him colorless. "Fuck me."

Nope, that was not happening tonight. She'd need an entire bottle of vodka and perhaps a few shots of tequila to ever get in the mood again. Ever.

"Okay, we need a new plan. Let's go back to Denver. Watch that cover band and pretend this whole thing never happened." Never, ever, ever.

He glanced uncertainly to the door. "We can't just leave them here."

She got it, she really did. The desire to barge in there and break up the party battled against the intense need to never see the gray hair and all that wrinkled skin ever again. "Do you really think they're gonna miss us if we take off? We'll just leave a note."

There, all solved.

Jase ran a hand over his face. "Let's go to Brek's Bar."

Chapter Thirteen

Brek's Bar was nothing like the cowboy joint. Oh sure, there were still neon beer signs on the wall, but Brek's was actually clean and the food smelled amazing. Burgers, buffalo chicken, and spicy cumin. The band blared a cover of Dimefront's latest hit, and a smattering of couples took advantage of the dance floor.

What had her life disintegrated to that her days had come to barhopping, elevator make-out sessions, and…nope, she was not thinking about what was probably still going on up at the casino.

Jase's hand grazed her waist in a totally proprietary way that made her want to sigh and lean into him.

"Heather!" someone called from the corner.

She turned and couldn't help but smile. Claire, Velma, and Candy had commandeered a corner booth.

Jase nodded to the group. "Why don't you go play with your friends? I'm going to go get shit-faced."

"That sounds like a healthy way to deal with what's happened tonight." Heather gave him her best don't-do-anything-you'll-regret look.

"Sometimes avoidance is key to survival," he said with a grunt and made a beeline for the bar.

From behind the bar, Brek initiated some kind of elaborate handshake with him and poured a glass of whiskey. Jase snagged the bottle out of his hand and took a long pull, ignoring the filled glass in front of him.

Heather's lungs deflated. This was not healthy processing. She made a mental note to keep tabs on him tonight. Not that she expected he'd get in a fight or something equally as stupid, but her intuition flashed warning signals that he could use a wingman. Or wing-woman, in her case.

Brek caught her eye and gave her a wink, like he'd read her mind and was already on it. Her insides twisted uncomfortably. She'd love to hand her concerns over to Brek, but something told her Jase needed her.

"Don't worry about Jase. Brek will handle whatever's going on." Velma came up beside her.

"I'm not sure that'll be possible." Heather bit at her lip and sent up a silent prayer that Brek really could handle his best friend.

"You'd be surprised what those boys manage." Velma slipped her arm through Heather's and pulled her to the table. "I've never seen him on a bottle-of-whiskey night, though."

"So, you and Jase? Round two?" Claire asked, toying with the cherry in the fruity concoction she held in one hand.

Heather squirmed. What were she and Jase doing? Having fun. Yeah. Making out all over Denver. Check. But, really, she wanted to throw her hands in the air and ask the universe for some clarity. "Was there ever really a round one?" she asked.

"Depends on who you ask." Velma giggle-snorted.

Three pairs of expectant eyes focused on Heather from around the booth.

"I have no idea what we're doing. We're just…going with it." Whatever *it* was.

"Uh-huh." Velma clearly wasn't drinking the Kool-Aid. "Dish."

"We were going at it in an elevator earlier," Heather supplied. She glanced around the table to her stunned friends. "I'm not one to kiss and tell, but I'm telling you that man can do things with his tongue that I didn't know were possible."

"Holy crap." Claire leaned forward. "How far did you two get?"

"Top floor. Then we were interrupted. Then we gave up and came here."

"Well, I'm glad you're here." Velma patted Heather's back.

"What's your poison?" Brek tossed a cocktail napkin down in front of her.

"Soda water. With lime." She forced a smile. Jase needed a grown-up around tonight, and, unfortunately, her instincts said she should be that grown-up. Which meant…sobriety.

Brek glanced around the table, his gaze landing on Velma. "Everyone else good?"

"Yup. Just your standard girls' night. Not talking about Heather and Jase," Claire chimed.

"Way to be smooth," Heather mumbled.

"What the hell happened tonight that has him drinking his way to the bottom of the bottle?" Brek asked.

"You do not want to know," Heather replied. Hell, she'd give anything for herself not to know.

"Go see what you can dig out of Jase, we'll keep working on her," Claire said before sipping on whatever concoction she had over ice.

"We'll dig it out of her. Now shoo, girls only." Velma made a go-away motion with her hand. Brek chuckled and headed back to the bar. "If I can't tease my husband, who can I tease?" Velma popped a cherry in her mouth.

"You can tease me." Eli, the fourth friend in the Jase-Brek-Dean-Eli quartet, slid a plate of nachos on the table and took the seat beside Candy.

"I thought it was girls only tonight?" Velma went for a loaded chip. "I just made my husband leave."

Claire shrugged. "Eh, Eli's just one of the girls. He can stay."

Brek returned and dropped Heather's sad little soda water in front of her. "Something happened in Blackhawk. He said you were at the casino."

"You don't want to know." She squeezed the lime into the fizzing water. "You don't want to know. I don't want to know. Jase doesn't want to know. And now I have to move away. Far, far away." She took a sip, the bubbles tickling her nose.

"Aw, c'mon, Jase can't have scared you away that quickly." Brek leaned against the side of the booth and crossed his arms so the muscles in his corded biceps bunched.

"Okay, fine." Might as well let everyone else in on their misery. "Babushka moved in with me because her family is all kinds of worked up that she has a boyfriend and she lent him some money." No need to share the details of how much. "She and said-boyfriend decided to go to a weekend away at a casino up in Blackhawk. Jase insisted we chaperone. And we're officially the worst chaperones in the history of chaperones." She took a long pull of not-vodka'd seltzer. "So, they went to a movie. We played slots. Then we…ah…we kind of walked in on his grandmother in a clinch with her boyfriend. The boyfriend that I'd defended shortly before the…um… exhibition." She took a quick glug of seltzer water and coughed.

"Holy crap." Candy paused her beer bottle halfway to her lips.

"What kind of a clinch?" Velma asked, tipping her head to the side. "Clothes or no?"

"Definitely no," Heather confirmed.

"What base?" Velma asked. "First, second?"

Heather let out a huge sigh, blowing through her lips. "I think they'd rounded home long before we got there."

Claire's expression froze. "I think that warrants running away."

Brek glanced back to the bar. "I don't think I have enough whiskey."

"Brek. Go away. Girls' night. We need to dissect this." Velma shooed him away again.

"Why does he get to stay?" Brek jerked his chin to Eli.

Eli grinned big and settled deeper into the booth. "'Cause they like me."

"I'll fill you in later." Velma smiled up at her husband. "You should probably go water down Jase's whiskey, anyway."

Brek grumbled and stalked back to the bar.

"Babushka? Seriously?" Velma asked. "Naked. She's like a hundred."

Not quite, but who was counting at that point?

"Oh yeah. I know what I saw." Geriatric porn. Heather glanced to where Jase and his bottle of whiskey brooded at the bar.

"And what *exactly* did you see?" Claire scooted forward and dropped her elbows on the table. "Without being graphic. Just enough details so we can understand if it's a one- or a two-bottle night for Jase."

Heather swallowed. Hard. "Everything."

"Everything?" Eli's expression pinched in obvious disbelief.

"Oh, if it's anatomy used to...you know..." Heather bit her lip and slid her gaze toward the wall.

"Have sex?" Claire pried.

"Yeah. We saw it all. The view from the doorway was right in line with the sofa, and they were...ah...you know... like she was on her hands and knees." Heather's entire neck and face heated at the thought.

"Doggie style?" Claire's jaw dropped open. "You saw old-man balls?"

"In action." Heather squeezed the lime and dropped it into her glass with a *plop*.

Velma scrunched up her eyebrows. "Babushka's a little old to hold that position. How—"

Heather dropped her head to her hands. She would never forget the image burned into her retinas. "They used the throw pillows as leverage."

"Holy shit." Claire, for once, apparently had no other words. No witty comeback. Nada. "Good for her."

"And that's the story of why I'll be stabbing out my eyes." Heather took another gulp of soda, wishing like hell that Brek had laced it with a touch of vodka.

"C'mon, you're not even kind of a prude. You can handle a little dash of old-man balls. You're the queen of the penis cookies." Velma rubbed at Heather's back.

"My penis cookies are not elderly."

"Jase is gonna get so blitzed." Eli scooted out of the booth. "I should go do the friend thing and drink with him while we don't talk about his grandmother getting laid."

"Oh sure, we let you in on girls' night and you abandon us for your boys." Claire pointed the stem of her cherry at him.

He shrugged. "What can I say? Bros before—"

"You're gonna not want to finish that thought." Velma shot him a you're-never-invited-again look.

"I was going to say bros before beautiful women." He grinned a wide smile and left for the bar—slipping onto the vacant barstool next to Jase.

"Do you think Babushka's going to move in with this guy? Now that they're…you know?" Velma asked.

Gah, Heather hoped not. Sure, Babushka helped her around the apartment. But more than that, it was kind of nice to have someone to come home to. Babushka was quirky—

and that was an understatement. But it was nice to have someone care about her.

"A week ago, I'd have hoped she would. Now? Now, I like having her around." Heather shook the fuzz from her brain. "Let's talk about something else. Anything else."

"Are you and Jase really getting together?" Candy asked. "I think that'd be great. I mean, you bring something out in him. I can't quite put my finger on it."

Anger? Sexual tension? Heather could start ticking off the myriad of emotions she seemed to bring out in Jase. And vice versa.

"I don't know what we're doing." Heather said—the honesty of her words an everlasting frustration. She dropped her head to the table and left it there.

"Maybe we should talk about something else," Velma suggested.

"I have news," Candy replied. "I got into design school. Finally." She did a squee jazz-hands number.

Heather jolted. Candy had been applying to fashion design school for years. It was her dream to design clothing professionally. But Heather had started to rely on her at the shop. This couldn't mean… "You're leaving the shop?"

"Eventually." Candy bit at her lip. "Probably soon. I figure we'll get a replacement and I'll help train them."

A replacement for the bakery, yes. Not a replacement for the fun they had together in the kitchen. Yeah, it was selfish, but Heather liked that she and Candy knew each other so well they could stand in the kitchen for hours and not say a word one day, and the next they'd jabber the whole time. That wasn't the kind of thing she could expect from just any employee. That's only the kind of thing she could expect from someone who had known her since she was three.

Heather tapped down her disappointment because Candy was clearly so excited.

"And I can stay on part-time through school, if you'll let me," Candy continued.

Of course Heather would. This was her sister's dream, and it was amazing she got to live it. Even if it meant they were moving in different directions. She glanced to Jase. The world was turning, everyone doing new things…maybe she should, too?

THEY SPENT an hour dissecting Candy's career plans, and then Velma had to head home to do the mom thing. The band finished their set and Jase had left his barstool for the jukebox. Heather followed him, nursing her second soda water of the night.

She stared at the electronic playlists Jase scrolled through. "What're you looking for?"

"I'm in the mood for some Belinda Carlisle." His words blended slightly together. Still, he managed to punch a few buttons, and the opening strains of "I Get Weak" blared over the speakers.

"You are intoxicated." Heather pointed her drink at him.

"You are perceptive." He smiled a slurred smile. "We should have that prom committee meeting now."

"Or maybe I should take you home." She set her empty glass on a nearby table and linked her arm through his, ready to lead him to a bottle of aspirin and a glass of water. She'd get him tucked in at home and go home to her vacant apartment.

"Let's have some fun, instead." He draped his arm over her shoulders and tucked her into his side.

"I think we've had enough fun for one day." One week. One lifetime.

"Is this the part where you want me to deal with my shit, then?" he asked, his tone light.

She tried to push him toward a booth. She should get some food in him, too. "Jase, dealing with your shit when you're drunk hardly counts."

"That's the best time to deal with anything. The problem I have is there's not enough alcohol in the world to erase the memories." He tucked his chin into the top of her hair and inhaled.

"Which memories?" She pulled back so she could see his face. Read his expression. Unfortunately, it was blank. A fissure of unease spread along her spine. The fine hair on her arms stood on end.

"All of them." He ran a hand over his face and dropped it to his side.

She glanced around for backup. Her friends had left, but Eli and Brek should still be around. Brek was pouring drinks for another customer. Eli wasn't anywhere nearby. Damn.

"Let's dance." He snapped out of his trance and snagged her hand, spinning her in a circle.

She cleared her throat, trying to keep up with him. "Er...Jase?"

"Yup." He popped the p at the end of the word and leaned in close. His hips did a slow gyration that made her mouth go dry and her tongue numb.

"You're going to give everyone the wrong impression about us. They'll think we're together."

"Don't care." He nuzzled her neck, the five-o'clock shadow on his cheek scraping against the sensitive skin.

"You'll care tomorrow."

"Heather." He pulled back and caught her gaze with his. "Shhhhhhh." He raised a finger to her lips dramatically. "Let's dance."

So, they did.

Chapter Fourteen
SENIOR "SENIOR" PROM COUNTDOWN:
19 DAYS

Jase should've had a headache. Hell, he'd earned one the night before. But, nope, he didn't get hangovers. Especially with Heather shoving water and aspirin down his throat as soon as they'd returned to his apartment above the flower shop. His gaze roamed to his bedroom where she currently slept. Did she sprawl out or did she curl into a ball? He'd bet his right arm she curled into a ball asleep. Now, he wanted to know. Dammit.

He'd offered her his bed when she'd poured him inside last night. She'd insisted on sticking around to check on him. He'd insisted she sleep there while he took the couch. His couch was a piece of shit. On cue, his neck cracked when he sat up, punctuating that thought.

At some point, Heather had tossed a blanket over him. He owed her for that. And getting him home.

He rolled off his sofa and clicked on the coffeepot in the kitchen. His coffee wasn't great, but it did the job.

Two full cups of fresh drip coffee in hand, he knocked lightly on the door.

"Come in." Her voice was early-morning groggy.

He pushed open the door and stepped into the room. "Morning."

Curled up in a ball. That's how he found her.

He couldn't help the smile tickling the corner of his lips. *Called it.*

"Morning." She sat up, and the gray Navy T-shirt she'd apparently borrowed from him slipped off one shoulder. Fuck, that was sexy as all hell.

When was the last time he'd wanted a woman like he wanted Heather Reese? It'd been a hell of a drought. Not that he didn't have the occasional hookup. He just hadn't felt the intense need to see a woman smile from the depths of her soul. Not for a long, long time. Not since…

Nope. He refused to think about his past.

The edge of the bed creaked as he sat down and handed her a mug. She took it. Held it between her palms. Couldn't meet his gaze.

The air between them weighed heavy.

Awkward. That's what this was.

"Glad you found something to sleep in." He gestured to his shirt.

Her face flamed red. "Oh. I hope it's okay… I was worried about you."

"Because I should be vomiting my guts out now?"

Her cheeks went even more red. She messed with the blanket, and it slipped, revealing creamy thigh.

His dick stretched, ready to come out and play. *Down, boy.*

The last thing he needed at the moment was for the captain in his pants to start making requests.

"I…uh…" he started.

More blanket slipped from her thigh. The T-shirt covered a good deal, but he couldn't pull his gaze from that sliver of pale skin.

"So." He scrubbed a hand over his hair.

She stared intently at the brown liquid in her cup. "So."

"What do you have planned—" he said at the same time she said, "How are you feel—"

"Not much, just working—" she replied at the same time he replied, "Good, thanks for the aspirin."

They both glanced to their respective mugs. She took a sip. He took a gulp.

He stood. This was one of the clumsiest mornings after ever, and he hadn't even gotten laid. "I can help you with committee stuff today."

And maybe keep my hands off you.

"That'd be great." She set her mug on the New Belgium beer crate he used as a makeshift nightstand and waved a hand between them. "This is weird. Why is it weird?"

Because he'd gotten trashed in front of her. They'd seen his grandmother getting laid. Why was it weird, she asked? He could go on and on. "Last night was one of those nights that—"

"Makes you question everything?" She finished for him.

He brushed a hand over his hair. "Right."

"Sit." She patted the bed beside her.

He sat. Not because he necessarily wanted to, but it was becoming clear he had no power around her.

His hand crept toward hers. The damn thing seemed to have a mind of its own.

She placed her palm over his knuckles. "Jase. I feel like where we're going with this could be a really bad idea."

"Where exactly are we going with this?" He set his mug beside hers. Communication sucked.

"Hooking up. Climbing each other in elevators."

He swallowed so hard his Adam's apple practically bobbed right out of his throat. Communication *definitely* sucked. They weren't even officially together, and she was giving him the brush-off. He slipped his hand away from hers. His dick pouted.

"I mean, I do *want* that. I just want the rest of it, too," she finished.

He cleared his throat. "What's the rest of it?"

"The idea that it could actually lead somewhere. I get it, you want to hook up and move on. I want the chance it might lead to more."

"Picket fence? Dog? Kids?" he asked.

She threaded her fingertips through the edge of the bedspread. "Well, yeah."

"Heather, I've done the forever shit. It's a lie. Had the picket fence. Had the dog. Wanted the kids. It doesn't work out." Because a wife eventually leaves and takes the dog with her. He couldn't open himself up to that. Not again.

Heather continued to look at him as though they were discussing the cumulus clouds in the sky and not his failed marriage. "Did it ever occur to you that maybe it didn't work out because you were with the wrong person?"

Every goddamned day.

He smashed his lips together. He did not want to talk about this.

"I like you, Jase. Maybe we should try this thing? Be open to us not ending. To us seeing where it goes. If it doesn't work out, it doesn't work out. But maybe we could try. Maybe it'd be good for both of us..."

"Maybe we could try." He echoed her words, but his were filled with frustration. How the hell was he supposed to try?

Elbows on his knees, he dropped his head to his hands.

Her hand came to his back and rubbed a particularly tense spot between his shoulder blades. "We don't have to. I won't be mad."

He glanced to her then. The loneliness in her eyes took his breath. No, she wouldn't be mad, just disappointed—and that was worse.

"Heather, I'm not good at the long-term gig. I'm just not." She had to understand that.

"I'm not asking you to be. I'm just asking that we both go into this without expecting it to end quickly. Or at all." She studied his blue bedspread.

"It's better to go into a hookup with your eyes wide open," he said.

"That's what we're doing, then? Just hooking up?"

"And hanging out."

"Exclusively?" she asked.

"Well, yeah."

"Jase?" she said. "That's called a relationship."

Noooooooo. Nope. It sure as hell wasn't. Relationships meant dinners with family and waking up together. Two things he did not partake in. Although, he wouldn't mind waking up next to Heather. If they spent any amount of time together, his family would be involved. Which meant…

Shit.

They were in the relationship zone.

"We could try," she whispered.

This time her words weren't frustrated. They were hope-ful. God, how long had it been since he'd felt any kind of hope?

"Only if you're ready." She leaned into him, her tits pressed into his back.

Fuck, no, he wasn't ready.

But she wasn't asking for promises, just hope.

His dick twitched, ready to come out and *try*. The disloyal bastard.

He could go into this thing they had going without looking toward an ending. It'd be hard as all fuck, but he could manage. His blood pressure skipped. He was going to do this. Really going to give it the effort.

With an exaggerated, resigned breath, he turned to her, caught her mouth with his. She wrapped her arms around his neck.

"You," he practically growled. "Make. Me. Crazy." He punctuated each word with a kiss against the skin of her neck.

"Ditto." Her chest pressed against his.

"We'll try this your way," he conceded, waiving his white flag in defeat.

Her breath caught, and her breasts heaved. "Really?"

He pulled his shirt off of her in one quick motion. "Really. I just have one request."

She gripped his arms and wrapped her legs around his torso, the heated core of her center rubbing against him. "Yeah?"

"Don't tell my family."

She paused, inhaled deep. Frown lines creased around the edges of her mouth. "What?"

"Just…let's have this for us. Just us. For a while." Because once his family got involved, it'd be a fucking free-for-all.

"Jase…" She started to pull away. "Babushka is going to know what's going on."

And that's what he worried about most. He'd like to put that off as long as possible.

"Just for now," he assured. Until the time was right.

She let out a deep breath. "Just for now?"

"I want this." He pressed himself against her. "Don't get me wrong."

"Okay." She kissed him, a light brush of her mouth against his.

"Can we have sex yet?" he asked.

"Yes, please." She pressed a deeper kiss to his lips.

He pushed her back onto the bed, pinned her arms over her head, holding them there with one hand while he kissed his way down her face. Her neck. Her chest.

She ground against him. The power had somehow shifted, but he couldn't be sure if she held it now, or if he did. All he knew for certain was that he wanted her.

For now, maybe that was enough.

"I'd tell you you're beautiful, but you should already know that."

"Something like that is always worth saying," she replied.

They pressed against each other, the barrier of her lace underwear and his boxers the only thing keeping them apart. He kissed down to her belly button, to the edge of her panties, and yanked them off. He skimmed his hands up her thighs, over the skin that had driven him crazy. Her knees fell apart.

He kissed her wet center. Diving in with his mouth, his tongue.

She bent her knees and lifted herself to him.

Sweetness. Her. He poured everything he had into her pleasure. Gripping her ass. Pulling her to him.

His dick literally wept at the beauty of all that was Heather.

He should probably say something, but his tongue was presently busy, and given the moaning coming from his pillow, she wasn't going to be talking for a while. Not if he had anything to say about it.

Her knees began to tremble as her orgasm took over. He continued to work as it wracked through her. He should've known she'd come fast and with her whole body. Heather Reese didn't do anything halfway.

"Jase." Her head lulled to the side as she came down. But he wasn't done with her yet.

A quick kiss to the inside of her thigh before he lifted himself to his knees and reached for the little wooden box he kept on his nightstand. "I'm not done."

Holding the condom in his hand, she pressed a kiss to his mouth and started humming something against his lips. A song he vaguely recognized. From a game show.

Wait, what the hell was she doing? He pulled back.

"Well, don't stop." She gripped his back, pulled him to her, and started humming again.

"Are you humming the theme song to *Jeopardy* during fore-play?" Women had done a lot of shit in bed with him, but he'd never had one do that.

"Uh-huh," she muttered, catching his mouth with hers in a kiss that defied all reason.

She pressed herself against him so there was nothing he wanted more than to be inside her.

She rolled him so she was on top and ran her palms over his bare abs, working her way down the muscles to his boxers. With a little help from him, she tugged his boxers off and tossed them on the floor beside the bed.

That was more like it.

She trailed little kisses along Jase's waist, down the little line of hair leading to his—she started humming again. The laugh that burst from his mouth was totally unexpected.

This time he hauled her up his chest, flipped her on her back, and fell on top of her, holding himself up on his fore-arms, effectively halting progress on his own orgasm as he laughed into the sheet beside her head. "What the hell are you doing?" he finally asked.

She lifted his head with her palms, catching his gaze with her own. "You don't like television. I figured I'd start condi-tioning you to enjoy it by humming theme songs while you do something enjoyable."

Serious? She was totally serious. Her expression was one of total sincerity. For the first time since *his* first time, he had a woman nearly naked in his bed and he had no idea what to do with her.

Then she burst out giggling. "Sorry. I'll be serious. Look, this is me being serious."

"I have no idea what to do with you, sugar." He pressed a kiss to her mouth, both of them chuckling against each other. She ran her hands down his back, and it took less than two seconds for things to heat back up. The laughter turned into a moan, and he made sure Alex Trebek was the furthest thing from her mind.

Condom still in hand, he slipped the latex over his ready-to-get-in-on-the-action dick.

Then he was inside her. And it was amazing, her body wrapped around him.

And screw it all…*trying* was fucking fun.

Chapter Fifteen

Heather burrowed under the covers of Jase's bed, his thigh between her legs, his arm draped across her belly. They'd spent the day together, and the night, and now Monday had arrived. She had to get home, showered, and to the shop before it opened.

She started to roll away from Jase, but his arm tightened.

"Stay." The word was muffled by his pillow.

"Work," she replied, brushing the hair from his forehead.

"Stay." His thigh began to rub against her core, the sparks between them burning bright. "Please," he muttered before turning his body along the length of hers.

"Cookies don't bake themselves." She pecked a kiss against his lips. "And I've got to meet with the retirement-home director in a few hours about prom logistics."

"You want to talk about prom decorations?" His hand trailed over her belly, and, oh, screw it. Talking about prom was basically like going to work while staying in bed.

She led his hand lower past the waistband of her panties. "Sure."

That was basically work, anyway. They could multitask.

He smiled and proceeded to move his fingers to the spot

that would definitely have her calling in for a personal day. "I was thinking about our garden theme. Drew some sketches of what I'm thinking for the event."

He withdrew his hand to grab a sketch pad from the crate nightstand.

The drawing was a basic sketch with the general layout of the room she'd provided. He'd marked where he'd put trellises and pillars and a crap load of flowers.

The idea was really good, but not the Jungle Safari theme she'd built up in her head. She did her best to let that go. "I like it."

He studied her, then the drawing. "What's wrong with it?"

"I said I like it."

"See, you said that, but your whole body tensed when you looked. And you got all distant."

"I did not. I said I like it, and I do." She did.

He rolled and raised himself over her, his forearms on either side of her shoulders. "Tell the truth. You hate the idea?"

"No." She didn't hate it. "I just had the jungle theme in my head. I need to adjust. That's all."

"Where'd the jungle theme idea come from, anyway?" he asked.

She lifted her head to kiss him. "It's not important. I like your idea. Let's do it."

Heather let out a moan as his mouth met hers, and his hand moved to where he'd had it before, and seriously, shouldn't every day start with a solid finger bang?

She whimpered in response, riding his hand as he took her higher, pausing and starting over, making it last. Drawing it out.

He kissed along the line of her lips, across her cheek, down the column of her throat, stopping to give attention to her breasts before moving down her belly. He moved his thumb, pulled her panties to her thighs, and dropped his mouth to her. Sucking, licking, and basically giving her the best morning she'd ever had.

He stopped for a moment. "Where'd the theme come from, Heather?"

What? "Jase?"

"The jungle theme, where'd it come from?"

"Are you holding my orgasm hostage until I tell you?"

He lowered his mouth in reply, bringing her just to the edge before stopping again. "Where'd the idea come from?" he asked again.

"This is torture, you know that, right?" She glared at him.

"Where'd the idea come from?"

Now it was a game. A game she absolutely didn't mind playing.

He started again. This time he took her closer, bringing her nearly to the edge before stopping. Again.

"High school." There, she'd said it. "That was the theme of the prom I didn't get to go to."

She swore he dropped an f-bomb, but then it didn't matter because he was doing his thing again. He made a come-here motion with the two fingers inside her and that was that. The orgasm took her. Noises were made. She pressed her head against the pillow, but his hand didn't stop, his mouth continued, until she rode the wave back down.

Jase made waking up the kind of experience a girl could really appreciate.

He reached for the box on the nightstand, but she got there first, grabbing a plastic-wrapped condom and tearing it open. She pulled her panties off and neither of them spoke. Jase, on his knees, his erection ready and waiting for her. She rolled the condom over his solid length, watching as his eyes dropped closed. He sucked in a breath. She squeezed the root and met him chest to chest, her hand still gripping him.

"Jase?" She kissed him, his mouth meeting hers, hungry.

"Hmm." He didn't stop the kiss, continued it as her hand stroked him over the latex.

"We don't have to keep doing it this way. We're exclusive. I'm clean. I'm on the pill," she said against the side of his mouth.

Something changed in his eyes when she mentioned the pill—she'd swear it was fear. But that wasn't right. This was Jase.

"As long as you're clean and all that," she continued.

He pulled back, his hands framing her face. "Yeah, I'm clean."

And then it didn't matter because he was kissing her again, rolling to his back so she could ride him like the cowgirl she was not.

Knees on both sides of his hips, he filled her, and she took him. Hard. Hard because he pushed her to. Head tossed back, she let him have everything. She pressed down, he pressed up. It was like all weekend he'd treated her like she was made of glass. But now? Maybe he realized she wasn't so fragile.

She brought herself to the edge, the orgasm tightening, ready to spring. Hands gripping her ass, he moved with her. Gripped her hard.

A groan fell from her as the coil inside cinched.

Midthrust, he sat up, still inside her, and shifted her to her back, him to his knees, never stopping. This was some kind of challenge. She scraped her fingernails over his chest, across his nipples. This time, he groaned, and she released.

Ankles around his shoulders, she arched her back as the orgasm started. He didn't pause as she clenched around him, the biggest orgasm she'd ever had consuming her as he continued pushing them both forward and over together.

This wasn't the gentle guy she'd been having sex with all weekend. This was a morning fuck, pure and simple.

And she loved it. Her body responded in a way she'd

never thought possible, clenching and pulsing around his erection.

Then he pressed inside her, stilled, and… Jase was a gorgeous man, but when he came? He wasn't just gorgeous, he was transcendent. She couldn't pull her gaze from him.

Yeah, being a partner to that was pretty exhilarating.

Both of them breathing hard, he dropped his forehead to hers. She kissed him and trailed her palms up the sides of his chest.

He'd just given her one of the best orgasms of her life.

"Catch up for dinner?" she asked.

"I can't." He brushed her hair behind her ear and pushed up off of her. Not even a kiss.

"How about tomorrow?"

He headed for the bathroom. "Tomorrow's out, too."

Her heart fell to her stomach.

"Ohh-kay," she said to the empty room, her voice shaky. It hit her what had just happened. He'd said what he needed to say to have a sex-filled weekend, and now it was time for him to scrap her from his life.

She pushed up and off the bed in an incredibly ungraceful dismount, digging through the sheets for her underwear.

"Tonight, the guys are coming to hang drywall," he said to her back. "I promised pizza."

Right. Drywall.

"We're behind schedule, and Eli's on my ass to get in his new kitchen," Jase continued.

He said it, but something was off. He was pulling away. Which made sense. This was Jase. She'd let herself forget this was Jase. He gave her the goodbye fuck and he'd send her on her way. This was the game.

"Okay," she repeated. "I have to catch up at the shop, anyway. I get it. Maybe the day after tomorrow?"

She didn't get it. But she'd opened up, she'd spent a

weekend in bed with him, and now it was Monday and he'd just said goodbye in the only way he knew how.

"I'm working on the renovation tomorrow, too," he continued.

Of course he was. Dammit, she knew better than to get involved like this. She. Knew. Better.

"Heather."

Where the hell were her underwear? She swallowed hard, willing her heart to stop beating so fast. She didn't need to be red-faced and embarrassed. There was nothing to be embarrassed about.

This was how it was meant to be.

Calm as she could, naked and post-amazing-orgasm, she dug through his bed. Seriously? It wasn't that big.

Screw it. She'd go commando.

Finger-combing her hair, she strode across the room to where she'd tossed her jeans. Bare-bottomed, she sat on the edge of his bed and pulled them on.

"Heather," he said again.

She couldn't do this. Not the actual goodbye. Maybe the note Logan had left made way more sense than she'd given him credit for. She'd never had to look at him, never had to turn red and cry when he told her it was over. She'd done all of that alone.

Not that she'd cry over Jase. It was a weekend fling. He hadn't earned her tears.

"Heather."

"Yeah?" she clipped, pulling her shirt over her head. She braced herself for what was coming. How he'd deliver the blow.

She glanced to him; he was totally naked in the doorway of his bedroom, his arms crossed across his chest, studying her.

His eyes absolutely soft.

She immediately regretted her tone.

"Tonight. Come over after I'm done downstairs?" he asked gently. "And lunch tomorrow? My brother's coming into town, so the family is doing a big dinner with him or I'd hang with you."

Oh.

He moved toward the bed, pulling back the blankets and handing her the panties she couldn't find before.

She took them. Stared at them.

He sat beside her on the bed, totally not caring that he didn't have a stitch of clothes on. He tilted her chin so she looked at him, treating her like she was as breakable as she felt in that moment.

"The pill thing. You really want that?" he asked.

"I do." She bit at her bottom lip.

He leaned forward and brushed a kiss over her lips. "Okay."

"Jase?" She pushed into him, her face pressed against his pec.

"Hmm?" he asked, his hand stroking the back of her hair.

"I'm all kinds of messed up."

"No, sugar. You're not." He pulled her tighter, held her against him.

He felt so good. Her breaths came easier. He didn't let her go. That wasn't breakup sex.

This was going to be all right. She hadn't made a mistake of epic proportions. No, things were okay. And Jase wasn't the man she'd convinced herself he was.

God, she hoped he wasn't the man she'd convinced herself he was.

Chapter Sixteen
SENIOR "SENIOR" PROM COUNTDOWN:
18 DAYS

"Well, hello there, boss lady." Candy's gaze traveled up and then down Heather's two-day-old clothes. She'd seen Heather wear them at the bar and leave with Jase in them. "I guess you decided the no-men thing isn't worth it, huh?"

"I don't..." *Know.* Heather didn't finish the thought. She shook her head and plopped onto a chair in the kitchen while Candy worked on a batch of race-car cookies.

"Did you have breakfast?" Candy asked.

Heather glanced up and caught the flash of concern in Candy's eyes. They'd been there for each other through every relationship and every breakup. Candy knew better than even Velma and Claire how hard Heather had taken the last hit.

"I'm gonna head up and shower and grab something." Still, Heather didn't move.

Candy set down the icing bag. "You wanna talk about it?" she asked gently.

Did she? "I slept with Jase."

Candy nodded. "Yeah, I got that much."

"And we're semiserious." Mostly. She was pretty sure. That's what they'd decided. "Exclusive" meant "semiserious."

They couldn't really be serious if he wasn't going to tell his family they were together.

"Okay…" Candy splayed her hands on the table. "What does that mean?"

"We're not seeing other people. But he doesn't want to tell his family." Heather stood. "I kind of get it. You've met his family. But how can we be really together if we're half hiding?"

Candy raised her eyebrows. "Uh…"

"It's fine. Because, you know, I know that they can really test him. But I don't want to keep the fact that we're together now a secret. And I'm torn, but I don't want to do something that will upset him. I mean, things are still new and weird and…really awesome. Like amazingly awesome." Case in point: that morning, before she'd made everything weird. "I'm so conflicted. But Jase and I are together now, and that's what matters, right?" Heather could really use a bit of confirmation on this.

Candy cleared her throat and pointed over Heather's shoulder.

"Who's standing behind me?" she asked, turning her head. Son of a bitch, Babushka stood in the doorway of the kitchen. Heather's heart dropped straight to the sealed concrete floor.

Jase was not going to be happy about this.

Babushka's eye's misted. "This is the best news."

Oh no. No. Shit. Damn. Fuck.

Babushka shuffled toward Heather, folding her into a Fels-Naptha-scented hug.

"Oh my God. He's going to kill me," Heather said to no one in particular. Their semi-relationship was over before it had even semi-started.

"No, he is good boy. I tell you this already. He makes good choice." Babushka patted Heather's cheek with her soft palm. "Now, I vill move in with Morty. You two can be private."

Oh no.

The air went solid and caught in Heather's chest. "Really, that's not what we want. You should stay with me or move back home… Moving in with your boyfriend so quickly? I don't think—"

"Hush. Ve vill make it vork."

"I thought you said you two weren't serious?" Because moving in together was pretty serious.

"Oh, ve are not. But you need space for Jason," Babushka insisted.

No, Jase definitely didn't want his grandmother moving in with Morty. It was an epically bad idea. "What if you didn't move in with Morty? I mean, you should have your own space. I help out up at the assisted-living center just a block away. They have really nice apartments." They were more like rooms, but they were lovely. "And then you and Morty can still see each other." With the chaperones. "But you'll have your own space."

Babushka stared at her, her eyebrows drawn together.

"Then you can still just walk over here or to Jase's whenever you want."

The wheels were obviously turning in the old woman's mind.

"And they take care of your meals. And they have a lady there who will do your hair, whenever you want. It's all included."

"You're overselling," Candy whispered.

"This place? It's close?" Babushka asked.

"I help out there sometimes, and it's just a block away. An easy walk." And it didn't involve moving in with a boyfriend.

"This apartment. Ve vill go look. I vill consider this choice," Babushka said firmly before she continued her shuffle to the back stairs that lead up to Heather's apartment.

"She hasn't been here all weekend, either. Has she?" Heather asked.

Candy shook her head. "Don't think so."

So Heather wasn't the only one walking the walk of shame that morning. She hated calling it that; there was literally nothing to be ashamed of.

Heather dropped her face to her palms. How the hell was she going to tell Jase that his whole family would know about them in approximately five seconds? And, the cherry on top? She'd just convinced his grandmother to move into the assisted-living facility for the elderly.

Heather sucked in a lungful of oxygen. It'd be fine. Totally fine. Jase was a good guy. He'd handle this okay.

Chapter Seventeen
SENIOR "SENIOR" PROM COUNTDOWN:
18 DAYS

He was an asshole of epic proportions.

It's not that he needed Heather around—he just felt human again when she was nearby. He had no idea what that was all about, but he had spent years numb inside while still acting fine on the outside. It beat the hell out of the guilt that took over whenever he started to feel. But with Heather, he wasn't numb. He also wasn't guilty. For the first time since everything had gone to shit, he felt like himself. An older, more tired version of himself, but he wasn't the shell of a man who'd lost his crew and then his wife.

Jase shoved a vase of freesias in the cooler beside the cash register and stalked to the back of the shop. Usually, he worked right up front. He had a table there because early on he'd realized how much customers loved to watch the finished product being created. And he liked it. He liked talking to them and being in the middle of it all.

Not today. Today he worked in the back. Today his staff didn't need a memo to steer clear of him. Today he was an asshole.

He'd screwed Heather senseless and got skittish with all the relationship-pill-long-term talk. And she knew it. She fucking knew he was questioning things. That's the kind of jerk he was.

He couldn't bring himself to let Heather go that morning, and a woman like her deserved happy. Happy he would fuck up. The crinkling was the sound of his balls shriveling at the thought of her lips against anyone's but his own. Nope, he wouldn't play along with that.

He shoved a rose too forcefully into the floral foam, breaking the stem.

He stared at it, clipped it and tossed it back in the bucket of water.

That morning he'd realized he really wanted to do this with her, the possible-forever gig. Shell-shocked, he'd just stood there. He was a goddamned bomb technician, trained to stay calm and clip the correct wire—even when he had no clue which one that might be. Trained to expect the unexpected. One bomb could be four. An insurgent could be waiting around the corner with an AK-47 and a truckload of attitude. Yet, he hadn't see this coming.

He couldn't end it. No, he couldn't bring himself to do it. Because he wanted more of her. He was a selfish prick.

So, no. She wasn't the one who was all kinds of messed up. Not even close. He wanted to hang on to her because he liked the way things were with them. Liked being around her. Even though he knew…he fucking knew it would end badly.

He picked up the brick of foam and threw it against the wall, a splat of water on the paint the only evidence of what he'd done when the foam hit the tile floor.

Hands braced on the side of the metal table, he took ten deep breaths, counting each one.

"You wanna talk about it?" Brek asked from the doorway that led to the shop.

Jase glanced up.

"Or you wanna throw shit? 'Cause I can be down with

either." Brek grabbed the foam from the floor and held it between his hands.

Jase didn't say anything, he just grabbed a new foam brick and started over.

Brek pulled a chair up to the side of the table, lounging like he had nothing better to do. Didn't he have a bar to run? And a kid to take care of? And a wife to do shit for?

Jase didn't look up. "I fucked Heather."

He'd also had lazy sex, and fun sex, and hot sex, and he'd kissed her and talked with her until one in the morning. He'd made her coffee and he'd held her hand. Yeah, he'd done all that.

"You did *what?*" Dean asked from the doorway.

Jase jolted. Another rose snapped in two.

He clipped it and tossed it into the bucket.

He'd fucked Heather and he'd fucked himself. Dean would not be as forgiving as Brek. But he might as well know, too. Their wives would be all over Jase like a grenade with the pin pulled when things went south. And he'd been around long enough to know things would eventually go south. "Figure you guys should know so, when shit blows up, you'll know why."

"She okay?" Brek asked, his expression blank. "Heather?"

"Yeah." She was fine. Right now, she was fine. This morning when she knew what was coming, she hadn't been fine. "We agreed to be exclusive. Then I asked her not to bring it up to my family. Now shit's weird."

"I think he caught the bug." Dean pulled up his own stool. "But he's fighting it."

"Don't fight it. Not worth it." Brek leaned his elbows on the table.

Eli strolled into the back room like he was there for a tea party. "What'd I miss?"

"He and Heather had sex," Dean supplied.

"And he's emotional about it," Brek said.

The hell he was.

"And they're together, but he's not telling his family," Dean added.

"Keeping track of your not-a-relationship is a full-time job," Eli grabbed a stool. "So your family wanted you to date, but you didn't want to, so you said that you and Heather broke up and you were too devastated to date. Now, you are dating her, but you don't want them to know…because…?"

"Because then they'll want to get involved and they'll start whispering in her ear and then shit will go sideways."

"Maybe shit won't go sideways." Brek toyed with the foam Jase had tossed earlier.

Jase moved his gaze between his three friends. "Why do I feel like this is a setup?"

"If it looks like a setup and it smells like a setup, it's probably a setup." Eli straddled the stool and took his place with the other traitors.

Son of a bitch. "Your wives talked to Heather, didn't they?"

"I don't think we're allowed to say." Dean grimaced.

"They have her back? They'll make sure she's fine?" Jase asked. She had to be okay.

"You just said she's fine," Brek replied.

"I mean when shit goes bad. They'll be there for her?" Jase asked. He should just give up on work for the day, let someone else finish up.

"Why is shit going to go bad?" Dean was apparently in shrink mode.

"'Cause he thinks shit always goes bad," Eli answered for him.

"Should we all hand in our balls, grab a pot of tea, and sit around processing my sex life?" Jase asked. "Because that sounds like shit I do not need."

"I'm game to talk about feelings, but I'm gonna need hard liquor if you're gonna cry," Eli said.

"You're being a dick." Jase pointed the end of a rose at him.

"It's my gift." Eli flashed a shit-eating smile. "Pull up a chair and tell me what's got the stick shoved up your ass."

"When's the last time he was this upset he got laid?" Dean kicked back in his stool, lounging against the wall.

"I can't recall a time he got some and wasn't happy about it," Eli replied. "Not that I know every time he gets a piece."

"She's special, okay, assholes?" Jase spit out the words before he had a moment to think it through. "She's special, and when I fuck it up, she's going to get hurt."

"Shit. We're doing this again." Eli scrubbed a hand over his face. "It's like I'm over here holding up the singles area all by myself."

"Your turn's comin', too," Brek replied.

Eli glared his way.

"You know? Let's not talk anymore." Jase did his best to ignore them.

The silence was unbearable.

"The thing is, I shouldn't want this with her."

The guys stayed silent.

"Aren't you going to say something?" Jase asked.

"Are we supposed to?" Eli asked, entirely too innocently.

"Fucker." Jase gave him a one-finger salute.

Eli leaned forward, elbows on the table. "You know what I miss? I'll tell you. I miss when we used to talk about Brek's bike, and you going on and on about shit that blows up, and what mountain I'm gonna climb next, and whatever the hell Dean does for work. Don't get me wrong, I dig a good lay just as much as the next guy. But ever since you all got lady issues, you're no fun."

"You're shit with advice." Brek shook his head.

"Then, Dean, you're up," Eli replied.

"Heather is special." Dean gave Jase a pointed look. "And

I think it's in everyone's best interest that you do not, in fact, fuck it up."

"She's not Angela," Brek said, quiet, eyes focused on his hands folded on top of the table.

No shit. Heather wasn't his ex-wife. He refused to do a comparison. The shit of it was, he and Angela had left things on a decent note. Despite everything. Hell, they'd even shared a divorce attorney. She'd moved on and she'd hoped he would, too. "Angela has nothing to do with anything."

"Just everything," Eli muttered.

Jase wanted to spend time with Heather. He wanted to get to know her. He never wanted to get to know a woman—not like he was craving her. His heart had been broken once and everyone said it'd heal.

They'd lied.

He used duct tape, super glue, and a heap of Frankenstein staples to hold the thing together. His resolve to keep it tucked away hardened. He couldn't let the past repeat itself. He wouldn't survive that again.

And the way she'd looked that morning?

Another staple had popped in his heart at the disappointment in her eyes.

"I think what these idiots are trying to say is that Heather may seem like the kind of woman who doesn't get hurt. That things don't bother her. But she's been through a pretty rough patch." Dean was all business. "You've been through a rough patch, too. Maybe the two of you can help each other past it. If that means you end up together, it makes Thanksgiving easier. But if you don't, at least maybe you'll learn something from one another."

The cowbell on the front door clanked and something shifted in the air, then he heard her voice and it effectively pressed the pause button on his heartbeat. Heather.

"Everyone act like we weren't talking about their sex life," Eli suggested.

Brek thumped him upside the head, and then she was there in the doorway and Jase was stripped raw.

"Sorry. I didn't realize everyone was here." Heather slid a glance between them all.

"What's up, sugar?" Jase asked, the endearment slipping through his lips like a buttered grenade.

Brek coughed into his hand. Eli dropped his head to the table. Dean just smiled like a candy-ass.

Heather took it all in, briefly, before shifting her gaze back to him. "The afternoon deliveries are ready, so I thought I'd come over and let Ethan know."

"He's not back yet, but I'll send him over when he gets here." That wasn't why she'd come by, though. That was a phone call Candy usually made. Not a trip across the asphalt for Heather.

"I also wanted to see which flowers you wanted to use for the prom, so I can coordinate the cookies." She shifted from foot to foot. "I want them to match."

"I'll text you some pictures." He couldn't help but notice the way her breaths were coming more quickly than usual.

Her hair was back in its ponytail and she'd changed clothes. No apron this time, so she obviously wasn't in a rush when she'd headed his way. "I need to talk to you about your grandmother. Have you talked to her?"

Shit. No, he hadn't even thought about Babushka since… Negative…he hadn't talked to her.

"I guess that's a no." Heather's chest started to heave like it had when she was upset that morning. "Okay, so she figured out that we're together. Back together. Just together. Whatever."

Fuck. If she knew, his mother knew… If his mother knew? Everyone knew.

Heather went on, "And I'm sorry, I know you didn't want to tell her. Yet. She just overheard…you know. She just…"

Heather had no idea what she'd just done. To both of

them. There would be no escape for either, once his family knew. He and Heather would get sucked into their vortex and they'd never get any time alone.

"We'll just step out," Dean stood and ticked his head toward the door. "Brek? Eli?"

"You might as well stay. I mean you'll hear all this anyway," Heather replied.

Dean slid his gaze between the two of them, finally settling back on the stool.

"Okay. She knows. I'll take care of it. Just…the family is going to descend."

"I can handle that." She nodded.

Ha. No one could handle a roomful of Dvornakovs.

"Also…there's another thing…"

"Maybe we should step out now." Dean stood again.

Heather took a deep breath. "Babushka wanted to move in with Morty, but I told her that's a bad idea and she should stay with me or move back in with your parents. But she was really not into those ideas, because she's still mad at your dad and she wants us to have our space. So I convinced her to consider the retirement home where we're hosting prom. She's got a tour later today and she's really excited—"

She kept talking, but Jase couldn't hear her over the buzzing in his ears. Her lips were moving, but he just stared at them, not really able to process what she was saying. When had his life spun so far out of control because he'd had a crush on a girl with a cute ponytail and a bouquet of erection cookies?

Oh, she'd stopped talking and was staring at him like he was supposed to respond.

"Jase?" she asked.

He opened his mouth, looked to his buddies, then back to the woman he'd committed to that weekend. He closed his mouth.

"She asked if you want to go," Brek chimed in.

"Go where?" He couldn't pull his gaze from Heather's red lips.

"To take the tour with her. With us," she replied.

"To take the tour. Right, because she's moving out because we're—" Jase coughed.

Awkward silence settled over the room.

"Together. That's the word you're looking for," Eli supplied.

"It's at four. If you want to come, you can. And I'll just wait and see what you decide." Heather was breathing funny and her cheeks were redder than normal. "I'm going to go now."

She turned and practically bolted through the shop.

"I have no idea what just happened," Jase said to the air she'd vacated.

"This would be the part where you go after her." Dean crossed his arms and nodded toward the front of the shop.

And do what?

"You gonna go after her?" Eli asked in his best ten-year-old-*duh* voice.

Was he?

Eli started to raise from his stool. "Or I can go?"

"Every second counts." Brek shoved a hand on Eli's shoulder, pushing him back down.

"What am I supposed to say?" Jase asked.

"Start with an apology, that usually works for me." Brek shrugged.

See? This was why Jase didn't do relationships. He always ended up apologizing for shit he didn't understand.

Eli started making a *ticktock* sound by clicking his tongue.

Fine, so he'd go find out what that was about without the audience around making shit uncomfortable.

He tossed off his rubber apron and hurried after Heather. What the hell was he going to say?

Somehow, he made it to the sidewalk. She was halfway across the street.

"Heather," he called.

She turned and paused. Frowned. Then she walked back toward him.

He jogged the distance between them, stopping in front of her. "I…"

She frowned deeper.

He tried again. "This whole thing…"

She raised her eyebrows.

"What I mean is…" He fixated on her lips and the words disappeared from his brain.

In the Navy, they'd taught Jase to control his emotions. Subdue his physiological responses to stress. He could enter a room with enough dynamite they wouldn't even find traces of his DNA. He never batted an eye. Throw him in the frigid waters of the Atlantic? He controlled his pulse to stay alive long enough for an extraction. But now? Every time he was around Heather, all the training Uncle Sam could throw at him went down the toilet. He couldn't control shit.

She was frowning, and that was unacceptable. That he'd made her frown. So, he did the one thing he could actually think of in that moment. He kissed her. Tongue and fire and his hands totally wrecking her ponytail. She fisted her hands in his tee and held on, kissing him back with everything he knew she had.

And they were on the sidewalk. In the middle of the day.

Slowly, he pulled back. Then leaned in and kissed her lightly.

She held his stare and his pulse swished faster.

"We're good?" he asked.

Now she smiled. "Yeah."

"Good." He brushed the pad of his thumb over her cheekbone.

"This whole thing between us is just so… I mean. I wasn't

doing this again. And you weren't. And now we are." She dropped her head to his shoulder.

His favorite place for it.

He rested his hand against her neck. "I'll be by in a few hours. Go with you and Babushka to check this place out. I need to check out the space, anyway, if I'm going to decorate it."

"That works," she said against his skin. "You're really okay with your family knowing about us?"

"Well, let's not get carried away." "Okay" was not the word he'd choose to describe his feelings, but he'd go with it. "We'll make it work."

She didn't move. He didn't move. Her hands still fisted in his shirt. "I guess I have to go back to work," she said.

"Then you have to let go, sugar." Now he was chuckling.

She glanced to where her hands still held on to his tee. She released him. "Right."

His insides started to go soft. Except one specific appendage that flew full staff whenever she was around. Her cheeks were pink, and his dick was hard, and somehow they'd figure out how to do this so it didn't go sideways. No one had to get hurt.

Chapter Eighteen
SENIOR "SENIOR" PROM COUNTDOWN:
18 DAYS

Heather followed behind Jase and Babushka as the director at the retirement home gave them a tour. After Logan left, Heather had found a volunteer notice and had started coming by. Turned out, she really liked the residents who lived here. They loved it when she stopped in and never got tired of the time she spent with them. When she got lonely, it was easier to come for a visit and chat with her new friends than spend the evenings alone. They were a balm to her fresh heartache —they understood loss and they didn't downplay her feelings. And they loved her cookies—especially the naughty ones. The book club ordered them weekly.

They also loved game shows, which was a huge plus. Ever since she was a kid, watching them with her grandmother, they'd become a permanent part of her routine. She loved the unpredictability of what would happen next. The strategy. The way they could take an average person and make their life better.

"Heather!" She turned when Harry, one of her favorite residents, hustled toward her. "How's my sweetheart?"

The retirement home was all decked out in pastel colors and a multitude of beiges. It was very subdued and meant to be calming. Harry was none of those things. He was a spry old man with a huge smile and an abundance of cologne.

She grinned. "I'm good. Bringing a friend who might want to live here for a tour." Heather gestured to Jase and Babushka, who were listening to the spiel about how the shuttle to downtown worked.

Harry's eyes twinkled. "Is she single?"

"No." Heather shook her head. "She's got a boyfriend."

He shrugged. "Eh. At our age, that status changes hourly."

Oh God, that's just what Jase needed. Another boyfriend for Babushka.

"The book club ladies and I want to ask you about a cookie-decorating class. We want to change things up." Harry rubbed his hands together. "What do you say?"

That sounded like a load of fun. "You all name the day."

"Aye-aye." Harry gave her a little salute and scooted off toward Babushka. Heather followed, slipping beside Jase. His hand found hers and he linked their fingers together.

And, dammit, she'd had sex with this man all weekend. But when he linked their fingers together? Butterflies danced through her stomach. She'd been out of the game for a while, so they were practically geriatric butterflies. But they still flitted, and she felt like a teenager who'd just been asked out to the movies.

Meanwhile, Harry was in total flirt mode—wide smile, freshly combed hair, animated talking. Babushka was eating it up, which didn't bode well for poor Morty.

"You wanna see the room where we're hosting the prom?" Heather whispered to Jase.

"Will we be alone, and does it smell like mothballs?" His breath played against her ear.

She turned so they were nose to nose. "Yes and no."

"Then I'm in." He unlinked their hands and laid his palm

on his grandmother's shoulder. "Heather's going to go show me some stuff. We'll catch up."

"Yes, yes. I'm good." Babushka brushed off his hand and linked her arm with Harry's outstretched elbow.

"I'm starting to think this retirement home might not be the best place for her." Jase glared in Harry's direction.

"It's this or Morty's."

Jase sighed heavily. "So, this place is looking better and better."

"C'mon. I'll show you." Heather pulled him toward the large rec room with a bank of windows along one wall that led out to a concrete patio with potted plants and benches. An abundance of white-plastic folding tables lined one wall next to a rack of metal chairs. They would set those up with table-cloths for the dance—given that the attendees likely wouldn't be able to stand for long periods. "I figured we'd put the DJ over there, and the dance floor here, and then snacks and punch right next to the door."

He took it all in. "You really like doing this stuff, don't you?"

"Well…yeah." She did. It gave her something to do and it made people happy. "I've got a little dance lesson planned, too. You wanna be my partner?"

"I'm in. Name the day." He pointed toward the patio. "What about an arch of flowers covering the doorway, and I can bring in some trellises and hang vines. We'll do it up with lots of flowers."

"That sounds expensive."

"We'll call it a write-off."

He would do that? Her chest heaved. In a good way. "Still. Maybe stick with carnations?"

Jase made a sour face. "I run a classy shop. We don't even let carnations in the door."

"And you don't mind doing this?" Heather gestured wide.

He tilted her chin up with his index finger. "I'd sell my left nut to have you look at me again the way you just did."

She leaned up on her tippy-toes and pressed a kiss to the edge of his mouth. "I like your nuts where they are, thank you."

He moved toward the windows, inspecting the walls around them. "Anything else you want for this thing? I'll have Elizabeth put together some corsages, and we can bring some single long-stemmed roses."

"I'm starting to rethink my stance on flowers." When it was just the two of them, it felt like no one else in the world existed.

He winked at her. "Then my plan is working."

"Vat are ve doing?" Babushka breezed into the rec room.

"Jase and I..." Heather glanced to him. "We're..."

And just like that, when another person showed up, she turned into a stammering mess.

"Heather's planning a prom for the residents here. I'm helping." Jase strode back, his hand caught hers, and he pulled her into his side.

"I vill live here. I have decided." Babushka clapped her hands, and apparently, that was that. "I vill start paperwork." She headed toward the offices at the front of the building.

Jase hadn't moved his arm, it was still slung around Heather, nestling her against his side.

"Are you good with this?" Heather asked, looking up at him from under her lashes. "Your grandmother living here?"

"The alternative is her living with that idiot from Blackhawk. So, yeah, I'm good with this." Jase gave her a side squeeze. "I'll talk to Eli, get him to do the food for this thing."

That would be amazing, but... "We really don't have that much of a budget, Jase. I was just thinking like cookies and punch or something."

"He owes me. I'll call in a favor." He caught her stare. "You're doing it again, sugar."

"Doing what?"

He traced the column of her neck with his fingertip. "Looking at me like that."

"I'll stop." She glanced around the room instead, doing a mental catalog of all that needed done.

Jase tilted her face back to him. "Don't stop. Don't ever stop."

Oh.

Well.

Oh.

Chapter Nineteen

Jase was working construction again, Babushka was settling into her new apartment, and Heather, Claire, and Velma were doing an impromptu let's-dissect-Heather's-life-choices at Velma's place.

"I thought you were off men." Velma settled into the white leather sofa.

"I was. But Jase and I... I don't even know what happened, it just did." Heather took an oversized gulp of chardonnay. "And mostly, it's been amazing."

"Mostly?" Claire asked.

"It's just, this morning I was pretty sure he was going to break up with me. Like we'd had our weekend of fun and he was done." And boy, was the weekend fun.

"But?" Claire pushed, her own glass of wine in hand.

"But then he didn't. And he's been really sweet." They'd gone to the assisted-living center with Babushka. She liked the place, Jase was okay with it, and she signed the lease.

"I feel like I have to be the one to say this." Velma paused and set her iced tea on a coaster. "I just think that for your first foray back into the world of dating, Jase may not be the best option."

Like Heather hadn't already thought that very same thing a thousand times.

"It's just that I don't think this is a healthy relationship when he didn't even want to acknowledge you to his family," Velma continued.

"I don't know." Claire sat taller. "Jase isn't Mr. Commitment, but neither was Brek. I mean, who would've called that one? Your relationship with him didn't exactly get off to a great start. It took time."

Claire made a good point—no one in their right mind would've expected a guy like Brek to settle down and enjoy married life. Or someone with Velma's particularities to be all in with a guy like him. And yet? He and Velma were happy. Blissfully so.

"What we need is a strategy for your heart." Velma was ready to make a list, Heather could feel it.

"V?" Brek hollered from the nursery where he was getting Lily changed.

"Hang on." Velma stood and pointed to both of them. "Don't say anything until I get back."

Velma scooted down the hallway.

"You think I need a strategy for my heart?" Heather asked Claire.

"I think you need to decide what you really want. If you really want to be alone, then do that. If you really don't want that, then don't. But don't be afraid to try with Jase."

"I'm back." Velma returned, baby in hand.

"And I'm out." Brek kissed his wife and sat to put on his motorcycle boots.

"Before you go. What do you think of the whole Jase-and-Heather-getting-together thing?" Velma asked. "It's the topic of conversation tonight."

Brek stood, stretched, and bent down to peck another kiss on Velma's lips. "My opinion is that I don't have an opinion."

"That's not helpful," Velma replied. "Did you hear Jase is helping Heather with the prom thing she's planning?"

"Nope." He grabbed his leather motorcycle jacket and pulled it on, zipping it up to the collar.

"Really?" Velma asked, unconvinced.

"Believe it or not, we don't sit around and gab all day," Brek replied.

"That is not entirely true," Heather said. From what she'd witnessed that afternoon, the boys talked a lot.

Brek grinned at her. "Don't spill the secrets."

"So, we're going to the prom," Velma told him.

He stared at her a beat. "Of course we are."

"I'm just wondering when you're going to ask me to be your date." Velma bounced Lily and grinned up at her husband.

"My ring on your finger?" he asked.

"Well, yeah."

"Done deal." He kissed her again, and then Lily's head.

"You should never just assume anything," Claire said to his back.

"Brek, did you get that DJ's name like we talked about?" Heather asked. "For my prom?"

"Shit, yeah," he said. "I'll text it. He said he's in."

"You know you're the best, right?" Heather asked.

Brek grunted and did a two-finger wave before heading out.

Claire stood to top off her glass. "I'm gonna make Dean ask me. He's gonna have to do a full promposal."

Cotton stuck in Heather's throat. Flashbacks to high school and a very uncomfortable prom night with no date. That wasn't now, though. She had a sort-of boyfriend, not that they'd labeled anything yet. But he was helping her plan prom, and they were sleeping together, and he was holding her hand. So, yeah, he was her prom date.

She'd just go with that.

Chapter Twenty
SENIOR "SENIOR" PROM COUNTDOWN:
3 DAYS

Heather was in Jase's bed, again. She'd met up with Jase at his apartment after her girls' night and then they'd continued their weekend fun late into Monday night. She ran her hand over his pillow. Around four a.m., he'd kissed her and told her he was heading down to the shop to get some work done. A few extra hours of sleep had done the trick, but it was time to get up and head to work.

She rolled from the bed, dressed, and headed downstairs.

Music blared from the speakers in the flower shop. Shirtless Jase was in his zone again—a private dance party to Warrant while he worked on a vase of gardenias. She paused at the foot of the stairs that led from his apartment to his shop, drinking him in.

He danced her way, and she knew the moment he saw her. His lips stopped moving to the beat of the song, and his eyes did that thing they did whenever he saw her—the instant soft thing. "Heather. Hey."

She couldn't hear the words, but she could read his lips well enough. Her blood heated, and she tingled all over, right up to the roots of her hair.

He turned off the stereo, Warrant singing about cherry

159

pie zipping to a stop. She moved to him, reaching up on her tiptoes to kiss him. He tilted his head, deepened the kiss, and held her close against him, his hands in her hair. Early mornings weren't so bad with Jase and a good make-out session.

"I guess this is the part where I tell you I have to go," she said once he broke the kiss, her mouth only millimeters from his. "The shop opens in an hour."

"Then this is the part where I tell you I'd rather you stay." He grinned.

"And this is when I remind you that you have work and then are spending the evening with your family."

He groaned. "Can't I just pretend I'm sick and come over to your place?"

"I'm watching game shows tonight. I'm way behind on my bingeing, and I need a dose of *Family Feud*."

"I guarantee if I come over, we won't be watching *Family Feud*." His hand slid down over her back, resting just below her waist.

Her fingertip seemed to trace circles on his pec on its own. "Don't make our first fight over Steve Harvey."

"Are we fighting? Do we get to make up later?" With the way he was looking at her, they'd need to go upstairs for another round before either of them would get anything done.

"Come by after you're done," she whispered against his lips.

The cowbell on the door clanked. They both glanced over.

His mom and sister stood there.

"Heather." Anna's eyes were bright. "I'm so glad you're here."

"Shit," Jase muttered under his breath. He dropped his hands and held them up in mock defense. "Whatever you two are about to do, knock it off."

"We came to invite Heather to tonight's family dinner,

Jason." His mother adjusted her purse over her shoulder. "Since we don't get together often."

"Only every other night," he mumbled under his breath.

"I figured she'd be here. I was totally right." Anna strutted over to Jase and held her hand up for a high five.

He didn't return it.

"Hi," Heather said cautiously.

The light in his eyes shut down. "Babushka would be the trifecta if she weren't pissed at everyone."

"Jase, it's okay." Heather gave his biceps a squeeze.

He pursed his lips. "Heather has plans tonight."

She did?

Were they back to this? Back to his walls around his family. A night with Steve Harvey hardly counted as plans.

"Heather?" Jase's mother asked.

"I've got to go to work." She chanced a glance to Jase, who had an unreadable expression etched on his face. "It's nice to see you again."

"Jase, quit being a dingbat. We'll be nice to Heather and we want to get to know her, too. Stop hogging her," Anna huffed. "Unless, you really have plans?" She turned her attention back to Heather.

Heather shifted on her feet.

"She does," Jase replied for her.

Plans that could easily change, but still, plans.

"Give us a second?" Heather asked. "Jase, will you walk me across the street?"

"Gladly." He grabbed her hand and marched across the street with her, not speaking.

"You don't talk much when you're angry, do you know that?" she asked when they got to the door of her shop.

He grunted.

She had to reach on her toes again so they were face-to-face. Well, face-to-face-ish. He was way taller than her, so it was more like chin-to-nose. She pressed her palms against his cheeks and tilted his face to hers. "If you don't want me there, I won't come. But I can hold my own with your family—if that's what this is all about."

He sighed. "You don't understand. They seem fine on the surface, but soon enough they'll be slipping under your skin and you'll be revealing your deepest secrets without realizing it ever happened."

"What am I going to say? Tell them that thing you did last night with your tongue?" His eyes flared. She went on, "Jase, we're just us. They're them. But they're a part of you, and I'd like to get to know that part."

"I went through training you can't even imagine. Training to prepare me for the worst of the worst this planet has to offer—people who thrive on breaking us down. People who take a Navy recruit and turn him into a pile of mush." He was totally serious. "Heather, they have nothing on my family. Because my family uses sweet saccharine to lure you in. Then they'll ruin everything."

"They cannot be that bad. I love your *babushka*. Your mom and sister seem great."

"Oh, they're great. They'll just involve themselves in our relationship."

"They're part of you." She pecked a kiss against his lips. "Let me in. Let me know them."

"You have no idea what you're getting yourself into." He stroked her cheekbone.

She unlocked the door, pushing it open. "We'll be in it together. It can't be that bad."

He grunted again. She glanced over his shoulder. His mom and Anna were on the sidewalk outside of their shop. They both waved.

"They're watching us," she whispered.

"Of course they are." He turned their direction and gave a little wave.

"Be serious for a minute." Heather gently grabbed his

arm. "Are you frustrated because I'm invited or because they're sticking their noses in?"

"I'm frustrated because I want you all to myself." The air between them got heavy.

She linked her arms around his neck. "I think that you're trying to be sweet."

"I'm trying to protect you."

"I'm a big girl. I can handle this." She glanced to his mom and sister. Yeah, she could handle this. They loved him and she…oh God….nope. Not going there. She really liked him a lot. So she already had something in common with his family.

Like…a whole lot of like.

Chapter Twenty-One

Heather held on to Jase's waist as he pulled his Ducati into the driveway of his family's huge Cherry Creek home. He parked, and she tossed her leg over the side, pulling her helmet off and hoping like hell her hair wasn't totally smashed. Jase had assured her the dress code was casual, but she still went with a summer dress and her hair down. She'd even curled it—not that it mattered with the way the helmet had likely smashed the curls.

Jase went with his perpetual jeans and T-shirt combo—this tee had his company logo on the front.

She retrieved the box of cookies she'd made from the saddlebags. Flower-shaped sugar cookies seemed appropriate, decorated with extra-sparkly sprinkles and a dash of edible luster dust. She'd added a dozen chocolate chip, because one could never go wrong with chocolate. "You ready?"

"No," he replied. "Let's do it, anyway."

He tucked her hand in his and headed for the front door. He didn't knock. Of course he didn't, he didn't have to.

"You're not even a little excited to see your brother?" she asked.

"Yeah, I'm excited to have a beer with him once all this

family bullshit is done." He squeezed her hand. "You want the tour?"

"You want to avoid the evening?" she replied, following him away from the sound of voices in the kitchen.

"Hell yes." He pulled her along with him as he showed her through the rooms of the house, carefully avoiding the area where his family chattered. She'd known that his family was loaded. Not just loaded, but like Molly-Brown-and-a-firepit-of-money loaded. Heather had been in the house once before, when Babushka texted her for the pickup, but she hadn't made it past the entryway.

The entryway was ornate, but the rest of the house was massive. High ceilings and one-of-a-kind signed Russian art on the walls. The whole house was decked out in cream and gold with marble accents. Heather had grown up in a small apartment in Arvada. Everything was thrift store and Walmart with linoleum accents. They might not have had a marble staircase, but there'd been a lot of love in that little second-story apartment.

Jase walked her through the bedroom wing of the house, taking his time showing her the different rooms. His old bedroom, his sister's, and both brothers. Zach, who still lived in Denver, and Roman, who was enlisted and rarely visited—the man of the night.

They paused at Jase's old bedroom.

"Didn't look like this when I lived here." He leaned against the dresser. "I wouldn't have let Mom put stupid pillows on my bed."

There were throw pillows at least a foot deep at the head of the bed. The whole room looked like it came from an interior design magazine spread. Still, there were little traces of Jase—framed photos on the nightstand of him with his family, and another of him with friends she'd never met before. It wasn't Brek and Dean and Eli—these guys had a military look to them.

She meandered to the closet and flicked on the light. A handful of dry-cleaning bags hung on the rack, his uniforms inside.

He'd come up behind her.

"You ever wear these?" she asked, turning so she could see him.

He shook his head. "Not anymore."

"Is that not allowed?" It would be a huge disservice to the world if Jase Dvornakov couldn't wear his uniform anymore. "'Cause uniforms are super sexy."

"They're allowed. Important events. Things like that. But I stick to a tux now." His expression had turned stoic.

Right. No more talk of sexy uniforms. She turned the closet light off and closed the door.

"You know what else is sexy?" she asked, ready to ease the heavy air that had taken over the room.

"What?"

"When you wear nothing." She pressed a quick kiss to his mouth.

He smiled against her lips. "Are you getting fresh with me in my parent's house?"

"Mm-hmm," Heather hummed as she deepened the kiss.

"Jason," a man who had to be his father said from the doorway.

Heather jolted and stepped away from Jase.

"Dad." Jase didn't seem at all fazed that his father had just walked in on them making out. "This is Heather."

Jase held his hand out to Heather. She grabbed it, tethering her to him in a gesture of reassurance she hadn't realized she needed.

"Hi." Heather held out her other hand.

Jase's dad shook it with a strong, warm grip. "It's nice to finally meet the woman who has cracked Jason's shell."

"I don't know that I'd go that far." Heather couldn't help the blush that was obviously creeping up her cheekbones.

"I guess Mom sent you to come find us?" Jase asked.

His father nodded. "Everyone is anxious to meet your girlfriend."

"We'll be right there." Jase continued holding Heather against his side as his father left. Clearly in no hurry to get to his family, he showed her to the open patio with a pool, an outside kitchen, and a table already set with a white tablecloth and bone china. *I'll take things that cost a bajillion dollars for two hundred, Alex.*

"Looks like we're eating outside tonight," Heather mused, running a finger along the length of the tablecloth.

"What do you think?" Jase tucked his hands in his pockets and rocked on his heels.

"I think you're holding out on me and I should've gone for the Mercedes version of my delivery van." Heather tucked her arm through his.

"Next week," he replied.

"What?"

"The van comes next week. I'm sure you'll be happy not to have to coordinate with Ethan anymore. They're painting it this week and then adding the cookie and then…delivery." He stroked the bare skin of her arm.

"Kind of crazy how this whole thing has played out, huh?" she asked.

He paused. "Yeah."

"You think this was her plan the whole time?" Heather stared at the wavy reflection of them on the surface of the pool. "Babushka."

"I don't even want to guess." They arrived at the patio door that led into the main kitchen. His parents, brothers, and sister were on the other side, unaware they stood there.

"What's your dad's name?" Heather stopped him before he pushed open the door.

"Alex. And you can call Mom Diana."

"Alex and Diana." Heather rehearsed their names. "And Zach and Anna."

"And Roman," Jase finished for her. "We call him Rome."

She sang the names under her breath. A little trick she used when she got nervous and needed to remember something.

"You're cute, you know that?" He pressed his hand to the small of her back and opened the door. All eyes turned to them. Heather was generally a confident woman, but five pairs of Dvornakov eyes trained on her at once and she was squirming in her sandals.

Zach and Roman looked a lot like Jase. Roman was built like a tank and sat tall—like Jase did. Zach lounged against the counter. Anna was all happy, perky smiles.

"Heather." Anna stood from her barstool. "Last time you were here we didn't even get to say hello." She turned her attention to Jase. "You're late, mister."

"Heather got the tour." He headed for a bottle of what appeared to be top-shelf Russian vodka next to a bottle of red wine and a bottle of white. He poured himself a small bit of vodka and held the bottle up to her.

She shook her head.

"I'll have a glass of white." Yes, it was definitely more of a wine evening, or they'd have to scrape her off the floor. And what kind of an impression would that make?

Jase poured her a glass.

"Heather, tell us about your busi—" Anna started.

"Ve can start. I am here." Babushka breezed into the room with Harry on her heels.

"Where's Morty?" Heather whispered to Jase.

"Fuck if I know," he answered.

"Morty couldn't be here," Babushka replied. "I brought Harry instead." Babushka brushed past everyone, beelining straight to her. "Heather. You are here. This is good thing."

Rome coughed into his hand. "Hey, Babushka."

She waved him away with a flick of her wrist.

Heather returned her hug, taking in the shocked expressions of the rest of the family.

"Heather is like the child I never had." Babushka patted her cheek.

Jase's dad cleared his throat at the comment. "You have a son. That would be me."

"I help her at her shop," Babushka ignored him. "We have vonderful time together. No judgement. Just happiness for me." She glared at her son. Man, when Babushka laid it on, she laid it on thick.

"I want happiness for you." Jase father's voice went softer. "I love you, Mama."

"You say this, but you forbid this and forbid that."

"I forbid because I do love you. Can't you see that?"

"No." She turned her attention to the rest of the room. "Now, vere is Rome? Ah, my boy. You come home."

"Babushka, I've missed you. I hear we're going to have another huge birthday party this year." He returned her hug.

Jase's dad shook Harry's hand. "You are the man who took money from my mother?"

Harry paled and glanced to Babushka.

"No, that's the other one," Jase mumbled under his breath.

"That is Morty. Different man." Babushka poured herself a tumbler of vodka. "This is Harry. We live together."

Oh God. Jase's father's face started to turn purple, but credit to him for keeping it together. "You live together?"

"I guess I'm off the hook, huh?" Heather muttered quietly to Jase.

"You live with this man?" his father asked again.

"I think she means, they live together at the retirement home," Heather tried to help.

"Details." Babushka waved a hand toward Heather.

"What the hell did I miss while I was gone?" Rome asked Zach.

"Babushka's having a very late midlife crisis." Zach went to work on his own glass of vodka.

Jase pulled at Heather's arm and shook his head. "Rules of combat in the Dvornakov house: stay low, don't say anything, don't let them see weakness."

"I think you're being a bit dramatic." Heather watched him over the rim of her wineglass.

"Also, if it's stupid but it works, then it isn't stupid." Rome lifted his glass to her.

"Heather, sweetheart, we missed you at book club last week." Harry strutted her way.

"You know this man?" Jase's father asked.

"Heather volunteers at the retirement home. She likes committees." Jase placed his hand at her back, a silent gesture of support that meant everything. "Mom likes committees, too."

So he'd said.

"What committees do you serve on?" his mother asked.

"Right now, I'm helping with the senior 'senior' prom at the retirement home up the street from our shops. I thought it'd be fun for everyone and help bring in some new potential residents."

"Nadzieja already agreed to go with me." Harry's eyes danced. "For part of the night. I'm sharing her with the man who owns Pistol Polly's. I get second shift."

"Pistol Polly's?" Anna asked.

Heather swallowed hard.

"Second shift?" Zach asked, eyes wide.

"Oh shit," Jase said under his breath.

"It vas Heather's idea for me to move in with Harry." Babushka picked at one of the appetizer trays.

"It was your idea for Nadzieja to move in with Harry?" Jase's mother asked Heather in total seriousness. There was definitely an edge to the words that hadn't been there before.

Heather choked on a sip of wine. "No…that's not—"

"Was this before or after they decided to take shifts with my mother?" Jase's dad asked, his expression a blank canvas.

The wine had gone sideways in her chest. She thumped at it with her fist.

Jase started to talk. "I think I can explain this—"

"Because she and Jase need their privacy at her apartment. She says I need my own space," Babushka continued. "That I should move in with Harry."

Okay, so that was not at all how the conversation had gone.

"This is what you say to my mother?" his father asked.

Shit. No. "Jase…" Heather said.

"This is getting twisted." Jase pulled her against his side. "Dad, Babushka wanted to move in with her boyfriend—the other one—so Heather was coming up with alternatives. This was a much better idea."

"And home is not an alternative?" His father glanced between Heather and Jase. "This is not an alternative you presented to my mother?"

So maybe she wasn't off the hook after all.

"Morty is vonderful, but he always vorks," Babushka babbled on. "Heather saw this when she took me to his restaurant."

"To Pistol Polly's? They have a restaurant?" His mother's eyebrows fell together. "I'm confused."

Heather tried to explain. "It was a total misunderstanding. I didn't realize where she wanted to go eat—"

"C'mon, Dad, it's not like Heather hasn't been helpful to Babushka," Anna tried to reason. "When you lost your temper, she let her stay with her."

"I lost my temper because she's handing out money to men we don't know."

"What the hell has been going on here?" Rome stood, apparently ready to join in the fray.

"Heather, let's go on the patio and sit by the pool." Jase snagged her hand and started toward the exit.

"When did you take my mother to the strip club?" Jase's dad asked.

Heather's heart stalled. "It wasn't like that. I mean, yes, that's where we ended up. And, sure, I was driving. But it was her idea and I didn't realize until we got there—"

"Hey. Where did Babushka go?" Zach asked.

Harry was missing, too. Heather glanced to Jase. "You don't think they'd…?"

"They'd what?" Anna asked.

Jase pinched his lips together and shook his head. "This is why we can't have nice dinners."

Jase's father bustled from the room, his mother following, both of them talking to each other in rapid-fire Russian.

"Ten bucks says they're making out in a closet somewhere." Jase's forehead was etched with lines, and the little lines around his mouth pointed straight down. "Let's get out of here."

Heather's hand in his, he started for the front door.

"My family doesn't really do dinners like this. We save it for Christmas and stuff," Heather said, trying a bit of small talk. Now she kind of understood why they only got together a few times a year. If this was the kind of family drama that getting together regularly brought, she'd stick with twice-a-year get-togethers.

Jase's mother shrieked from down the hallway. His father boomed what sounded to be Russian profanity.

Heather heaved a breath and chanced a look to Jase. "Yup. Making out in a closet. At least they didn't have time to do what we caught them doing."

"What did you catch her doing?" Anna's expression was of total confusion.

Heather's nerves had all gone numb, like when you're in a car and it's about to hit a telephone pole. Not that it had ever happened to her, but if it did, this is what she imagined it would feel like.

"We caught Babushka with her other boyfriend," Jase replied. "They were…having…"

"Sex," Heather finished for him.

"Serious?" Anna asked.

Jase nodded.

"Well. Shit." Zach stood and refilled his tumbler of vodka. "Dad might just stroke out if he finds out."

Heather's shoulder slumped. "I don't think this is going well."

The muscles in Jase's jaw clenched. "Welcome to my personal hell." He dropped his untouched vodka tumbler on the counter. "Another rule of Dvornakov combat? Evacuate and get the hell out."

Heather was 110 percent on board with that.

"Oh, hell no." Rome jumped to block the exit. "If we have to stay, you have to stay."

Jase widened his stance. "Heather, how do you feel about waiting by my bike?"

"What?" Heather slid her gaze to him.

He pressed his hands in his pockets, like they were at the zoo waiting in line to see the zebras. "You wanna get out of here?"

She nodded.

"I have a plan to get us out of here. Do you trust me?"

Uh. "Sure."

"Then when I say go, you go. Wait by my bike. I'll be right there."

"That's how this is going to go?" Rome asked, a sly smile stretching across his lips.

"Shit." Zach stood and started moving the wineglasses off the kitchen island.

Heather gripped his forearm. "Jase, what are you doing?"

"Don't get in the middle of it," Anna said, hopping up on a barstool by the sink. "You'll get a collateral-damage-black-eye, and they'll both feel bad."

"Jase…" Heather's heart started to pound. "Whatever you're going to do—"

"Trust me," Jase said before she could finish. Then he stared straight at Roman. "You really want to block my way?"

The ominous air that had taken over the room intensified. Heather pulled at his arm. "Jase," she said, her voice low.

She was already on the short list of things his parents hated, she didn't need whatever Jase was planning with his brother.

"Be ready to move. I'll be right behind you." He turned his entire focus back to Roman.

Roman made a little c'mere motion with his fingers, licked them, and crouched. Like, he actually licked his fingers.

Well, crap.

"Go." Jase said it so low that she barely heard it. But she hurried into the hallway to the front door, tossing it open. Anna squealed. Zach let out a "whoooop." Something shattered. Something large shattered. There was… Was that fist on flesh? It sounded like someone was taking hits. She started to turn back, this was ridiculous.

"What are they doing?" Jase's mother hurried beside her.

Heather glanced to her and opened her mouth to tell her she had no idea, but Diana clearly got the message, what with the telltale thuds and cracks coming from the kitchen.

"Why didn't you stop them?" Diana whisked herself in to the kitchen. More Russian cursing. She must've learned that from Jase's dad.

Heather didn't need to stick around to figure out what Jase and Roman had done. She'd take his rules of combat and evacuate as directed.

She bolted to the Ducati. She'd barely made it there when

the front door opened and Jase strolled out like nothing had happened. No crashes, no thuds.

He grabbed her helmet. Tossed it to her. And dealt with his own.

And he didn't say a word.

The light in his eyes said it all.

"Do I need to go check on your brother?" she asked.

"Nope," he replied, clicking her chinstrap for her.

"What did you do to him?" She slid her gaze back to the house. It looked totally normal. Fine. Like nothing had happened.

"He wouldn't let us leave." Jase tossed his leg over the bike, kicking on the motor.

"Jase…" She crossed her arms. Maybe she should go in and check on Roman.

He turned to her. "I didn't hurt him. I just tied him to the refrigerator."

How on earth?

He raised his eyebrows and tilted his head to the seat behind him. "You'll want to get on, because if we're not out of here before Mom comes out, we'll end up staying. I can't tie her to the refrigerator."

Who was this guy?

You know what? She didn't need to know. If this was the kind of thing people in big mansions did, she'd just be glad she'd grown up in a tiny apartment. A small, totally normal apartment.

JASE WAS PRETTY SURE his mother was blowing up his phone. Not that he'd check tonight; he'd turned it off before he tied Roman to the fridge. His own fucking fault for trying to block Jase and Heather in.

On a good night, his family went a little bonkers at these

things, but with Roman home and Babushka off her rocker, the last thing he needed was for Heather to see just how crazy his family could be. And he could tell from the way things were going, they were just greasing the gears for the real bizarre to come out.

He pulled up behind Heather's shop, parking his bike in the alley next to the door leading to her kitchen. He turned off the engine and helped Heather to her feet.

"Is this how dinners with your family usually go?" She pulled off her helmet.

"Yes and no." He tucked the keys in his pocket.

She leaned into him, whispering in his ear, "A little more, Jase."

Shit, he didn't want to dissect this. "Yes, it's usually crazy. No, I don't usually get to leave."

She shifted on her feet, clearly unsure. "Why'd we leave, then?"

"Because I would like, at the end of the night, for you to still be speaking to me." And possibly doing other things with him. He also didn't particularly want to be around the table with Babushka and Harry while they acted like teenagers.

"I won't judge you based on your family." She stepped forward, placing her arms on his shoulders. "They're them. You're you."

"See? You say that now. But..." He did a little one-sided lip curl, shaking his head.

She dropped her hands, unlocked the heavy exterior door, and pushed inside. "Do you want to place bets on what happened with Babushka and Harry after your parents caught them?"

"I want to not discuss my family anymore." He paused to trace the edge of her forehead with his thumb.

"You want a cookie?" she asked, letting him by.

He heaved a breath from his lungs. "Is that code for something? Because either way, I definitely want a cookie."

She gave a deep, throaty laugh before flicking on the lights in her kitchen. The kitchen was immaculate. He'd never seen it without her staff. Usually, it was bustling, with flour and icing flying.

"I can fix you a sandwich?" she asked.

"I'm good with cookies."

She grabbed a bin of undecorated sugar cookies, pulling off the lid. "I know you don't want to talk about your family anymore, but for some reason, you kicking someone's ass is totally a turn-on."

"How much of a turn-on?" he asked as she opened another bin filled with pastry bags of icing. She must've meant real cookies. That was fine, but later he wanted the figurative ones, too.

"Like, I'm in the showcase showdown on *The Price is Right* and my showcase is the one with a trip to Tuscany, a boat, and"—she went into game-show-announcer mode—

"*a brand-new car.*"

God, she was funny. He pressed his lips together so he wouldn't bust out laughing and ruin the mood he was attempting to set.

"What do you, ah, want to do about that?" Jase dropped his voice lower.

She glanced up from icing his name on a cookie, obviously catching his vibe. "I suppose I'd like you to teach me to tie you up. Seems like that's a skill you've been holding out on me about."

His pulse skipped. Well, folks, he had not expected that. "I could teach you. First, I'd have to show you. I'd need you to volunteer."

"That sounds fun. I could do that. But don't lose focus, I want to learn the ropes. As they say."

He moved closer to her, not in her space, but close enough he caught her scent. "You get me tied up, what are you going to do next?"

"How do you feel about frosting? Because I love frosting." She piped a bit on her fingertip.

"You are not icing my dick." He had very few things he wouldn't do, but he drew the line there.

"I'm really good at icing dicks."

"I repeat. You are not icing my dick."

"I'll lick it off." She illustrated what she'd do with her tongue and her lips until there was no more icing on her finger. Well, hello, there, Heather.

Fuck it all, he no longer had that limit. Go figure.

"All right, so we get a little frosting involved. I get to have fun, too."

"Where would you like to put it, Mr. Dvornakov?" she asked, the epitome of innocence.

He turned her so she faced the table, her back to his chest. Hands on her shoulders, he moved them to her collarbone, slowly down to her breasts, stopping at her nipples to rub circles there. "Maybe here?"

"Hmm…" She dropped her head against his pecs.

He continued lower, his hands pulling her against him. He stopped at her navel, rubbing more circles. "Here."

"You're getting warmer," she said in a singsong voice.

"And it'll feel so good, but your hands will be like this." He pulled the pastry bag from her grip. Then he raised her arms so they stretched around his neck. "Don't move them," he whispered in her ear. "See, they'll be here. And you'll want to touch yourself, but you'll have to wait, because I'm going to be enjoying the frosting." His hands continued their lazy journey down to the skirt covering her outer thighs. Stopping there.

"Where would you like me to put the frosting, sugar?" He brushed his lips against her ear.

She moaned, her hands still at his neck, her back still pressed against him. "Jase," she said quietly.

Carefully, he lifted the edge of her dress so it was up around her hips before returning his hands to her thighs.

"Little to the left." She squirmed against him.

"Then do I get my cookie?" His voice was rough.

"Then you can have all the cookies," she replied.

He moved his hands to her inner thighs, rubbing there with the pads of his fingertips—just inches away from where he knew she wanted it. Drawing it out, making them both squirm. His erection pressed against the seam of his jeans, right against the outline of her ass.

Whatever this game was they were playing, he wasn't ready for it to end.

She started to pull her arms away from his neck. Quickly, he moved his hands from her thighs to adjust her hands back to his neck again. He held them there. "Now we have to start over. It's a good thing I like frosting."

She made a gurgle sound in the back of her throat.

"Let's go back to the beginning. And this time"—he began his slow descent down her body once more—"don't move your hands."

He brushed the hair from her shoulders, a light touch down the inside of her arms with his knuckles, over the slope of her breasts, pausing at her waist. She parted her thighs, but her arms didn't move.

"See, you're good with games. You learn fast." He nipped at her earlobe. "Be a good girl, and drop your arms to the table, but don't move them once they're there."

She did as directed.

"Do you want to do this here or upstairs?" He lifted her skirt, tracing the edge of her thong with his index finger.

"Here." She gripped the table harder, grinding her core against his finger.

"Good choice." He removed his hand from her skirt so he could free his erection.

He didn't go right back to the heat of her, first he pulled

her thong down to her knees, then he grabbed the pastry bag and squeezed a dollop of frosting onto his fingertip.

"Jase, please."

She didn't have to ask more than once. With his not-frosted hand, he tested to be sure she was ready, and thanked the gods of kitchen fucks that she was. Slowly, because that seemed to be the name of the game that night, he entered her.

He'd never been so ready for a woman before.

She moaned, dropping her head. But she knew the game and she didn't move her hands from where he'd directed. He lifted the frosting on his fingertips to her lips. She opened her mouth, licking at the icing before he slid them into her mouth. She sucked harder and he started moving inside her to the rhythm she set with her mouth.

Time slowed further. The only thing that mattered was the two of them.

He panted along with her, on the precipice of something he knew was big but that he couldn't understand. She flexed her internal muscles around him, nearly sending him spiraling.

With his free hand, he reached to her sweet spot, massaging the place he knew drove her crazy. Pushing her over the edge.

She fell first, and he followed.

Wrapping his arms around her, burying his face in her neck, he held her steady as she clamped around him over and over. Still, she didn't move her hands. Her knuckles were nearly white from gripping the table.

Both of them out of breath, he withdrew and straight-ened her panties back where they went. "Sugar, you can move your hands now."

"I don't think I'm ever going to be able to move again," she replied, breathing hard.

He lifted her palms from the table, kissing each fingertip.

"We can go upstairs, and it'll be your turn to play with the frosting."

A wry grin spread across her lips. "You are so on."

Pastry bag in hand, she sauntered toward the stairs to her apartment. He took his time putting himself back together. She paused at the corner of the room, raising her eyebrows. He snagged the cookie with his name from the tray on the table and bit into it.

Tonight, he was getting all the cookies.

Jase sat by the cash register in his shop and did a quick inventory of the raspberry-ice-carrousel roses he'd managed to track down. After the clusterfuck of a dinner party the night before, he and Heather had ended up not-sleeping at her apartment. He had a whole new fondness for icing uses in bedroom adventures. He liked Heather's place. It was comfortable and had real furniture. Unlike his makeshift bachelor pad with crates as end tables.

Then Dean had texted him that Claire was requiring he do a full-out promposal for her and he needed ideas. Fuck that. If Jase was going to plan a promposal, it'd be for Heather. Thus, the hunt for every raspberry-ice rose in the Denver metro area.

So far, he was pretty sure he'd come up with enough. Ten dozen ought to do it. And another few hundred rose petals for the bed. He'd already asked Babushka for her key so he could slip in before Heather returned from work.

Babushka had given him the third degree about what he was doing and why. Then he heard her tell Harry that he needed to step up and ask her before Morty did. Then Harry had called and ordered a bouquet of two dozen red roses and a box of chocolates the size of Babushka's Buick. Apparently, that's what Babushka required to agree to be his date.

Yeah, prom season brought out the crazies.

The cowbell on his door clunked and he glanced up. His mother, father, and Anna.

Fuck.

"Mom. Dad. Anna." He tucked the slip of paper with the rough design of how he'd pull this off in his pocket. "Didn't expect to see you so soon."

His mother was pretty pissed about the whole refrigerator situation. He knew because she had left him a multitude of voice messages over the past eighteen hours informing him.

"We came to talk to you about Heather." His mother was wringing her hands, but he knew it was all for show. She didn't get nervous, but she put on a good show.

"Talking about Heather is off the table." He strode to the cooler and did a quick adjustment to the display—anything to avoid the discussion about his love life that was sure to follow.

"We're just worried about some of the things that she's done with Babushka." Anna flicked her hair over her shoulder. "The strip club and moving her to the retirement home without talking to us about it."

"Well, one, the strip club was all Babushka. Two, it was either the retirement community or moving in with the man who owns Pistol Polly's. And, three, I like her so lay off."

"Son, we'd like to open a conversation about this with you. We want you to move on, find a nice girl, but we don't think that's Heather." His father crossed and uncrossed his arms.

His mother sighed. "It's not that *we* don't like her. We just worry about her influence. So far, it hasn't been…"

"Great. It hasn't been great," Anna finished.

"You wanted me to date someone," he reminded them. Hell, it was all they'd talked about for a year. They had meetings about that shit.

"We wanted you to meet someone. But Heather's…" His mother twisted her face in illustration of how she felt about her.

And that was unacceptable.

"Look, Babushka is in some strange midlife crisis forty years too late. She's pulled Heather into her crazy. You can't blame Heather." He pointed to Anna. "And you don't get a say about who I'm dating or why or when." And now his blood pressure was rising. "You all wanted me to start dating." He stabbed the air between them. "And I didn't want to, but then I met Heather and she's fun and we're enjoying each other."

"You two already broke up once, can't you just go back to that?" Anna asked. "Just think of all the reasons it didn't work the first time. Saves a whole lot of trouble."

Jase glared at the lot of them. "You are my family, and I care about you. But if you don't knock this shit off, we're going to have some serious issues. The kind that a family therapist won't even be able to fix."

Anna raised her hands. "I didn't realize you felt so strongly about it."

"Yeah. Well. I do." Apparently, he did.

"Do you remember when you came home?" his mother asked. "From over there."

Of course he remembered. He'd been overseas on a mission for Uncle Sam. There were multiple explosives. He'd gone to work on one, his crew on the others. One of theirs had gone off. He was only steps outside the kill zone. He'd survived. They hadn't.

Then he came home, and he found his wife had created a life without him. She'd moved on. He couldn't.

"We all stepped in to help you. Set you up here at the shop. Made sure you were eating. Made sure you had a place to sleep—because you didn't care. We made sure you found your way back to us," his father said, repeating what Jase already knew. Hell, he'd lived it once. He didn't need a reminder. "Your friends died. Your wife left. Life was hard… but we didn't let you disappear, even when you checked out."

Jase gulped at the realization of all his family had done for him. And all the time he'd thought they were meddling. Thought they were being intrusive.

They'd known exactly what they were doing—not letting him disappear into his own head forever.

"You trusted us then," his father continued. "Trust us now."

He had trusted them then. But they were wrong now. They were wrong about Heather.

"I am grateful for everything you all have done for me." Jase hooked his thumbs in his belt loops and stared at the ground for a moment. Reminding himself where he was, what he was seeing, what he was doing—so he didn't go back to that place. "But I'm ready to take over my own life. And that's going to include Heather."

It was 100 percent going to include Heather. Because he was 100 percent into her.

Shit, when had that happened?

He thought back and…if he were honest with himself, it'd happened long before she'd walked into his shop with a stack of posters.

A length of silence hung in the air.

"If she means this much to you, and to Babushka, we'd like to get to know her," his mother finally said.

Maybe his mother could be reasonable.

"For real get to know her, or so you can try to control us get to know her?" he asked.

"Jason, believe it or not, our entire lives are not spent trying to control yours," his mother said.

He begged to differ. Believe it or not, he could count all the times they hadn't tried to control what he did on less than one finger.

He glanced out the shop window just as Babushka marched up the sidewalk to Heather's shop. She was leading a parade of the elderly. *What the hell?* He counted ten of them with her—walkers, canes, even a woman in an electric scooter. All Babushka was missing was a baton and her marching-band uniform.

He shook his head.

He did not need to know what his grandmother had planned.

"You should apologize to her, Mom." He'd be firm on that one. Heather may not have understood what his mom and dad had said when they'd left the kitchen, but he hadn't missed it.

"For what?" A mask of confusion fell over her face.

He shoved his hands on his hips. "She can't speak Russian, but I can. And I heard what you and Dad said last night."

At least his mother had the decency to look flustered. "It was a rough night."

No kidding. Not all of their family gatherings ended with one of their children tied to an appliance, but when they did, it was because Babushka was stirring up shit.

He chanced a glance across the street, but they'd all gone inside.

"Mom, Heather does seem really nice," Anna tried. At least one of them was coming around to his side. "And Jase seems happy. We should fix this. Make sure she knows she's always welcome at the house."

"She's at her shop. I'll walk over with you. Elizabeth?" Jase hollered over his shoulder. "I'm running out for a bit."

He led his reluctant parents and sister to the front of Heather's shop.

Anna laid a hand on his shoulder. "Jase, we really want you to be happy. That's what all of this is about."

"Then lay off and just let things be." He pulled open the door and gave a wave to the cashier. He'd been around enough lately, she didn't even question him going straight to the back.

Heather glanced up and her smile lit her whole face. It wasn't lost on him that she was smiling like that for him. His mother, father, and Anna followed behind. Heather's smile disintegrated.

It was apparently cockie day at the shop because she had trays and trays of them on the table in front of her. All the blood in his body dropped to his toes. He sucked in a breath.

Babushka and her comrades were decorating cockies.

"Jase, you brought your parents. And your sister. To my kitchen." Heather stared daggers at him.

Some of the cockies were even decorated like policemen and firemen and…no. No more looking, because what he saw his mother saw. And his mother was not going to be okay with the penis-shaped firemen cockies on Heather's tray. Although, he had to give it to Heather, the way she did that helmet was very creative.

He tilted his head. Yeah, he never would've thought to do it that way.

"We're supposed to be making flower cookies for prom," Heather said, unmoving. "But I have orders…and they were more excited about these."

"Ve need to vork on the foreskins." Babushka emerged from behind a rack of trays. "They look better in the bouquets."

"What on earth?" His mother stared at the trays of cookies.

"They insisted," Heather said, her face pale. "Babushka's idea."

Of course it was.

One of the elderly women icing veins onto her cockie glanced to his mother. "The thick ones are easier to handle. Go for those."

"She means the cookie," Heather said quickly. "They don't break as easily."

His father said nothing, his mouth simply opened and closed with no sound emerging. That was a first.

"They came to apologize for the other night." He scrubbed a hand at his neck. "I didn't realize it was bachelorette party day."

Anna didn't say anything, she just stood there, eyes wide. "Why are they decorated like policemen?"

"It's a new thing I'm trying. So far customers love the unique icing." Heather started strong with her enthusiasm, but she lost all her steam there at the end. Probably because his mother's expression was equal parts horror and anger.

"This isn't all I make," Heather said quickly. "I mean, obviously, because I brought you the flower ones. We do all shapes. For weddings. Kids' birthday parties. And different flavors. Lemon, chocolate chip, snickerdoodle. But these pay a lot of the bills. And they're just for fun—"

"Vould you like to try one?" Babushka held up one that… yes, it was a foreskin penis. "They are delicious."

And that's the story of how his grandmother bit off the tip of a dick cookie in front of his mother.

Heather gasped. His father paled. Anna's jaw dipped further, her mouth the shape of an O. His mother didn't seem to be breathing.

And Jase? Well. There's that moment one realizes they are utterly and truly fucked between their mother's wish for them to be happy and the girlfriend who could not catch a break. This was that moment.

His girlfriend made policemen penis cookies. How was he going to get his mother past *that?* "It's like I love your brain," Jase said to Heather. "And then I don't understand it at all."

She shook her head at him, her eyes squinted in the most adorable what-the-fuck look he'd ever seen. Okay, perhaps he should've kept his trap shut.

"Mom, you totally have to apologize to Heather now." Anna linked arms with his mother and pushed her forward. "Because when we get together for Thanksgiving this year, it's going to be epic."

Thanksgiving was the furthest thing from his mind. Turkey-shaped cookies, and Babushka, and her two boyfriends. It'd be a Russian-flavored Griswold celebration. He glanced to his mother. If he wasn't mistaken, she still hadn't taken a breath.

"Mom." Anna tapped her on the back.

His mother gulped. She closed her eyes. Counted to five in Russian. Then, without another word, she turned on her heel and left the kitchen. His father followed without saying a word.

"Shit," Jase said. He didn't even say it under his breath. There was no need.

Heather stayed in place, piping bag in hand, staring at the space his mother had vacated.

"Vat?" Babushka asked, a little penis crumb falling to the floor.

Yes, he'd been well and truly fucked by a penis-shaped sugar cookie dressed like a policeman.

"Well, I don't know what it takes to get involved in this, but I definitely want to participate." Anna sidled up next to the woman in the scooter and grabbed a cookie.

Chapter Twenty-Three

By the time Heather slogged up the stairs to her apartment, it was already eight o'clock at night, and if she had to look at another sugar cookie, she might stab her eyes out. Apparently, every bachelorette party in eastern Colorado was that week. She'd spent the entire day icing dicks. And freaking out Jase's family. He assured her they'd come around, they just needed time. But given the look on his mother's face, Heather was pretty sure time wasn't going to fix what was broken.

After his mother walked out, Anna had stuck around and chatted. Turned out Anna was pretty fun. Also, she had a flair for using the flood icing and an inventive idea for prickly peckers decorated like a cactus.

Needless to say, it'd been a long day, and all Heather wanted was a bowl of Cheerios, a shower, *The Price is Right* on repeat, and bed.

And Jase, she wanted Jase.

But Jase was busy with his renovations, and she was too spent to even walk across the street to hang out with him.

She stuck her key in the keyhole, but it was already unlocked. She pushed open the door.

"Candy?" she called. Candy was the only one with a key.

Well, Babushka had one, too. But Babushka was tucked away with Harry at the retirement home for the night.

"Hey." Jase was lounging on the couch, some book—it looked like the retirement home's June book club pick—in his hands. He knifed off the sofa and dropped the novel on the coffee table. "I wanted to surprise you. Didn't realize you'd have to work so late."

"How'd you get in?" she asked, hanging her purse on the hook.

"Babushka lent me her key. I hope that's okay." His hands fell to his hips. He hadn't changed after work—same *The Flower Pot* tee and pair of jeans he'd been wearing earlier.

She dropped her keys in the bowl by the door. "It's always all right."

Were they at the key-swap stage of their relationship? She should ask. See if he wanted to.

"Long day?" he asked. As though he hadn't been there when his mom and sister had shown up in her kitchen.

She ran a hand over her forehead, probably making her bangs stick straight up. She did her best to fluff them. "If I see another penis today, I'll lose my mind."

He raised an eyebrow. "That doesn't sound promising for our night. I brought you dinner." He did his chin-jerk thing to her table.

If she wasn't into the man before, the fact that he'd brought her a chicken bake did her in. He could totally have a key.

"Don't worry, Eli made it. I wouldn't subject you to my cooking," he continued.

"I'm glad you're here." She kicked off her shoes and walked straight to him.

His arms encircled her and the crazy of the day drifted away.

"You look spent." He brushed a kiss at the crown of her head.

She glanced up at him. "You have no idea."

He scooped her up in his arms and started toward the bedroom. "Jase, what are you doing?"

"I'm going to get you a bath started. I'll bring you dinner, and then put you to bed," he said with military-like precision.

Okay, that sounded pretty good. Arms around his neck, she relaxed against him.

He pushed open the door, and she saw that the whole room was filled with candles and the pink and white roses he'd been bringing her. He called them carrousel something. She sucked in a breath. There were vases and vases of the roses, and rose petals were scattered all over her bedspread. Her heart skipped. Then she realized they spelled out something, and she looked closer.

Prom?

She couldn't hold back the giggle. "Are you asking me to prom?"

"I am." He set her feet down and held her hands in his. "Heather Reese, will you go to prom with me?"

"Did Babushka know you were doing this? Is that why she gave you the key?"

"I have to have some secrets, don't I?"

She pressed the back of her hand against her lips. "I can't believe you left a massacre of flowers in my bedroom."

"That doesn't answer my question," he said on a growl.

"Of course I'll be your date, you loony tune." She pressed a kiss against his lips.

"Okay, good. Because otherwise it'd be really awkward." He pecked a kiss on her nose. "Now, bath for you."

He started toward her bathroom. *Deep breaths, Heather.* She took in the room: he'd also added a bottle of champagne and two champagne glasses to her nightstand. Funny, when she'd come up from work, she'd been exhausted. Now? Now, she was exhilarated.

He'd asked her to prom. And his promposal was fantastic.

She did a twirl that would've made teenage Heather proud.

The bathtub faucet turned on behind the closed door. And now he was filling a tub for her? She practically had to pinch herself.

She followed him, latching the door behind her. He was on his knees filling her soaker bathtub. He'd lit her candles in there, too. The whole place smelled like jasmine.

Hands at her sides, she moved to him and ran her palms over his back. "This is really amazing, Jase."

He grinned up at her and something shifted in his eyes. It was almost unnoticeable, but she seemed to be so tuned into him lately, even the smallest change affected her.

She pulled her polo work shirt over her head and tugged the band from her hair, finger-combing it. He hadn't stopped looking at her. She undid the clasp on her bra and let it fall to the ground. As the bra hit the bath mat, his pupils dilated in anticipation of what would come next.

She continued her striptease, unzipping her jeans and pulling them over her hips, down her thighs, past her calves, and kicking them away. He continued to drink her in. The bathtub continued filling, but she wasn't done. She pulled her panties down, pushing them aside with her toe, so she was completely bare in front of him.

His nostrils flared, but still he didn't say anything. A step into the bath and she tested the water—of course it was perfect. She slid beneath the water and glanced at him. He still hadn't moved. Hadn't said anything.

"Aren't you coming?" she asked.

"I should ask you to prom every night." He pulled his shirt over his head and made quick work of removing his jeans and boxers.

"Front or back?" she asked as he stepped into her soaker tub.

"Can't go down on you from the back." He knelt between her legs, pulling them around his hips.

"We're in a bathtub, pretty sure you'll drown if you try." She sat up and wrapped her arms around his neck, then traced a fingertip along the anchor tattoo on his arm.

"I do believe you just dared me." He grinned against her mouth and started kissing his way down the column of her neck. "I used to defuse bombs underwater. The difference was I didn't want them to go off when I was done."

Oh.

He continued kissing down her chest, over her nipples, and just as he got to the waterline, he took a deep breath, and, holy shit, he was actually going to go down on her underwater in a bathtub. He gripped her hips, positioned her under his mouth, and…he was doing an amazing job. How was he able to do that with his tongue and no oxygen? Well, she'd never know.

Back pressed against the tub, she ran a hand over her breasts and down to his shoulders, ready to pull him up from the water. He released his grip on her hips only long enough to pull her hands from where she was tugging him up by his shoulders.

Okay, so he wasn't wanting to be done yet. That was fine. She could keep doing this. Really, if he could hold his breath this long, she'd just appreciate it for the feat it was. Everyone had their skill set, and if this was his, she was a very, very lucky woman.

He licked and sucked and then he released her hips to get his hand in on the action. Breathing hard, she wrapped her ankles around his back, careful not to press down. But he was Jase, and he did what he wanted when he wanted. If he wanted to come up for air, there was nothing she would be able to do to prevent that.

At the moment, he apparently didn't require oxygen

because he was doing things with his mouth and tongue that she'd only read about in books.

He pulled away from her, emerged from the water, grinned, took a deep breath, and without a word, he disappeared under the water again.

This was such a better way to unwind than watching *Jeopardy*. All those months she'd decided to go off men, apparently, she'd just not picked the right one.

The coil inside her began to tense, and she relaxed against his mouth, ready to let him take her over the edge. And he was really giving it his all as he kissed and licked and, really, how did he do that thing with his finger? He pressed her sweet spot with his thumb—at exactly the right place. She moaned as the orgasm took over, her head falling against the side of the bathtub.

Best. Promposal. Ever.

She was still coming when he finally came up for air.

He pressed a kiss against her mouth.

She toyed with the close-cropped hair at the base of his neck. "The last time a guy asked me to prom, all I got was a dozen roses." And a night alone when prom came.

Jase was kissing her neck—the sensitive skin right under her ear. She pressed her palms against his hips, moving them to his…yup, he was hard as a rock. Reaching around him, she snagged a bottle of bath oil and poured it into her palm.

He watched her, his eyes heavy-lidded while she got to her knees, her hand between them gripping his dick, rubbing up and down the length of him. So maybe she could deal with one more dick that day. If she could hold her breath longer than twenty seconds, then, yeah, maybe she would've tried the underwater thing. As it was, they'd have to go with her hand.

He gripped her hair, tipping her face up to him, leaning down to kiss her while she continued working his shaft. He urged her on with his tongue. She moved her hand faster, splashing against the water until he finished—both of them breathing hard, his mouth still pressed to hers.

He closed his eyes. She released him. He shifted behind her, settling her on his lap in the water. Using her toe, she turned on the hot water knob to heat it up again. The water trickled, and he held her against his chest, and everything felt right.

"Are you going to stick around and watch game shows with me?" she asked.

He scooped water up and over her chest, trailing his fingertips along her skin. "I don't do TV."

She settled more firmly against him, her back to his chest. "I don't do roses, but that seems to be changing."

"Really, TV's not my thing. But you can watch." He was totally snuggling her in the bathtub.

She relaxed against him, linking her fingers with his.

He cleared his throat. "TV gives me flashbacks."

She stilled. What the hell had happened to him over there, anyway? He continued toying with her fingers, as though he hadn't just cracked the shell on taking their relationship deeper. Sharing things like this.

She pulled his hands in hers and squeezed. "We don't need to watch, then. We can just hang out."

"I want to watch with you." His voice had gone husky in a way she hadn't heard before. "But the way the lights on the TV flash and the way they cut the commercials—I don't sleep after."

"Okay, you don't need to." She held his hand tight, unsure what the right thing to say or do was. No way would she push him on this. And she didn't know how to tell him how much it meant to her that he'd shared.

The silence wrapped them both. The only sound was the trickle of hot water coming from the faucet.

"You like games, though. We can do board games," he said finally.

Did she even have any board games? They could buy some. She'd do that tomorrow. First thing. "That wouldn't really be fair. I mean, I'd win all the time."

She turned off the faucet with her toe, and the silence was back. Not an awkward silence, just the quiet of two people together.

"Thank you," he said softly against her ear.

"For what?"

"For not pushing."

Well, given what she'd seen of his family, she'd bet he wasn't used to someone choosing not to push him. "I like you, Jase. If something bothers you, we don't have to do it."

He squeezed her closer. "I like you, too, Heather Reese."

She turned on his lap so they were face-to-face, readjusting herself so her knees were on either side of him, her core pressed against him. And, dammit all, if he wasn't ready for round two.

"You like me?" she asked.

"Uh-huh." He pushed her hair from her face.

"Like, *like me* like me?" She giggled.

"Uh-huh." Damn, he was hard before, but now his erection full on pressed against her. "Do you *like me* like me?"

"Will you go down on me in the bathtub again sometime?"

"Anytime you want."

"Then, yeah. I *like you* like you."

He smiled big. "You want to go steady?"

She laughed and dropped her forehead to his. "Yes."

"Ladies and gentleman, she said yes." He kissed her hard, the heat between them intensifying. This was so much better than *The Price is Right*.

Chapter Twenty-Four
SENIOR "SENIOR" PROM COUNTDOWN:
1 DAY

Jase was late to work. Well, late by his standards. But Heather had made his tardiness worth the effort. Usually, he got to work before dawn, unable to sleep. With Heather, sleep wasn't an issue. They played hard. They slept hard. Then they played hard again. And after the night he'd had with her, there wasn't much that could ruin his morning. When he walked into his shop, both brothers and his sister were lounging around his arranging table, a half-eaten box of doughnuts in the center and a to-go carafe of coffee next to it. His heart dropped.

Early-morning family wake-up calls were never a good thing.

"Glad to see you let yourselves in." He snagged a chocolate-frosted doughnut and bit into it, but the glazed dough held no taste. Not when he was prepping himself for whatever shit his family was about to sling.

"We needed to escape Mom." Anna flicked sprinkles off of her own doughnut. "We figured the one place she wouldn't look for us is here."

"It's like the tree fort when we were kids, but with flowers," Zach said.

"Remember when we all sardined in there because Jase accidentally lit the roof on fire?"

"I put it out."

"Still, when Mom found out?" Zach grimaced. "She was ma-ah-ad."

"What's her beef this time?" As if he didn't already know that Heather and her fireman penis cookies were the culprit.

Zach stared him down. "Puh-lease. You're dense, but you're not stupid."

"You've got a girlfriend taking Babushka to naughty places and making naughtier cookies. Do you need me to spell it out?" Anna continued her assault on the sprinkles. "It's kind of fun that it's you and not me this time."

His sister had been through a bit of a phase in her early twenties. The good part about that was Jase had been the favorite child for a while.

"She is on a tear." Roman tossed back a slug of coffee. "I haven't seen her this worked up since she got kicked off the Parade of Lights committee for telling the mayor to shove his foot up his own ass."

"Ahh…memories." Jase pulled a stool up to the table and straddled it. "She's pissed at Heather. She's pissed at Babushka. I'm sure there's some left in there for me. And I do not care."

Because he had an amazing night wrapped up in Heather.

"What would it take to break up with your girlfriend?" Zach asked, totally serious.

No. Not going to happen. "More than Mom being pissed off, that's for sure."

"Can't we just tell her that you two broke up?" Anna asked. "I mean, I'm pretty sure Heather isn't going to want to come by the house anytime soon."

"And by the time Mom figures out you two are still

together, you'll already be broken up." Zach sat taller. "Actually, this isn't a bad idea."

Right. It was an epically idiotic idea.

"No." Jase poured himself a cup of coffee.

"What if I tell her?" Roman asked. "If I tell her, then I get my two weeks of peace while I'm here and you all can deal with the fallout after."

"Or we can just make sure she never finds out," Anna suggested.

"And in a few years when Heather has her grandkid, you don't think she'll realize we're hooking up?" Whoa. Why was his mind and his mouth going to kids? He was having fun with her. They were together. That was enough. Besides, Jase had played the fake breakup game already; convincing Heather to do it again would probably cost him a Mercedes Coupe S 550 and any hope of more Heather bathtub time.

Anna seemed to choke on her coffee. "You're having kids with Heather?"

Well, not yet, but maybe someday.

Seriously, why was his mind going there?

"He's not having kids with Heather, he can barely keep a pet mouse alive." Roman toyed with his coffee mug.

"I'm not lying about my relationship with Heather." Jase may be willing to change his personal limits regarding frosting on certain appendages, but he wasn't going to lie about what was going on with Heather.

"That's the beauty of my suggestion," Roman said. "You don't say anything. And as long as you don't say anything, everyone is happy."

Seeing as he wasn't particularly speaking to his mother at the moment, talking to her about his relationship status wasn't a big deal.

"If Roman tells her, then I don't have to hear any more about penis cookies and strip-club steaks?" Zach asked. He held his fist out to Roman. "Dude, I will owe you."

"Perfect. Problem solved." Anna hopped off her stool. "I'm so glad we solved this."

"You guys are idiots," Jase muttered, clearing the box of doughnuts and coffee so he could get some actual work done.

"Yeah, well, we're idiots who won't have to listen to Mom rant, aren't we?" Roman slid from his stool and headed toward the door. "And the next time you tie me to a fucking appliance, I'm going to kick your ass."

"Big talk for a guy who ended up hugging a refrigerator." Jase wiped off the table.

Roman tossed him a one-finger salute.

"I've gotta head to work, too." Zach followed Roman. "For what it's worth, I actually like Heather. Anyone who visits strip clubs and can make a cookie look like a fireman cock is my kind of person."

Jase pointed at Zach with the spray bottle of cleaner. "Stay away from her."

"That'll be easy because officially you two are no longer together." Zach rubbed his hands together.

Jase ignored him. Whatever, he was happy in his bubble. Let his family do whatever they were going to do. His siblings were a bucket of stupid in a sea of dumbass, and he'd protect Heather by keeping her out of it.

Chapter Twenty-Five
SENIOR "SENIOR" PROM COUNTDOWN:
0 DAYS

Heather rolled another round folding table into place, pulling the legs open as she propped it on its side. Then she hefted it up into position.

The room was coming together. Prom was going to happen, and she was pretty sure this time her date was going to show. She looked to where he stood on a ladder stuffing flowers into a trellis, the defined muscles of his arms bunching as he worked. As though he felt the weight of her stare, he glanced to her, his eyes warming on contact. She still got that fluttery new-relationship feeling in her stomach whenever he looked at her like that. The little flutter of anticipation of what was coming next.

"Heather?" Velma asked from where she was ironing tablecloths. "I think we're short a few?"

"That's not right. I know I counted." Heather grabbed the box of supplies and rummaged through, certain they were there.

She'd recruited Velma and Candy for help with setup. Jase had recruited Eli and Brek. They'd all been at work for a few hours already, but the tables were now set, the trellises were placed, and Jase was looping a bazillion flowers onto them.

Heather found the missing cloths in the bottom of the box. "Got them."

"This one's ready." Velma began covering the table Heather had just set up.

"Hold off on those," Jase said from his position on the ladder. "We're going to want to move the tables a bit."

Eli pulled off the tablecloth. "What's wrong with the tables?"

Yeah, what he said.

Jase rubbed the back of his arm over his forehead. "They're too close to the dance floor. If we move them about two ticks to the left, we'll utilize the space better."

"But then the walkers won't fit." Heather tried to envision his suggestion. Yeah, the flow would be better, but the aisles wouldn't be big enough. "Forget about the wheelchairs getting through. We need the extra space between." She moved her gaze to him. "If we move those trellises along the side of the dance floor, that'll open a few more feet."

Brek groaned. "Don't do that. It took us an hour to get them stable."

She pinched her lips together. Hard. That wouldn't work, either.

"We could just leave the tables where they are," Velma said from where she ironed another tablecloth. "Then everyone gets through and less work for us."

Jase climbed down his ladder, surveying the space. "Let's move this one to that corner, and that one over right next to the DJ."

"But then the DJ won't have any space around that side of his station," Heather replied.

"Let's just try it. It'll work." Jase was already tilting one of the tables to roll it into place. "Eli, grab the other one, would you?"

"Brek, would you go find a walker so we can see if it'll be enough space to get through?" Heather asked.

"Serious?" he asked.

"She seems pretty serious." Velma had paused her ironing.

"Hey, Candy, can you help Brek find a walker?" Heather asked her sister.

Candy paused where she was setting up the food table. "Um…sure."

"We're going to need to have some chairs in place, and they're going to shrink the walkway." Heather started setting the chairs around the tables in question. "There's no way this is enough room."

"It's plenty of room." Two of the chairs clanked as Jase flicked them open simultaneously.

"Got 'em." Candy pushed a walker through the door—hers was the Cadillac model with the hand brakes and an attached seat. Brek had one, too, which he carried his over his shoulder. His was basic aluminum with the bright-yellow tennis balls attached to the feet.

"Okay, see if they'll fit." Heather nodded toward the aisles.

Brek paused midstride. "You want me to actually use the walker?"

Well, yeah. How else were they going to see if they'd fit?

"Hold on, I need to grab my phone. There needs to be photographic evidence that this happened." Velma pulled her phone from the side pocket of her purse.

Candy pushed hers to Jase. "Why don't you go, too."

It was the hot-guy brigade…with walkers.

Walkers in hand, Brek and Jase started down the aisle. Two hands on his walker, Brek bumped into one of the tables. He gave Heather a there-you-go look; it was not going to work.

Crap. "I think we need to put them back how I had them."

"No, it'll fit." Jase was using his walker to shove the chairs out of the way à la Babushka. "See, it's fine."

It so was not fine. "Jase."

He wasn't listening, he was too busy fitting the walker through the aisle space by any force necessary.

Her stomach twisted around the ham sandwich she'd scarfed for a quick lunch.

"Maybe we need to get one of the motorized scooters," Velma said as she held her phone and clicked photos. "Really check things out."

"Send Eli, I'm not driving one of those." Brek lifted his walker and held it over his shoulder like a backpack.

"Or"—Heather rubbed at her temples—"we could just put the tables back how I had them."

That would be her choice. Thank you very much.

"Nope, this is going to work." Jase was rearranging chairs to only one side of the table, leaving the other side bare.

It looked very asymmetrical.

"Jase, that's even worse than before." Heather's head started to throb. "Let's just put them back where I had them, and we can finish. Then I can go get my hair fixed. And you can go do whatever boys do before a big dance."

Jase stared at the space, clearly trying to play a game of Tetris that was not in his favor. "Let me think on it."

Heather was torn between the desire to have Jase as her date for the evening and the desire to throttle him for being so stubborn. "I'm going to go return the walkers."

She grabbed the tennis-ball-embellished one from Brek and pulled it behind Candy's in an exit that was anything but smooth. The aluminum frame banged against her calves as she wrangled them down the hallway.

"Heather." Jase was jogging behind her.

"What?" She brushed a stray hair that had fallen from her ponytail.

He put both hands on her shoulders. "It's just some tables."

It wasn't. This was her prom. This was what she'd never gotten to have. This was her opportunity to share how awesome this place was with new residents. This was not just some tables. "I want it to be perfect," she said finally.

He expression softened. His eyes went warm. He squeezed her shoulders. "Do you trust me?"

Did she? Yes, in theory. Though, not when it came to table arrangements.

"Answer the question," he said. "Do you trust me?"

She placed her hands at his waist. "Of course I do."

"Then go get your hair done. Let me do this for you." He kissed her forehead, letting his lips linger there. "Do what you need to do this afternoon. I'll be by to pick you up, just like we talked about."

"Jase…" She couldn't just leave her project behind.

"Trust me," he said, his breath brushing against her bangs.

In that moment, everything in her shifted. She trusted him. And if the tables were wrong, they would still be right.

"I trust you."

And she meant it.

THE LAST TIME Jase went to prom, he got drunk on spiked punch and made it to third base with Shelby Mitchell before his mother caught them on the back patio and took the keys to his Mustang for two months. He had high hopes this evening would be substantially better. Of course it would. Heather was his date.

She'd taken off to fix her hair and change her clothes while he wrapped up everything. He'd called in Elizabeth and finished up. He'd told Heather everything was done. He'd lied. And he'd gone slightly overboard with vines, water features, and other accents. He called the revised theme "Garden Jungle."

He hoped to hell she didn't hate it.

The surprise mattered, and he'd needed that line of space she was so insistent on setting tables in for a few jungle-themed water features that involved koi fish and running water.

He rushed to pull on his tuxedo jacket, affixing the boutonniere he'd made to match her corsage. He'd spent way too much time staring at the dress whites he'd brought home to wear to prom. In the end, he couldn't bring himself to put them on. So a tuxedo it would be. A glance in the mirror, and, yeah, not too bad for a guy in a penguin costume. Corsage in hand, he hurried to her apartment.

He knocked. His heart rate started to kick around in his veins, like the teenager he was not. Genetic memory perhaps of all the men before him who'd stood on the other side of a slab of wood waiting for the girl they loved to open it up.

His breath caught. *Hold up.* He had no business thinking about words like "love." Love was not what he'd signed up for. He didn't do love.

He did "like" and "going steady" and as many kinky things as she'd allow. But love? His heart started to thump, ready to get in the game.

Shit.

"Hang on," Heather called.

He hung on, engaging tactical breathing to reduce his heart rate.

She pulled the door open. Her dress was practically painted on, low-cut light-blue satin that hugged her in all the places he'd frosted. Maybe not all the places. That would be indecent. But enough of them to make his mouth literally water and his dick want in the game that his heart was already trying to play.

Tactical breathing wasn't going to control shit at the moment.

"Is it okay?" She shifted the strap on her shoulder.

Earlier, when she'd been helping decorate, she'd been wearing an oversized sweater and shorts that he fucking loved because they showed off her legs. Now? She'd curled the hell out of her hair and piled it on the crown of her head. He'd seen her all dressed up for two weddings—Dean's and Brek's. He'd danced with her both times. Thought she was pretty. Wished she wasn't with the idiot she'd been dating.

Tonight, though? She was fucking beautiful. Because tonight she was his.

"Jase?" she asked, her expression turning serious. "Is it okay?" She shifted again, glancing down at the satin. "You're not saying anything."

"Wow," he finally said. "You look…"

She was waiting for him to finish the sentence, but he didn't have the right ending. Everything he came up with didn't do her justice. Instead, he traced the line of her cheek with his knuckles, letting the air between them go still. Because if he moved, he'd kiss the lipstick right off her lips and then she'd probably be pissed.

"I look…?" The lips he wanted to kiss turned into a frown.

That was unacceptable.

"You look like the most beautiful woman I've ever seen." There, that seemed about right.

The smile she gave him lit up her whole face. "You're being a goober." She glanced to the plastic box in his hands. "Is that mine?"

"Yeah." He fumbled to open the box. "Sorry. I got distracted by that dress."

"Do you want to come in?" She moved to let him through.

He stepped into her apartment, a line of sweat forming at

his collar. Was it hot? Or was this just what it felt like when emotions took over?

Somehow, he managed to open the clear plastic corsage box. Carefully, he lifted the wristlet—a silver cuff that was all the rage with the seventeen-year-olds this year—and slipped it on her arm.

"It's beautiful." She held it up.

He'd used her roses and silver beads. It was simple.

But stunning.

It fit her perfectly.

"We should go, huh?" She tilted her head toward the door.

"Yeah."

"Are you okay?" She held the back of her hand to his cheek. "You're acting weird."

"Fine. I'm fine. Let's go." Since her dress wasn't made for the back of a Ducati, they'd agreed to walk the block to the retirement home. But he'd circumvented that and hired a stretch black Lincoln limousine.

She turned toward the sidewalk.

He grabbed her hand. "This way." He led her to the street where the chauffer waited.

The limo came into view and she stopped. When he turned to her, she had two fingers pressed over her lips. "You rented a limo?"

"It *is* prom night. And since you didn't get to go to the last one, I figured you should get the entire Dvornakov experience." Minus getting caught in a make-out session on his parents' patio. Not to say he didn't hope there would be lip action later in the evening. Just not the kind that involved any parentals barging in.

She was wearing heels this time, so her lips were right at his level. Which was ideal, because when she pressed them to his, he didn't have to lean over, and she didn't have to stand on her toes.

What he wanted to do was shove his hands in her hair and kiss her like she deserved. But she was all wrapped up like a present, and he didn't want to ruin that. So instead he kept it the light brush that she instigated, his hands appropriately at her waist.

"Thank you," she whispered.

The chauffer opened the limousine door and Jase helped her in, then slid onto the seat.

Brek had made him up a pitcher of spiked punch. He poured it into a champagne glass and handed it to her, the pink liquid pitching against the side of the glass as the limo pulled into the street.

"What's this?" She held up the glass.

"This is step two in the 'Dvornakov prom night' experience. Spiked punch." He poured himself a glass.

She clinked her glass against his and took a sip. She half coughed, half swallowed. "Holy shit, what's in this?"

He had no idea. He took a slug of his own. Motor oil. Brek had not gone easy with the spikeage. "Brek made it. I think that's a mixture of vodka, juice, and a fuck ton of rum. I believe it's called jungle juice."

A little nod toward the evening.

"Oh my God, I haven't had jungle juice in years." She giggled and sipped again. "Brek made us jungle juice."

"Glad to see you approve."

She traced a hand along the collar of his tux jacket. "The Dvornakov prom package is really something else."

If he touched her, he might not be able to stop. Not in that dress.

He touched her anyway, his fingertips on satin. "What's your favorite part so far?"

"Definitely you." She scooted toward him. "Did you know we're going the wrong direction?"

Yeah, he did. He'd instructed the chauffer to take the long

way. Otherwise, it would've been a two-minute ride. Heather deserved more than that.

"We're taking the scenic route," he replied.

She raised her champagne flute to his and clinked it before taking another sip.

The limousine pulled up to the retirement home. Jase waited for the chauffer to open the door before he helped Heather out. The crew was waiting outside for them—Brek, Velma, Claire, Dean, and Eli.

The guys all in tuxedos, except Brek, who had issued a personal moratorium on them after Claire and Dean got hitched. His jeans didn't have holes in them that night, so that was something.

"He got her a limo," Claire said to Dean. "Why didn't you get me a limo?"

"He didn't mention he was getting her a limo," Dean grumbled.

Jase glanced to Dean and shrugged.

"He's not married to her," Eli replied. "They're still in the limo phase."

"Are we out of the limo phase?" Velma asked Brek.

"Not after what we did in the last limo. Pretty sure we're gonna always be in the limo phase," he replied.

"I'm just glad we get a few hours away." Velma snuggled next to him.

"She'll still be checking her phone every five minutes to see if Grandma and Lily are gettin' along," Brek said to Jase.

"For the record," Jase whispered to Heather. "Even if we were married, I'd have gotten you a limo."

Heather glanced to him, her face full sunshine. "I like your Dvornakov prom package."

"Eli, couldn't find someone to put up with you?" Jase raised his hand toward his buddy for a high five.

Eli smacked it in return. "Someone's got to hold up the singles area."

Jase held his arm to Heather. She took it, and they led the way into the rec room.

TURNED out prom in your thirties was a billion times better than prom in your teens, Heather mused. It helped when your date for the night actually showed up. Her arm linked with Jase's, he pushed the entrance to the rec room open.

When she'd left the place earlier that day to get ready, Jase had arranged the trellises along the wall and had added a load of foliage and flowers. Apparently, he'd been busy after her departure, because now there were water features. Live fish. And he'd added vines.

It was a jungle-themed garden party.

She sucked in a deep breath.

He'd made her a jungle—because he knew it was important to her.

Fountains bubbled in the background, the DJ was setting up his area, the dance floor was ready to go, and Candy had laid out a bunch of cookies from the shop. Jase had even added large arrangements to each table that matched the flowers on the trellises.

Before she left, it was awesome. Now? With the jungle-themed additions? It was freaking stunning.

She gasped and gripped the fabric of his tuxedo jacket sleeve. "You did all this?"

He squeezed her against his side. "Hope you like it."

"I love it." She gulped, refusing to cry and ruin her mascara.

"Ve are here," Babushka announced herself.

She bustled into the room, Morty trailing behind her, and a group of elderly women following him. Babushka had decked herself out for the evening in a floral mumu. She had a corsage on her wrist and wore bright-red lipstick with sky-blue eyeshadow. Morty took her arm, strutting alongside her like a peacock.

"When do you suppose Harry's turn starts?" Heather asked Jase.

He shook his head. "No idea, but I'm choosing to ignore her antics tonight."

Er…that didn't seem like the best idea.

Jase snatched the bundles of red roses he'd brought for the ladies, and passed out handfuls to Brek, Eli, and Dean to distribute.

The residents started to pour in. Heather gestured for the DJ to turn on the music. On cue, big band music played through the speakers.

"Vere is Eli?" Babushka pushed through the throng to them. She'd lost Morty somewhere along the way. "You have no date, yes?"

"That's right." Eli handed her a rose. "Tonight, I'm every-one's date."

She didn't take the rose. "No, no. Vait. This is my friend Doris." She waved over one of the women. Doris was pushing eighty. She was also pushing a walker. "Doris, this is Eli. He is here stag. Isn't that vonderful?"

"Hello, Doris." Eli handed her a rose.

"I do believe stags and cougars can get along very well." Babushka pushed Eli toward Doris. "You vill dance vith her?"

Eli glared daggers at Jase. "Of course I will." He focused on the other woman. "Doris? Let's go find a spot on the dance floor."

"Did she just…?" Jase side-eyed Heather.

"I believe your grandmother found Eli a date." Heather giggled and buried her face against the side of Jase's arm.

"You fuckin' owe me, Dvornakov," Eli said under his breath. Still, he extended his arm to Doris, grinning like he was about to give her a prom to remember.

"Very good." Babushka clapped her hands.

Harry entered the rec room in a tuxedo, a bouquet of roses in his hands. "Nadzieja, my dear."

Alarm bells started dinging in Heather's head over "Mack the Knife" playing through the speakers.

"You are early," Babushka admonished Harry. "Ve agreed you get the second half of the evening." She reached for the bouquet.

He held it back. "These are for Carol, my first date."

Oh geez. Heather held on to Jase's arm, in case he decided to go rogue on one of Babushka's dates.

"You both have two dates tonight?" Jase held up two fingers in illustration.

"Morty first. Then Harry after eight," Babushka said as though it were the most normal thing in the world.

"Nadzieja had plans until eight, and I didn't want to miss out on the fun." Harry bounced on the balls of his feet. "But tomorrow she's all mine."

Babushka blushed.

Heather had spent a lot of time with Babushka—in the shop, up at the casino, taking her to appointments. But she'd never, not once, seen the woman blush.

And there had been plenty of opportunity for blushing.

"If you'll excuse me." Harry rubbed his hands together, smoothed his comb-over, and hurried to the woman Heather could only assume was Carol.

"Tomorrow vill be vonderful. Jason, you and Heather will be there, yes?" Babushka asked.

What was tomorrow? All Heather had on her schedule was work, laundry, and starting the search for Candy's replacement. She couldn't fault her sister for wanting to follow her dreams. Hell, that's what Heather had done herself. She just wished the timing was a bit better. That things were more established at the shop.

"Nadzieja, come have punch." Morty held up a cup of

the punch. Babushka bustled to him before Jase could answer about tomorrow.

"What's tomorrow?" Heather asked him.

"Family shit. Trust me, you don't want to be there." He adjusted his hand at her waist. He also didn't meet her eyes.

The little hairs on her arms stood on end. "What kind of family shit?" And why was Babushka inviting her when Jase clearly didn't want her there?

"The kind you don't want to get in the middle of." He kissed her forehead. "Promise."

Her stomach felt uneasy, and not from the spiked punch in the limo. Like she'd pulled the big wheel on *The Price is Right* and she was shouting, *Big money! Big money!* But she knew, deep down, she was only going to win a quarter and there was no hope of a showcase showdown.

"Is this because your mother hates me?" she asked, cautious.

"My mother doesn't hate you." He said it, but he didn't sound convincing. "C'mon, let's go dance." He did his chin-jerk thing toward the dance floor. "Eli and Doris look all alone out there."

"Jase." Heather released his arm.

He stopped.

"I want to make things right with your mom and dad," she continued.

It meant a lot to her that his family was on board with them as a couple. Given her past track record, she wanted a guy who was all in with her. He knew this.

He sighed. "My parents will come around. But for now, I think it's best if we avoid family gatherings. Until things blow over."

She let out a breath. They were seeing each other. They were seeing each other exclusively. They were seeing each other with the hope of more...weren't they? Or was she making what they were doing into more? Like she had always done before?

He wanted to keep her separate from his family, keep that part of him away from her.

Her history had proven she wasn't exactly the best at getting a read on men. But she was certain she and Jase were more than just a passing fling.

"Dance with me?" Jase asked, holding his hand out to her. She nodded. She took his hand, and they'd made it to the edge of the dance floor when the music changed from big band to the golden oldies. "Great Balls of Fire" filled the air. Jase spun her in a circle, catching her against his chest and tracing his hand over her waist just a tad too low for public consumption.

A buzz of awareness sizzled through her. Jase did a spin/turn combo move, pulling Heather along with him, ending with her back against his chest and giving her a view of Harry and Carol getting their groove on.

Harry was really into his moves. Heather's stomach dropped. Holy shit, if he kept that up, he'd break his hip.

They didn't need an ambulance extraction that night.

Apparently, Morty wasn't one to be upstaged, and given that he owned a gentlemen's club, he also had some moves. Moves that involved an abundance of pelvis action.

Heather looked to Jase. "Are they—?"

"You know, just when I think my life can't get any weirder, Babushka's two boyfriends have a dance off." He shook his head.

Morty did a slow air hump.

"That's my cue to leave." Jase evacuated to the cookie table where Brek and Dean had already taken up residence.

Heather should've followed, but her eyes were glued to Morty's attempts at sultry. She was worried Harry might bust a hip, but really, it was Morty who was using every bit of his body. All he needed was a pole to grind on.

Velma and Claire hurried toward Heather.

"You got a limo." Velma grasped Heather's arm.

Claire took the other arm. "And things look to be going really well with Jase."

Really well, unless his family got involved. And his family always seemed to get involved. Heather swallowed the lump in her throat. "Things are okay."

"Uh-oh." Velma pulled her away from the Harry and Morty dance contest. Claire followed.

"What happened?" Claire pulled out a chair at a nearby table for Heather.

Heather sat. "Honestly? Nothing. But Babushka mentioned a family thing tomorrow that I was supposed to know about, but Jase said it'd be better if I didn't go."

"Is this because his mother knows you make penis cookies?" Claire leaned her elbows on the table.

"I don't really know." Heather slumped in her chair. "I feel like he's blocking me out of part of his life. And that's fine. I mean, it's fine, right?"

She'd ruined many relationships by pushing too hard, too fast, but Velma and Claire did not look like it was fine.

"It's just that I really like him. And I think…" *He's the one.*

"Think what?" Velma asked.

She couldn't say it out loud. Not when he was in the midst of building walls around certain parts of his life. And, yes, she knew his family drove him nuts. She also wasn't so dense as to think that they weren't the most important thing to him. When they called, he came. When Babushka needed anything, he was there. They were everything to him. But he'd also made this prom night special for her. He'd put a load of effort into it. And she was overthinking things. Per the usual.

"Think what?" Velma asked again.

"You know how I meet a guy, and then I start thinking that things are getting serious. I start to fall for him." She waved her hand like they should know exactly where she was going with this.

"And?" Claire asked.

"And then I find out that it's one-sided and it's really only me who's taking things seriously, and they're really only into fun Heather, not forever Heather?"

"She's scared." Claire gripped Heather's hands. "Don't be scared of it."

"I'm at the starting-to-fall-for-him stage," Heather said. There it was, all out in the open.

"Have you seen how he looks at you?" Velma asked.

"What do you mean?"

Claire scooted closer. "That boy looks at you like you're everything. Dean said that he didn't even have that look around his ex."

"Brek said he thinks you're good for Jase." Velma tucked a lock of hair behind her ear. "And Brek doesn't say much about anything when it comes to his buddies, but he likes that you two are together."

"Since Jase's been back, he's been in a weird bubble. He's fun, but he doesn't let anyone get too close," Claire continued. "That's what Dean says."

"He's letting you get close." Velma looked over to the refreshments table where the boys huddled.

He *was* letting her get close. Heather had to let go of the past and all the things that had happened with her other relationships. Jase wasn't pulling away, they were just forging ahead in a new way. If he needed to go slower, she could do that.

"So I'll let whatever this is pass." Heather reaffirmed it to herself with a glance to where Jase was still hanging out by the cookie table. He caught her stare and winked.

Her insides warmed.

"It'll pass. His family will come around." Velma stood, smoothing the skirt of her dress.

"'Cause you're you. They'll see how good you are for each other." Claire stood, too. "C'mon, I think Harry and Morty are through. Let's get back out there."

Claire grabbed Heather's hand, tugging her along to the dance floor and the elderly mosh pit to jam to some Don McLean. Heather raised her arms, shaking her booty along with Velma and Claire. Like they were teenagers again.

A sizzle went through the air behind her. She didn't need to turn to know Jase was there. Her stomach dipped, like it did whenever he was there. She spun to him. He'd ditched the tuxedo jacket and had rolled up his sleeves. The thing about Jase was that, when he committed to dancing, he was all in. The moves that would make most people cringe and worry they'd screw up, he pulled off without hesitation. She'd give it to him, his dancing rivaled Harry's and Morty's. He didn't even need to air hump to make it happen.

Yeah, the Dvornakov prom package was pretty awesome.

Chapter Twenty-Six

Heather was still riding high on the fumes from her prom night with Jase—even though they'd had three other nights since. Three nights wrapped up in each other. He'd done his family thing, said it was fine, dodged any questions. So she didn't ask. Didn't push.

Now it was a new work week. A week where she had to start her search for Candy's replacement. She pushed another tray of cookies into the oven.

"Heather?" Jase asked from the door to her kitchen.

"Hey, what're you doing here?" she asked.

"I have something for you." He strode toward her, brushed his hand to her jaw, lifting her lips to his. The sensitive skin of her lips met his. The kiss deepened. Well, that was a nice way to say good morning. Not that they hadn't already said good morning once that day. The world around them bopped along, but they were holding on to each other. Mouth, tongue, and everything all wrapped up together.

His hand found hers, and he slid something into it. Cool metal. She broke the kiss, looking at the key fob he'd placed in her hand.

"Your van's done." He traced circles on her neck. "It's parked out front."

"Serious?" Heather asked. She hugged him.

"Serious." He kissed her forehead.

"Candy, I'm checking out the new van," she hollered on her way out the front door.

She skidded to a halt. Her breath caught.

It was perfect. Brand new, bright pink, with the cookie perched on top. "I love it."

Jase pulled her to his side. "Thanks for not sending my grandmother to the pokey."

Speaking of his grandmother, Babushka shuffled up the sidewalk toward them. "I am not speaking to you." She glared at Heather. Glared at the van. Nodded at Jase.

"Sorry?" Heather asked.

Jase tensed. Dropped his arm.

"I am not speaking to you," Babushka said in a louder voice.

Heather stepped toward Babushka. "What did I do this time?" she asked carefully.

Babushka planted her hands on her hips. "You can't even make time for an old woman's birthday party."

"Shit," Jase said.

What on earth was Babushka talking about? "Okay, I'm missing something."

Heather glanced to Jase. He'd gone pale.

"My birthday party. You vere not there," Babushka huffed. "Jason said you vere too busy to come."

He said what?

"I missed your birthday party?" Heather asked. She looked to Jase. "You told her *what*?"

He didn't meet her gaze. The family shit Jase was talking about was Babushka's birthday party?

Heather's heart did a dive to her stomach. "I didn't know. He didn't tell me."

Jase still didn't meet her gaze.

"You said you invited her," Babushka huffed.

"No, what I said was she had other plans. I also encouraged you not to make her feel bad about it."

Heather ground her back teeth together. "I didn't have other plans, Jase."

"Everyone else was there." Babushka waved her hand. "All my friends." She paused. "Except the girl who is like my own daughter."

"Laying it on a little thick there." Jase ran his thumb over his bottom lip. "Heather, I was protecting you from all the family drama."

The numb realization that he'd lied to keep her away from his family settled over her. He'd given her a fantastic prom. An amazing weekend. And he'd still tucked part of himself aside.

She couldn't do this. Not again. Not jump into the deep end and discover she was the only one actually in the water.

Her lips parted. Her fingers went cold.

The anger didn't come. The fast breaths. The threat of tears. She was just numb. No feeling. Because she was certain that once she started to feel it was going to hurt.

A lot.

"I think I need a walk." She pushed past him.

"Heather," he called.

She just shook her head and kept walking. He didn't follow. She hit the corner of the block. Her breaths came in sharp exhales.

She was Heather Reese. A sexy florist couldn't ruin her morning. A hunky guy couldn't ruin her day. And another bad decision couldn't ruin her life.

Was that what this was with him? A bad decision?

She lapped the city block once, twice, three times.

Her focus had slipped. That's all. Steely resolve held her up as she came around the corner to her street. She paused at the window to the jewelry store. She'd lost her focus. She'd spent how many months looking for that talisman of a promise ring to herself? Since she'd been with Jase, she'd slipped.

She pushed open the door to the jewelry shop.

"Heather, how is the cookie business?" Chandra asked, her tone off.

Of course it was, she was friends with Jase's mother. Jase's mother, who hated her.

That didn't matter now. "I came back for that ring." She paused. Fingertips to forehead, she pulled herself together. "Except I left my purse at the shop. I'll be right back."

She didn't wait for Chandra's response. She just hurried back to the sidewalk, heading toward her storefront. The bleat of a smoke alarm echoed down the street. Candy stood near the open door of her shop, ushering customers outside.

Heather's feet wouldn't move.

No. Shit. She'd forgotten the cookies.

She sprinted to the building. The soles of her shoes slapped the sidewalk like punctuation to a poorly written business plan. Nothing was on fire, she was just burning the shit out of some cookies. She passed Babushka by her van and skidded through the door, the scent of burnt sugar scorching her nostrils. A thick arm wrapped around her belly, pulling her back outside. She'd know that scent anywhere—cinnamon, cloves, and freshly cut flowers.

"The cookies." Her breasts heaved against the muscled forearm acting as a vise. "The cookies, Jase."

"Fire department is on their way." His tone was off. Clipped. Like he was giving orders.

Gah, no.

"That's what's burning." She tried to wriggle out of his grasp. "There's not a fire. It's the cookies."

He held tighter. Something was wrong with him, something had changed.

She pushed harder against his arm, but he clearly wasn't going anywhere. He shifted her, lifting her just an inch off the ground as he backed away from everything that mattered to her.

"Let go, Jase," she said over the rushing in her ears. "I have to get in there."

The fire alarm taunted her. *Your cookies are burning. Your cookies are burning.*

He held her tighter. "You're not going in."

"It's just the cookies." She fought against his grip.

He stepped backward, farther from the shop.

"Negative." His tone was all military. She'd never heard him like this, never experienced who he'd once been.

She forced her body to go from limp to dead weight.

"Nice try," he mumbled close to her ear.

The place wasn't on fire. The stupid, stupid, stupid cockies were burning. Though if she didn't get inside soon there *would* be a fire.

"Where's your grandmother?" Heather asked. She knew Babushka was behind her, but maybe the distraction would make him release his grip.

"Son of a bitch," he clipped.

It worked. He let her go, setting her to the concrete.

Her feet hit the ground and she did a *Risky Business* slide through the door, bolting to the kitchen. Smoke flowed from the seam of the oven door. She hit the switch to turn on the stove hood, the vacuum instantly sucking the thin gray air up through the vent and outside.

Her lungs itched with a compressed cough she refused to let out. Shoving her hands in industrial oven mitts, she squinted against her watering tear ducts to pull open the oven. Head turned to the side, she snatched a pan of black cookie bricks and tossed the whole thing in the sink.

She reached for the faucet, but a very male hand covered her oven mitt and turned the knob. Jase.

Not just Jase. Ticked-off Jase, with a murderous expression traced on his face and stone eyes holding no emotion.

She went back for the second tray of scorched cookies and tossed them into the sink, too, the cold water turning the black chunks to burnt mush.

The alarm still blared, but with the emergency averted, she let the cough she held rack her chest. Doubled over, her lungs continued convulsing. Eyes closed, she let the entire morning wash over her, effectively turning her to the same burnt mush as her cookies. She shoved open the back door to the kitchen, embracing the cool air with deep, broken breaths.

Hands braced on her knees, she sucked in oxygen. A shadow crossed in front of her, and a cool, damp kitchen towel pressed to her forehead.

Jase held the same expression from inside, but it had frayed around the edges. Little lines that had nothing to do with laughter crinkled around his eyes. His perpetual cocky demeanor had evaporated.

"Thank you." She held the towel to her forehead and wiped her eyes.

"You okay?" he asked.

Physically? "Yes."

"Good." He leaned in so she had no choice but to meet his gaze. "What. The. Fuck. Was. That?"

"I panicked." She pressed against the towel. "The cookies were burning."

"You don't run into a building when there might be a fire. That's how people die." His voice cracked, and the words pierced the anger she carried from earlier.

"Well, I didn't. Because I knew it was only a tray of cookies—"

"It might not have been." His words were clipped again. Tense. He tipped her chin to force her gaze to meet his.

She blinked against the sun behind him. "It was."

His eyes remained fierce, his fingertips still on her chin. "You take a stupid risk and people die."

"People? I'm only a person."

His eyes clouded. "You could've died, and I would've had to live with that, too."

She couldn't turn her head, his grip on her steady, so she followed the path of a dust mote in her periphery. Anything to keep her from meeting his inspection again, because all she wanted to do at the moment was hug the guy she needed to distance herself from. Hang on for all she was worth. Trust him.

"What happened to you over there, Jase?" she whispered instead.

"Everybody died." He leaned in, his expression unreadable. "Because I wasn't there in time."

She gasped. Her back pressed against the brick exterior of the building. She wished in equal parts it would swallow her whole and set her free.

He dropped his fingers from her chin and straightened.

The wail of a fire truck sliced the moment in two. He withdrew and his hands dropped to his sides. "The firemen will want to talk to you."

She nodded. This was her business and she should handle it, but right now she felt as fragile as one of his porcelain vases filled with roses. "Jase?"

He paused.

"I am sorry I scared you." She gulped. "But I don't want to go back where we started." Now she was sounding desperate. *Deep breaths, Heather.* "I don't want to have to pretend we're not together, because your parents hate me." She took another breath. *Get it all out.* "Before you, I thought I wanted to be alone, but it turns out I just want someone who wants me, too. As much as I want them. Someone who is all in. I think I deserve that, you know?"

"Heather—"

"I don't think this has to hurt so bad. Maybe we should just call it for what it was—a really good shot at something that didn't work out."

The light in his eyes went out. "That's what you want? To be done?"

"I want to stop feeling like you're not one hundred percent in this." Fingertips gripping the no-longer-cool cloth, she slid down the wall, ass to ankles, forehead to knees, heart to throat.

"This is what happens. Shit gets complicated." He cursed under his breath, kneeling to her level.

"Maybe that's why we should stop. It doesn't have to be complicated." She said the words, but she didn't mean them.

She waited for him to reply with something to make everything better. He didn't. He stood. She pinched her eyes closed. The kitchen door flung open.

"Something's wrong with Babushka." Candy was frantic. "You need to come quick."

Heather hurried to stand, following Jase as he rushed through the shop.

Chapter Twenty-Seven

Heather pinched her lips together, waiting for the fireman to finish his report. She needed to get to the hospital. Make things right with Babushka. God, Babushka had to be okay. She'd had some kind of episode. When Heather and Jase got to her, her face was chalky and she was having a hard time catching her breath.

The ambulance had just pulled up for the "fire"—Heather used the term loosely. The paramedics took no time in rushing Babushka to the hospital.

Heather checked her phone, hoping for an update from Jase.

Nothing.

"Candy?" she called. "Can you handle the rest?"

Candy stepped beside Heather. "I've got this. Go."

Heather didn't need to be told twice. She scooted out to her new delivery van. Key in the ignition, she squealed the tires pulling onto the street. Rose Medical was only a mile away, but it felt like it took an eternity to get there. She parked the van and dashed into the ER.

Jase stood near the nurse's desk with Anna. Heather's heart seemed to stop beating. How would she be able to see him and not be able to touch him? How would she be able to go back to who she was before Babushka took out her delivery van?

"Jase," she called his name. He glanced to her, his expression tense.

She wasn't close enough to hear him, but he mouthed her name. She hustled toward him. "Is she okay?"

"She's fine," Anna answered for him. "Not a heart attack, just a blip. That's what the doctor said."

Heather let out the breath she'd been holding since the fire alarm went off.

"She's been asking for you." Jase shoved his hands in his pockets.

Heather's rib cage seemed to cinch tighter. She hated that. The hands-in-the-pockets thing. Normally, he'd pull her to his side. The beginning of the end…that's what this was. And she'd started it. She'd brought it up. She'd have to own it.

JASE HAD WELL and truly screwed the pooch. He didn't want to lose Heather. Didn't want her to believe he was anything less than all in.

So, he'd fix it. He'd make it right.

According to the rules of Dvornakov engagement, if you're off the hook, don't screw with it. Jase had been certain he'd be off the hook. He'd decided to keep his Heather life and his family life separate. Everyone would win. He'd dug himself a bunker too deep to escape. All because his brother lied to his mother and Jase was going along with it because it made his life easier.

"Where is she?" Heather asked.

"This way." He jerked his head toward the curtain where Babushka was being evaluated.

Heather started that way. He strode beside her, letting his hand brush hers. She turned her palm so he could grasp it.

His blood pressure started to return to normal.

They'd be okay. He'd fix it.

"Why's she here, Jason?" his mom asked from behind.

Or not.

Heather dropped his hand. She bit at her lip. "Mrs. Dvornakov, I wanted to apologize for all of the"—she paused—"mishaps with Babushka. I think you and I got off on the wrong foot."

"Heather!" Babushka yelled from behind the curtain. "You vill come in."

Jase pulled open the curtain, letting Heather and his mother through.

"Nadzieja." Jase's mother brushed past Heather. "I think since she and Jason broke up, it's inappropriate that she's here."

Heather did a double take. Her eyes focused on Jase. "That's what you decided you want?"

No, that's not at all what he'd decided.

"Jase said you two broke up." His mother enunciated each word as though Heather hadn't caught it the first time.

No, that's not what he'd said, Jase thought. That's what Roman had said.

"What are you talking about?" Babushka frowned. "This is why you didn't come to my party?"

"Jase?" Heather asked him. Her eyes didn't spark with anger. No, this time it was disappointment.

"No, I never said that." He shook his head.

"I said it," Roman chimed in from behind them.

"I'm so confused." His mother looked between Roman and Jase. "I asked you. You said you broke up."

He could actually feel the moment he lost control of any aspect of a situation. This would be that moment. "Technically, you said that. I didn't correct you."

"Seriously, Jase?" Heather whispered.

Time to end this bullshit. "Mom, Heather's my girlfriend. Roman wanted you to quit ranting about it, so he told you we broke up."

"But you knew he was telling her that?" Heather was holding it together, but he could see the way she was shattering beneath the surface. All because he'd taken the easy way.

"Yeah." He hooked his fingertips at his waist.

"And you didn't think you should correct it?" Heather had tightened her mask, he knew the second she did it. Closed it down.

But her lip trembled just a tad.

He'd fucked up. Hurt feelings. Deep ones.

"That's why you didn't tell me about the party," she concluded.

The whole day was spiraling and all he could do was watch.

"You could've just told me what was going on," she continued.

"This is on me." Roman stood. "Also, Zach. He backed me up."

"So, you boys lied?" their mother asked, shocked. Which was total bullshit, because it wasn't the first time her kids had told her a fib.

"You were seriously an unhappy person to be around." Roman dropped to the chair next to Babushka's bed.

Heather hadn't spoken again. She just stared at Jase. Stared at him like he'd crushed her heart.

He took a step toward her.

She shook her head, backing up.

"Sugar," he started.

"Don't 'sugar' me here," she whispered, her voice wobbling slightly. "You don't get to do that."

She took the four steps to Babushka and gave her a hug.

"I have to go now, but I'm really sorry that I missed your party. Please let me know that you're okay. And take it easy, don't do too much."

Heather was barely holding it together. Jase knew her well enough to know this was killing her.

Babushka caught on, too. Patting her back and glaring at Jase. If looks could kill, he'd be flayed open right there by her oxygen tank.

Heather started for the exit.

"I'll walk you out," Jase said quickly.

She did the little head shake again. "I'm good. You should stay with your family."

He wasn't going to let it end this way. "Heather—"

She held up her hand. "Really, you should stay."

Turning on her heel, she left for the parking lot. He followed her to her new van.

"Don't do this," he heard himself say.

"Do what, Jase? Lie about our relationship? Tell people I care about that we aren't together? Worry about my own comfort over everyone else's? Fall in love with a guy who isn't all in? What, Jase? What exactly am I not supposed to do?"

Wait.

The fuck?

"You fell in love with me?" he asked.

"We all make mistakes." She unlocked the door, pulled it open, and climbed inside.

He caught the door with his palm. "Don't make this one."

Please don't make this one.

"I think you made it for me." She turned the engine over.

"Let's just take a step back." He'd fucked up, he got that.

"You want to take a step back? Fine. We're stepping back. This is us stepping back." She reached for the handle on the door.

That's not what he meant at all. "Heather."

"No, Jase. I don't want to do that. I don't want to step

back. I don't want to go backward. I'm done with that. It's time to go forward. With or without you." She pressed her fingers against her eyelids. "And you've made it clear it's without you."

She pulled the door closed. He couldn't move, just watched as she backed out of the lot. He returned to Babushka's curtained room.

"You let her go." Babushka pursed her lips. "I thought you were smart boy. But you let her go."

"Nadzieja," his mother said. "This is best."

"No." Jase shoved his hands on his hips. "It's not. But thank you for ensuring that the best thing in my life just walked out."

"Jason." His mother gave him her look. The one that nearly always got her whatever she wanted.

"I am not speaking to either of you." Babushka held her head high.

Somehow, he had to figure out how to make things right.

"Your problem"—Babushka shoved a finger toward him —"is that you let your mother and your father, and your brothers and your sister, tell you vat you vill do."

Also, his grandmother. She forgot to add herself to the list.

"You come home from combat and you are a mess. Ve help you. Ve make decisions for you. I vait for you to be ready to make your own. But you don't." Her moratorium on speaking to him apparently hadn't started yet. "A little shove I give. And still you don't choose for yourself."

A little shove? She'd totaled Heather's van.

That was her little shove?

He could admit he'd been a wreck when he'd returned home four years ago. He'd lost most of his team in an explosion. He'd come home ready to retire from a life of defusing crude roadside bombs and IEDs. Ready to stay.

He'd given it his best effort, but he wasn't the same guy

who had left. The shit that happened changed him. One night he'd shown up with flowers and chocolates only to find his house vacant. Divorce papers laid out on the counter.

The last time he'd reenlisted, Angela had told him she was done if he went through with it, but he hadn't believed her. Hadn't believed she'd actually leave. And she hadn't. Not right away, anyway. But she'd never forgiven him, either. And that shit ate through their marriage.

He'd taken the flowers to his mother. The chocolates to Babushka. Bought himself a bottle of Jim Beam and tracked down his wife. Her mind was made up. Time to move on. He had downed the whiskey and signed the papers. Pretended to feel nothing. But inside? Inside he'd been shredded. A pile of mush stomped down with no hope for the future.

And, yeah, that's when his family had started making decisions for him. He'd let them. They told him to be a florist? He agreed. They moved him back into the family home? He let them. He appreciated not having to think about shit. When they encouraged him to move into the apartment above the flower shop, he'd embraced that too.

But, fuck it all, he was ready to start making his own choices. Now he was ready to handle his own life. With gratitude for all they'd done, but with an eye for the future.

"When I convince her I'm all in, you will apologize." He stared at his mother. "And then you'll welcome her to the family, because she's going to be part of it."

The chains he'd wrapped around himself started to break free. He looked to Babushka. She nodded.

"She's going to be part of it, even if we don't work out. Even if she decides she wants someone else." Now he was really on a roll. It'd have to be her who left, because there was no way he could choose to be away from her. "Because she loves Babushka. And Babushka loves her."

He mother didn't meet his stare.

"And I love her," he continued over the lump in his throat.

And it'd taken him too long to realize that bit.

His mother's expression softened. "Jason, if she means that much to you, then—"

"Then you'll accept her. You'll accept her, or you'll lose me, too." He didn't need her acknowledgment. He knew she'd heard.

He had to get back to Heather. Back to her shop. He bolted to the ER entrance. Since he'd taken the ambulance with Babushka, he started to request a car on his phone app.

"I got you." Roman stepped beside him, jingling his keys. "And I'm sorry I fucked this up."

"You didn't fuck it up." Jase had done that all on his own.

Now he had to fix it. Stop running and letting life happen to him, and start taking it back. They piled into Roman's rental and Jase dialed Heather's number. The line went straight to voice mail, which was bullshit because she never turned off her phone. She'd leave it in her purse or around her apartment or in her office—but he never went straight to voice mail.

He'd hurt her and that was unacceptable.

Roman dropped him at her store. Jase shoved the front door open. She wasn't up front.

"Where's Heather?" he asked Candy.

Candy glanced up from ringing up a customer. "I thought she was with you?"

Fuck it. No.

He bolted through the kitchen, taking the stairs two at a time to her apartment. He knocked on her door.

She didn't answer.

There was no tactical breathing now. He needed to find her. Needed to make this right.

He pounded harder.

Nothing.

Chapter Twenty-Eight

She'd broken it off. Heather refused to cry.

What she needed was a night with her best friends. After she left the hospital, she drove her fancy new cookie van straight to Velma's Washington Park apartment.

Brek answered the door.

One look at Heather and he turned full glower. "The fuck did he do?"

"I was hoping Velma's around?" Heather asked.

Brek stepped back to let her through. "She's shoppin' with her mom. Should be back soon. You can hang with Lily and me while you wait."

"You don't mind?" The last place she wanted to go was back to work to deal with staff and customers, or back home where she'd be alone.

"Wouldn't invite you in if I minded." He ticked his head, effectively inviting her in a second time.

Heather slipped by him.

"I'd like to know what the fuckwit did." Brek went to the kitchen and poured her a glass of white.

He slid it across the island before pulling out his phone and typing something on the screen.

Heather hopped up onto a barstool. Then she spilled her guts to Brek—everything from the cockies in flames to Babushka's birthday to the hospital. She should've waited for Velma, but Brek was, actually, a good listener.

"You want me to kick his ass?" he asked. "He's my buddy, but I'll do it."

Heather shook her head. She didn't want that. What she wanted was to rewind to a month prior and park her van somewhere else. She wanted to rewind and not fall for him.

Not fall in love with him.

Because, if she were being honest, that's exactly what she'd done.

She thought she'd been in love before. With her latest ex and a few guys before him, she'd been certain what she felt was love.

But it was nothing compared to the way Jase made her feel. Or the way it killed her that they had to end. She wiped a stray tear from her cheek. Dammit, she'd promised herself she wouldn't cry.

She was not a crier.

Brek leaned forward, elbows on the counter. "Shit fucked him up good before he came back. Don't know what. Don't need to. All I know is the buddy who went over wasn't the buddy who came back. Something big happened and part of him shut off. With you around, he started to come back for real."

"You don't think I should've ended it?" The tears flowed freely now.

Brek handed her a paper towel. Velma must've bought the roll because it was soft like cotton.

She wiped her eyes.

"Nah, think he's had his head shoved up his own ass. He'll need the kick to knock it free."

"And if it doesn't?" She ran the paper towel between her fingers. "Doesn't come loose?"

"Then I think you'll still be okay. You're a strong one. It's him I'm worried about."

Velma burst through the door. "I'm here. Where is she?"

She beelined straight to Heather, barely pausing to acknowledge Brek. Then she hugged Heather, and Heather knew she would be okay. Because she was Heather Reese.

JASE WORKED ALONE in the construction zone that would soon be the bridal shop. Having hung the drywall, they were down to only needing to paint all the spaces. Eli would be in before his current lease expired, and the other spaces would be ready soon after. It was finally all coming together. Business-wise, at least.

He waited for his phone to ring. Waited for the lights to go on at Heather's apartment.

His phone buzzed.

"Brek," he said in greeting.

"Heather came by," Brek said.

"She broke it off."

"I heard."

"I fucked up."

"Yup."

Neither said anything for a moment.

Finally, Brek broke the silence. "She's still here. Talkin' with Velma and Claire. Figured you'd be lookin' for her."

Yes. Yes, he was.

Jase stood, confident in what needed to be done.

He was going to convince her to give him another shot.

Chapter Twenty-Nine

Heather had moved to lemonade. Sad drunk wasn't fun, and she wasn't ready to head home alone yet.

Velma had put on a rom-com, but Heather was only mildly watching from the periphery, bundled on one end of the white leather sofa. Claire was curled up on the other end. Mostly, Heather was planning how she could go through life with as little contact with Jase as possible.

It'd be easier that way.

She toyed with the edge of the blanket, the movie soft in the background.

"Heather," Jase said her name.

She glanced up over the edge of the sofa. The world pressed pause on her heartbeat.

Jase stood in the doorway, Brek holding the door wide.

She'd never even heard him knock.

But he didn't just stand there. No, he stood there in his Navy dress whites, his hat under his arm, a stack of papers in his other hand.

"Holy crap," Velma said.

"Whoa." That was Claire.

Heather's heart ached just looking at him. She couldn't

bring herself to say anything. Couldn't bring herself to move at all, because this was obviously a hallucination.

"Heather," he said again. "Hey."

He shifted the cap under his arm and strode toward her with a military precision that seemed so appropriate with his uniform.

"I'm working on a project," he said when she didn't say anything. "I was hoping you might hang a poster for me." He set the stack on the edge of the sofa and tapped the top copy.

"Jase…" she said.

God, this killed.

"It's for a dance I'm helping out with. Planning," he continued.

She glanced to the stack. *Jase and Heather Love Dance* was written in black Sharpie, the date, time, and details underneath.

"Why are you doing this?" she asked. Why couldn't they just be done? Why did it have to hurt so bad to look at him?

"The thing is, I think it could work out between us." He pushed the stack toward her.

She gripped the blanket tighter, unable to do this. Not again. "No, we tried it, it didn't."

"Then let's try again." He set his hat on the sofa and braced his arms there. "And again. Until we get it right."

If he wanted to play, she'd have to play. It didn't matter; the game they'd played to start this whole thing always ended with heartbreak. But if he wanted to do it once more…what the hell. "Your family would get involved. Things would get messy. We'd both end up resenting each other."

He, apparently, wasn't going to let it go so simply. "See, my grandmother might get involved. But she's kind of fun and she's got a good heart."

"And she'd crash her Buick into my cookie delivery van." In a fit of elderly, misplaced rage.

His expression gentled. "It's okay, I'd promise to buy you a new one."

"Then she'd decide she's going to work for me." Despite her best efforts, Heather's chin trembled.

Dammit, she didn't want to change any of this. And yet, she wanted to change all of it.

"And you'd take her to lunch at Pistol Polly's."

"You'd be furious." Maybe she should look at the posters. She pulled them to her. He'd drawn a little drawing of two stick figures next to the words he'd printed.

"I'd get over it." He didn't touch her, but his hand inched toward where she sat.

"This is the sweetest thing I think I've ever heard," Claire said to Velma.

Velma shushed her.

"Then we'd end up at a casino with her and her boyfriend." Heather only had eyes for Jase. The outside world didn't matter, it was just the two of them.

"I think we should skip this part." The edges of his lips twitched.

"We'd end up at your apartment." Her body warmed, like a switch she'd turned off earlier flicking back on.

"That's when the fun would start." His hand crept close to hers.

She released the blanket. Sat taller. "After which, you'd be ready to break up with me."

"But I wouldn't, because I'd realize what I had was worth fighting for."

Did he mean that?

"Then your family would get involved again and everything would go to hell." She glanced to the hardwood. This was where it would end. This was where things would fall apart.

"After my family fucked everything up, I'd politely tell

them to fuck off. Then I'd come to you in my dress whites and ask you to forgive me for being an idiot."

Her breath caught. He'd told his family to fuck off?

She kicked her legs over the edge of the sofa, her head in her hands. "I know you think I'm strong, but I can't keep doing this. I want forever, but I want it with someone who wants what I do." A tear trailed down her cheek. Twice in one day. What the hell? She batted it away with the back of her hand.

"If you aren't ready to hear it, and you aren't ready to do it…" His voice went husky. Effectively breaking her heart and her resolve. "I'll ask if I can come back every day until you are."

She hiccupped.

"And if you tell me it's really over, I'll turn and leave. Because that's what you want." His voice broke on the last word. "Please tell me that's not what you want."

"It's not what I want," she whispered.

"Then we'll work through this, because I love you."

He loved her? She glanced to him then.

"And eventually, we'd get married," he continued. "Or we can just live together. I'll be good with whatever you want." He took a long breath. "And if you want kids, we'll have kids. If you don't want kids, I can live with that, too." He paused. "Because I'll be the luckiest man in the world if I get to sleep next to you every night."

"Oh my gosh…" Claire said, reminding Heather they weren't alone.

Brek shushed her.

"And we won't break up?" Heather stood, facing him, letting the blanket drop to the floor.

"Not as long as you'll have me." He trailed a fingertip along her jawline.

"Okay." She nodded. They'd do this. All of it.

He kissed her then—lips and tongue and heat and fire.

"Why the uniform?" she asked when he broke the kiss. "I thought you didn't wear it anymore?"

"You said you liked a guy in uniform, and I figured it's time to stop running from my past."

She touched the air over one of the medals attached to the jacket, afraid to actually place her hand on it. "But isn't this breaking the rules? It's not a wedding or a funeral or an important event."

"Heather." He pulled her hand against his heart, pressing her palm against the medal she'd admired. "Convincing you to give me another chance definitely counts as an important event."

She gulped, her throat suddenly thick with an emotion she couldn't quite name.

He lifted a shoulder. "Also, figured since you are into uniforms, I could use all the help I could get."

She buried her face in his chest. "You're such a goober."

"Yeah." He raised his hand to the back of her neck, holding it there. "Your goober."

He was hers.

She traced the line of his abs through the poly-cotton blend. Yes, abs like the ones on Jase Dvornakov definitely made her reconsider swearing off men.

"I love you, Jase."

"That's what I was counting on." And he kissed her again.

<hr>

Epilogue

<hr>

"Are you sure you want to do this?" Heather sat next to Jase on her sofa. Their sofa.

He'd moved in shortly after they'd agreed to give it another try. It made sense. They spent all their nights together, anyway.

"Positive," he replied.

He said it, but she couldn't help but notice the way his fingers tapped against his knee. He was nervous. He never got nervous. Not like this.

She grabbed the remote control for the television. Since he'd moved in, she'd only watched when he wasn't around. The night he showed up in his dress whites he'd shared everything about the accident overseas. The accident that had changed it all for him.

"Trust me?" she asked.

He stilled his fingertips. "Always."

"We can just go in the bedroom and I'll tie you up or something?" That might be more fun, anyway.

A slight grin lifted the edges of his mouth. "Let's do this."

She snuggled against him and turned on *The Price Is Right*. His hand found hers just as the first contestant ran down the aisle to Contestant Row. His face turned hard, but he didn't glance away. She squeezed his hand. He traced the line of her ring with his thumb—she'd gone back for it after they patched things up. The ring represented the promise to herself that, no matter what, no matter how things went, she'd be okay alone.

She'd be okay by herself, but life was pretty fantastic when she had Jase next to her.

"You're still doing all right?" she asked as a contestant bid way too high on a Pentax digital camera.

He released her hand and wrapped his arm around her. "You're more wound up than I am."

"I'll relax." She forced herself to watch as Drew Carey named the winner and called him onto the stage.

"I like *Jeopardy* the best, but *The Price is Right* comes in at a close second." She wasn't a talker when she watched television, but she found herself wanting to distract Jase from whatever was going on in his head. "My favorite is Plinko. I think that's everyone's favorite. No one really likes the golf game, but they play that one all the time."

Jase slipped something hard and cool into Heather's hand. A box.

She lifted it up.

A ring box.

Her heart skipped. Drew Carey was announcing Punch a Bunch in the background as the first game, and Jase's fingertips were tapping against his knee again.

Everything about the moment imprinted in her memory as she lifted open the top. An engagement ring sat between the two tiny silk pillows. Her mouth dropped open. She turned to him and tucked her feet under her thighs, but she didn't look up, her gaze pinned on the ring before her.

"Figured you might want to." He lifted the ring from the box.

She snapped her gaze from the diamond solitaire to Jase.

He was breathing harder than normal. When he'd asked if she'd watch with him, she had no idea this was what he had planned.

"Do you?" He held the ring to her.

"Do I?"

"Want to?" He picked up her hand in his.

Her chest started to pulse with laughter. She bit her lip. "That's your proposal?"

"You're not supposed to laugh." His eyes sparkled.

She held her hand out to him, spreading her fingers so he could slip the ring in place. "Yes, Jase. Yes, I want to."

"Good." He turned back to the television.

She snuggled into his side. "Your marriage proposal could use a little work."

"You said yes, so it couldn't have been that bad." He lifted her chin with his fingertip, pressing a light kiss to her lips. She liked all his kisses—the hot ones, the fast ones, the slow ones, but she liked the light ones the best, because he saved those for important moments, the ones he wanted her to remember.

"Whatever the question, if it's about us being together, the answer is always yes." Heather caught his hand with her own and squeezed. She swore his eyes misted.

"Always?" he asked.

"Always and forever." She held his gaze and they stayed that way. Neither of them moved. "That's not to say a dash of what you did for me with the promposal wouldn't be welcomed."

"Because you love flowers now?"

"Because I love you." She studied the way her engagement ring caught the light. "Also, flowers."

"Heather?" he asked.

"Hmm?"

"Will you marry me?"

She threw her arms around his neck. "Yes."

He grinned at that. "You should know, I talked to my

family before tonight. Let them know I'd be popping the question. They're having a big welcome-to-the-family dinner for you tomorrow. I invited your parents and Candy."

Heather slid her glance to him. "Seriously?"

"There'll be vodka. We'll all manage."

"Which boyfriend do you think Babushka will bring?" she asked finally.

"Probably both, just to piss off my dad," Jase said.

Babushka still threatened to die every time she wanted something, but the doctors promised her health was fine.

Which was perfect, because Heather wanted to give her those great-grandchildren Babushka wanted so desperately.

Someday. Not yet, though.

Right now, she had Jase.

And that was enough.

There's more Jase & Heather!

A special bonus scene Christina created especially for newsletter subscribers!

Sign up for the bonus scene at:
ChristinaHovland.com/blowmeaway-bonus

Stay in Touch

Stay in touch with Christina by signing up for her newsletter!

ChristinaHovland.com/newsletter

Acknowledgments

Without the following people, this dream would not have been possible:

Angela, who first introduced me to cockies. Girl, I owe you.

My husband Steve and my kids for being so supportive of me on this journey. I couldn't be living my dream without you.

My mom, Shirley, and my sister, Sereneti. Your love of my books makes writing them worthwhile.

My critique partners and first line beta readers: Serena Bell, Ana Morgan, A.Y. Chao, Susannah Erwin, C.R. Grissom, Colette Dixon, Deb Smolha, Karie, Paige, and Amy.

Todd for answering random questions about the legal needs of fictional characters.

Beth for being the best author assistant ever.

L.A. Mitchell for making me believe this dream is possible.

My agent, Emily Sylvan Kim, who continues to support and encourage me. I am so blessed to have you in my corner. And Lynn at Prospect Agency, thank you for everything you're doing for my books!

Holly Ingraham for being an awesome, awesome, awesome editor! I adore working with you.

Michelle Hope for being the eagle eyes I needed on this manuscript. Thank you so much.

Shasta Schafer for being a friend and my final proofreader. We're both following our dreams and I love that we get to work together.

Kristi Yanta for always being supportive and awesome.

The amazing Rebelles. I am so blessed to be part of your group.

And, finally, the Romance Chicks: Dylann Crush, Jody Holford, and Renee Ann Miller.

Also by Christina Hovland

The Mile High Matched Series

Rock Hard Cowboy
Going Down on One Knee
Blow Me Away
Take It Off the Menu
Do Me a Favor
Ball Sacked

The Mile High Rocked Series

Played by the Rockstar

From Entangled Publishing

The Honeymoon Trap
Rachel, Out of Office
April May Fall

About the Author

Christina Hovland lives her own version of a fairy tale—an artisan chocolatier by day and romance writer by night. Born in Colorado, Christina received a degree in journalism from Colorado State University. Before opening her chocolate company, Christina's career spanned from the television newsroom to managing an award-winning public relations firm. She's a recovering overachiever and perfectionist with a love of cupcakes and dinner she doesn't have to cook herself. A 2017 Golden Heart® finalist, she lives in Colorado with her first-boyfriend-turned-husband, four children, and the sweetest dogs around.

ChristinaHovland.com
    Twitter.com/HovlandWrites
    Facebook.com/HovlandWrites
    Instagram.com/HovlandWrites
    Goodreads.com/HovlandWrites
    bookbub.com/profile/christina-hovland

Enjoyed the Story?

**Turn the page for a sample of
Take It Off the Menu!**

Saying "I Do" has never been such a mess.

Marlee Medford just got dumped. Yes, things have become ho-hum in her longtime relationship, but she was two days away from walking down the aisle with the man she thought was her forever when he called it off. Convincing herself that they'd be able to reignite their spark once the wedding craziness settled? That was easy. Suddenly finding herself without a fiancé? Not so much. Marlee needs to regain control of her life, and a weekend away with her friends is a solid first step.

One of Denver's best up-and-coming chefs, perpetual bachelor Eli Howard, isn't into serious relationships—especially the kind that ends in marriage. As if to prove his point that they aren't worth the trouble, the wedding he was supposed to be catering just fell apart. Feeling oddly protective of the jilted bride—his little sister's best friend—his weekend plans now involve a trip to Sin City with her group of friends. But it looks like he had a bit too much fun in Vegas when he wakes up married…wedding night included.

Marlee's attempts at getting her life back together are failing miserably. Her ex-fiancé is taking the house, her chihuahua is intent on a love affair with Eli's sneakers, and she's now accidentally hitched to the guy who can't even say the word *marriage*. With their quickie annulment denied, Eli and Marlee just have to hang tight until the divorce goes through. It's just a little divorce amongst friends, what's the worst that could happen?

Chapter One
TWO DAYS BEFORE THE WEDDING

"Lothario, stop humping the angora," Marlee Medford—
soon-to-be Bishop—stepped onto the patio of her Denver
townhome. Her pure-white-haired chihuahua tipped his head
to the side, stopped humping her fiancé's angora sweater that
had fallen to the ground, and whined.

Leaves from their two aspen trees rustled beside her—red
and orange and ready to break free from their branches in
preparation for winter.

She snatched the sweater, brushed a couple of fallen
leaves from the sleeve, and hung it over the arm of the empty
chair next to Scotty. He was immersed in his phone, apparently oblivious to the defiling of his clothes.

Lothario had a thing for Scotty's shirts, and it drove
Scotty absolutely nuts. Aside from Scotty's clothing, Lothario
literally humped anything that moved. Except Marlee. She'd
put a stop to that early on. One would've thought that
Lothario's recent unfortunate experience with a moving
bicycle tire would've stopped the behavior, but all it got him
was a cast on his right leg and a rededication to defiling all
things.

She turned her focus from the dog to Scotty. He had his serious face on that morning.

"Hey, sweetie." She squeezed his shoulders and kissed his cheek before sitting next to him with her morning coffee. "I've only got a second. I have a bajillion things to do today for the wedding."

Their wedding.

Their forty-eight-hours-away nuptials.

"Leelee." He set his phone down beside his coffee mug. "We need to talk about the wedding."

"Okay." She squeezed his hands. "What's up?"

"I don't want to do it." He glanced to the side, not meeting her eyes.

That wasn't exactly a choice anymore. Not with four hundred of their closest friends coming to Denver for their wedding.

"We're not getting married, Leelee." He heaved a huge breath. "I'm sorry."

She dropped his hands. *What?*

"We're not getting married?" she asked.

"No." He shook his head. "I'm so sorry."

He was sorry? *He* was sorry?

Marlee's stomach dropped.

"It's been this way for a while." Scotty's eyes were kind as he spoke. "I've been thinking we should take a break, but with the wedding planning and your dad, I figured we'd see it through." He sighed. "It was the wrong decision."

He'd asked her to sit on their patio with him and have a cup of morning coffee so he could end their relationship? What. The. Hell?

No. This was just cold feet. They'd get through it.

"I know we haven't exactly been connecting lately, but that's totally normal. We're in a committed, long-term relationship. It's not supposed to be exciting," Marlee said. It's not like she hadn't noticed the lack of spark. "We're just supposed to stick with it, so we have someone to grow old with, right?"

They'd settled into a routine with each other that was just about as comfortable as lukewarm bathwater. Not awful. Definitely not great. Once they were married, things would heat up again. They'd get back to Jacuzzi level.

"I don't just want someone to grow old with." Scotty gulped. "I want someone who lights a fire inside of me. Like we used to do for each other."

"Look, if you want a fire, I can try to cook something." Marlee was the queen of burning the shit out of anything she tried to make.

He chuckled. Then his expression broke. "I think we should stop now, while we still like each other. Not wait until we can't stand to be in the same room together."

While she waited for her heart to break, she focused on the milky brown liquid in her mug. Her best friends had flown in from all over the country. Her family owned two of Denver's most prized sports teams, so the wedding had even made headlines in the *Denver Post*. The breakup would undoubtedly be devastatingly public. The panic she felt wasn't from all that, though. She felt like she'd been dropped out of a plane but landed on a mountain of soft pillows. What she was feeling was…relief. Relief that was starting to make her panic. And that didn't even make any sense.

"Marlee?" Scotty kept his focus on her. "Say something."

Her gaze caught Lothario pulling Scotty's sweater off the chair again. "Seriously, stop having sex with Scotty's sweater."

"That's not what I wanted you to say." Scotty rubbed his forehead.

"What do you want me to say?" Marlee asked. "It's fine?"

"Just say what you're feeling."

Staring at him, she really tried to see the man she'd fallen in love with. But that man was gone—he had been for a while —and she wasn't the woman he'd fallen in love with, either.

She opened her mouth to speak. Then she closed it again.

How was she supposed to be done with the guy who had been there for her since she was twenty? They'd spent a decade together. A decent decade. There were good parts to that decade.

"Scotty, I…"

Her throat started to close up, her chest went tight—and not from an asthma attack. No. This was the panic portion of their breakup.

"You said you loved me more," she said on a breath. Just last night, he'd said that very thing.

He dropped his gaze to the table, not responding.

They sat together in the silence of their broken relationship.

"I meant it. I just don't think you love me very much anymore, either," he finally said.

No, not really, but she figured they'd get back to that. She'd figured that's what a relationship was—two people who fell in and out of love over and over again. They just hadn't gotten around to falling back in love yet.

Marlee couldn't draw a breath. Four hundred guests to notify. The task would be mammoth. She had to call her wedding planner ASAP. Her lungs had seemingly collapsed against her ribs, the pillows of relief deflating to spikes of *holy shit*.

Keep it together, Marlee.

"You want a relationship break, or you want to move on?" she asked. Clarification at this point was a good thing.

A relationship break would be like twenty-four hours, and then they'd still have a wedding. The moving on? Totally different. Besides, wasn't a break just something people said to ease the bandage from the wound of an eventual breakup?

A vein in his forehead pulsed. It always did when he was agitated. Which she did not understand at all at the moment, given that he was the one messing everything up.

He didn't say anything. He didn't have to.

"This isn't a break," she said. Scotty was way too decisive for that. "You're ending us."

It wasn't a question, because she knew the answer.

"Yes." The word hung in the air around Scotty's lips.

"Seriously, Lothario, leave the sweater alone," she said firmly. The dog clearly had no idea her life was in a free fall and it was not the time to have a fling with angora. He was getting more action during her breakup than she'd had in weeks.

There seemed to be no feeling in her body. She couldn't get her limbs to move. Her lips were numb. Her fingertips had no feeling.

This was happening.

What was she going to do about all the filet mignon they'd already purchased for the reception? The cake she'd picked out? The final hair trial with her stylist scheduled for that afternoon? She glanced toward the French doors of their townhome, itching to get inside and start making the calls that needed to happen. And what did that say about the state of their relationship?

"There are four hundred people coming." She leaned forward, pressing her palms against the glass-topped patio table. "You didn't think to tell me this yesterday? Or last week? Or last month? Or whenever it hit you that you didn't want to spend forever with me?" She stabbed her finger at her own chest.

"It's not that cut and dry." Scotty fidgeted with his mug. "I had to get my own feelings straight." He shook his head, then quickly added, "But there's not anyone else, I promise."

She stared at him like he'd shown up to their wedding in Bermuda shorts and a Hawaiian shirt.

Of course, there was no one else. They worked together, lived together, exercised together—okay, he hit the weights, she scrolled through her phone while she walked on the treadmill. In any case, *duh*, he didn't have someone else. He wouldn't have time for that.

"I'm sorry, Leelee." He studied his coffee. "So sorry. I think we've both been feeling a little lost in the relationship for a while now," Scotty continued like he needed to keep explaining something that really didn't need explaining. "I know you feel it, too."

He wasn't wrong—the little flare that had started their fling dimmed way past the ember stage years after they'd entered full-blown relationship status. But then he'd proposed. And they'd—she'd—planned an elaborate wedding. Scotty worked with her father. Her father who would not be happy about the amount of cash he'd already poured into Denver society's event of the season.

"What are you going to do for a job?" Marlee asked as gently as she could. It's not like Scotty could keep working for her father after they split. She'd gotten him the job as vice president of operations and personally worked as director of events in the office. It'd be way too awkward for them to continue working there together. He'd have to sort out his job, and they'd have to figure out what to do with the townhome they'd purchased together. The logistics were starting to tug at a migraine brewing behind her eyes.

Scotty gave her his what-are-you-talking-about look. "I'll still work for your dad."

For a really smart guy, Scotty was being very dense.

"Even after we break up?" she asked.

"Yeah, Marlee, it's my job."

No, that wouldn't work. It was the job he got because he was with her. "But I work there."

"And?"

"And we won't be a couple. I don't think Dad will be okay with—"

"He's fine. We discussed it yesterday."

Wait. What?

There was that free fall feeling again.

"You told him we were breaking up before you told me?" Her cheeks heated, but not with embarrassment. "You knew you were ending things yesterday? And you didn't mention it?"

"Leelee." Scotty used that tone that never failed to piss her off. "He's my boss. He's my friend. Of course, I talked with him."

Her blood pounded through her heart, echoing in her eardrums. "You told him before you told me? And if he'd have said you couldn't keep the job, would we be getting married?"

She'd never have known.

Scotty pinched his lips into a flat line.

So that's how it was. This was all amicable, but if Dad would have said no, then Marlee would be getting married to a guy who didn't really love her.

The moral of this story? Never trust someone who says they love you more.

"You and I... We haven't connected in a while," Scotty said again.

She was sad, too. Sad that she understood about the not connecting. Their lives were more than intertwined, but their hearts? Once upon a time, they had been. Lately? Not so much.

Maybe that's why the breakup didn't burn the way it should've. The wound had broken open and healed long ago.

"You're right. We haven't connected lately," she finally said.

They hadn't. And she'd tried. Tried hard to catch his attention the way she used to, but after so much time together, things just... They just felt like one of those drums that you strike with the top of your palm. So, instead of a good tap, the sound was more of a thud.

She blew a breath into her cheeks. Scotty hated when she

did that—it annoyed the ever-loving snot out of him. But what Scotty thought didn't matter anymore. The breath escaped her lips slowly.

"When are you leaving?" she asked. Wasn't that the way this worked? The one who called it off was the one to leave?

"I'm not leaving. We'll sort through the logistics together. No need to rush."

Okay, so she would be the one leaving. At least for now, until she could figure out the legalities of homeownership after a breakup.

"I'll start making calls to cancel the ceremony and reception." She paused, waiting for that feeling of dread to take over like it should. A relationship was dying, but all she could think about was what she should do about the food that had been purchased.

"I'm sorry." His forehead relaxed, and he stared at his reflection in the table.

Her chair scraped against the concrete patio as she pushed from the table. "Me, too."

The soles of her bare feet padded across the cold concrete, through the door, past the kitchen. Lothario followed her inside, his cast thumping with each step. She paused at the bottom of the stairway, her gaze snagging on the open office door. He'd moved in there over a month ago. Sworn it was because he wanted their wedding night to be special, a little time apart in the bedroom would heat things up again. She'd thought it was odd at the time, but she'd gone along with it because… Why had she gone along with it? Right. Because she was thigh-deep in wedding planning and didn't have a thought to give about the *why* of Scotty's decision.

His decision to break up.

The pull of gravity seemed stronger than it had thirty seconds before. Oh God. They were really over. All her limbs doubled in weight. She gripped the railing, hefting herself up the beige carpeting of the staircase. There wasn't time for a breakdown. There were calls to make. Hurrying to the bedroom, she closed and locked the door.

"This is fine. Everything is fine," she said to Lothario. "We're going to stay at a hotel for a little while. Just until we figure everything out."

She grabbed her cell from her nightstand. Her father had called twice. She ignored his voicemails. "Hey, Siri, call Sadie."

Marlee fell to the edge of the bed, tucking her feet under herself. Sadie, former maid of honor, picked up on the second ring. "Soon you'll be Mrs.—"

"I'm not getting married. Scotty called it off and I'm about twenty minutes from a full-blown meltdown, so if you could come help me pack a few bags, that would be amazing." The words spilled from her lips.

"Uh," Sadie said. Shocked Sadie's silence filled the line.

"Sadie?" Marlee finally asked.

"Coming," Sadie said. "I'm coming. Literally calling a car right now."

"'kay." Marlee hung up the phone without saying anything else because she was afraid of what she'd say if she kept talking. She pressed her forehead to the phone screen. She needed a list. Lists were good for the times when a fiancé called off a wedding with less than two days to go. Yes, she'd make a list right after she got her bags together.

She pulled out the suitcases she'd been packing for their honeymoon and dumped the contents of each on the bedspread. There wouldn't be a honeymoon now. No need for swimsuits and summer wraps for an autumn in Denver. Hurrying to the closet, she started pulling clothes from hangers and tossing them into a suitcase.

She should fold them.

There wasn't time to fold them.

She needed to get everything together. Then she needed

to call Aspen, her wedding planner, so she could start the cancellation calls. That should happen first. Cell in hand, Marlee pulled up Aspen's number. She tried to force her fingers to tap on the phone number, her gaze catching the diamond engagement ring Scotty had slipped on to her left hand.

She couldn't bring herself to make the call. This was ridiculous. Yes, she was sad Scotty had called things off. Yes, she was disappointed in his timing. But no, this would not wreck her.

Still, she couldn't bring herself to make the call.

She pulled off the ring, dropping it on the nightstand. Then she pressed the message button and tapped out a note to Aspen. *Wedding not happening. Need to cancel everything. Call Scotty, he can handle this. He broke it off.*

There. That was better. Scotty could deal with the aftermath.

Since he loved her more and all that.

The garage underneath her bedroom opened. She moved to the window. Scotty backed out of the driveway in his black Sport BMW.

She did the cheek thing again, blowing out air through her lips.

Her phone pinged with a response, but she didn't read it. She held the off button until the screen went black. Then she shoved clothes into her suitcases. Sadie would be here in just a little bit and she only had to hold out until then.

Clearing her mind while she packed, she did her best to ignore thoughts of anything other than the task in front of her.

"Marlee?" Sadie's voice carried through the foyer and up the stairs to the master bedroom. Lothario yipped and jumped from the bed, limping through the doorway on his tripod legs.

"Up here." Marlee's voice cracked on the last word. Unacceptable. She coughed. "Here. I'm in the bedroom."

"I brought help," Sadie hollered.

Marlee met her at the doorway.

Sadie wrapped her in a hug. "I brought Eli to kill Scotty for you, but we passed him on the street. Eli will be lifting all the heavy things instead."

Marlee looked over Sadie's shoulder to where Sadie's brother, Eli, stood on the top stair. His talent as a chef would now be wasted since he wouldn't be catering the wedding anymore.

"Hey, Mar." He said her nickname so softly it hardly seemed fitting coming from a guy who looked like he had driven there from a UFC fight. A cross between Joe Manganiello and Jason Mamoa, Eli had the tall, dark, and scary-as-hell bit down. The scary-as-hell bit was only to those who didn't know him. Everyone who really knew him knew he was all pudding and marshmallow fluff inside.

"I'm here to lug suitcases and crack skulls, whatever you need," he said.

"Thanks." She cleared the emotion that was starting to lodge in her throat. No emotions. Scotty didn't deserve them.

"You're on Marlee duty." Sadie released Marlee from her hug and shoved her toward Eli. "I'm on getting-everything-sorted duty. Becca and Kellie are on their way."

Eli pulled Marlee in for a hug and...well...this was nice. She had her friends, she'd be fine. So why were her eyes leaking all over Eli's gray tee? She started to pull back, a hiccup wrestling its way out. She'd left tear-stained mascara smudges all over his shoulder.

There was no reason to cry. She was practically already over Scotty. He'd done her a favor.

"Hey." Eli's thumbs wiped her tears from her cheeks. "Let's let Sadie deal with the packing. Aspen already called to cancel everything, so she's got that covered."

"I need a place to live for a while." Marlee swallowed another hiccup before it could escape. "I was thinking a hotel. And I'd like to get out of here before my parents show up. Dad will talk about what a great guy Scotty is, and Mom will make the breakup all about herself."

Her parents meant well, but they were nothing if not predictable.

"Why are you the one leaving?" Eli asked, his thumbs resting on both sides of her cheeks.

"Because I know he won't." And when was the last time Scotty had comforted her when she was upset?

"Then we'll start with finding the hotel." Eli pulled her in for another hug. "And evacuate to it after."

She nodded. This was good. Sadie and Eli had a plan. They'd probably even written it down somewhere. The release of years of wedding planning, the official death of her relationship with Scotty—it had all just bubbled up in her chest and flowed out of her eyelids. That's all.

She wiped at her cheeks with the backs of her hands. "I'm a mess."

"You're practically part of the family. We're here for you," Eli whispered against the top of her hair. Then he let her cry all over his shoulder. He didn't even balk when she snorted. Somehow, he managed to produce a handful of tissues she could only believe Sadie had slipped to him.

He shifted, readjusting her in his embrace. One thing Marlee had never noticed about Eli before was how really nice he smelled. Not cologne, per se. That morning, he smelled like pancakes and bacon and man. Eli shifted again.

"Were you working this morning?" she asked.

"Yeah, we catered a thing before Sadie caught me." His voice was comforting, warm syrup over pancakes.

"You smell really nice," she said through a sniffle. "Like breakfast."

He shifted again.

"Sorry." She pulled back. "I'm making you uncomfortable." Probably because she was smelling him up.

"It's not you." He rubbed the spot between her shoulder blades with his palm. "But what do I need to do to get your dog to stop humping my shoe?"

She looked down and, sure enough, Lothario was going to town on one of Eli's trainers.

"Shit." She leaned down and lifted the pup. "This is Lothario."

"We've met." Eli nodded toward her lecherous dog. "Nice to put a name to the feeling in my toes."

"I'll just…uh…I'll just put him outside." Squirming dog in hand, she hurried down the stairs and dropped him off on the patio. She pointed at him. "Stay."

He whined.

"And no humping Eli," she continued.

"Listen to your mom, kid," Eli said from behind her.

She closed the door. "Can I get you coffee? Tea?" *Deep breaths, Marlee.* "Vodka?"

"Tell you what, you grab a cup of whatever you'd like, and I'll start looking for a hotel."

Everything was going to be fine.

No wedding. No fiancé. But things would be fine.

Just. Fine.

Chapter Two

There was not a single vacant hotel room in Denver. Eli hung up the phone after talking to the front desk clerk of yet another downtown hotel. The online booking companies had nothing, but he'd hoped if he called around, something would maybe pop up.

No, a huge outdoors show had booked everything east of Breckenridge. The block of rooms Marlee had reserved for wedding guests was totally filled.

He glanced to the former bride-to-be perched on the other side of the sofa with her notepad. She was, apparently, a quick crier. On it and then over it. Sadie was packing. He made calls and Marlee made lists.

"We're here," Becca called from the front door.

Kellie followed her into the living room with an armful of collapsed cardboard boxes and packing tape. She gasped. "Eli's here."

"If it's Eli serious, it's worse than I thought." Becca helped Kellie get more boxes through the doorway.

Yes, Eli was there. He'd spent a good part of his senior year of high school playing referee as these girls navigated their freshman year. They officially made up the rest of Sadie's girl posse, and they'd all moved away from Denver. Marlee was the only one who had stuck around. They were back for the now-not-happening wedding.

He might grump about them suffocating him, but deep down, he actually did enjoy having them around. Most of the time. Especially now that he wasn't personally responsible for their well-being.

"Hey." Marlee padded over to them and did the thing where they hugged and commiserated on what assholes men could be. Frankly, he could relate. Men really could be assholes. Scotty was a perfect example. What kind of a dick called off a wedding with two days to go? Not that Eli had his sights on marriage—hell no—he was perfectly content looking out for number one and number one alone. That was a lesson he'd learned long before he even graduated high school. But once Scotty had slid that ring on Marlee's finger, he should've been prepared to follow through. Not be a dick and call it off with the day in sight and the dinner all but plated.

"Is the rest of the bridal party coming?" Becca asked.

"You mean Scotty's sisters?" Marlee wrinkled her nose. "That's a negative." She pursed her lips into a thin line but then quickly covered it with a smile. "Eli's helping me find a hotel."

"With no luck," he added. "But you can stay at my place until the convention is over." Sadie was already sleeping in his bedroom, but he'd use a sleeping bag so Marlee could take the sofa bed.

"There's a convention?" Kellie asked.

"Some outdoor thing." He shrugged.

"Okay, you'll think I'm crazy, but you should go on your honeymoon," Sadie suggested, marching down the stairs to join the party. "Leave Scotty behind to deal with the fallout and take one of us along instead."

"By one of us, she means all of us." Kellie ran a length of tape along the side of a box.

Nope. Not Eli. All of us meant all of them.

"Going on your honeymoon after calling off the wedding is so cliché." Becca went to work folding another length of corrugated cardboard for Kellie to tape. "Let's go someplace else."

"You know where they have hotel rooms?" Kellie asked. "Vegas."

Shit.

"I'm not going to Vegas." Marlee fidgeted with one of the boxes.

"I'm with Mar on this one," Eli said.

"Getting out of town for the weekend isn't a bad idea," Becca mused. "I mean, of all the places to go after an epic breakup, Vegas is an excellent choice."

"The breakup wasn't epic. No one threw glassware," Marlee mumbled.

Broken glass was a requirement for "epic"?

There was the time Marlee and her senior-year boyfriend had called it quits, and she and the girls had covered his prized '69 Chevy Camaro Super Sport in toilet paper. Eli had thought that was pretty epic. He'd also been the one to explain to the police that his sister and her friends were not, in fact, perpetual rule breakers. Then he'd been the one to threaten to take away all their mascara if they ever pulled shit like that again.

"But you wanted to throw something," Kellie said. "I know you wanted to. Right at his head."

"Not really." Marlee dropped to the sofa beside Eli. "We grew apart."

The side of her thigh touched the fabric of Eli's jeans, her warmth seeping straight into his skin. In the good way when one actually likes someone and doesn't mind their thighs touching.

"I mean," Marlee continued, "at this point, I *do* think a quick divorce would be easier than cancelling it all, but Scotty's right, things between us haven't been awesome for a long time. I just hadn't realized it yet. Not out loud."

One thing about Marlee? She was a toucher. Always had been. So it wasn't a shock to him when she dropped her hand against his and pulled her calves underneath herself. No, that wasn't the shock. The shock was that he liked how at ease she was with him. How her hand felt on him. It was one of those endearing Marlee things that helped make her everyone's friend. Everyone loved Marlee. He wasn't that kind of person. He had his friends, but he didn't have the gravitational pull of Marlee.

It's not that he was standoffish. But he wasn't obtuse. He worked out a lot of frustration at the gym. He was six-foot-four, and the amount of space he took up—he'd been told—could sometimes be interpreted as intimidating. Hell, Sadie had told him just that morning she needed to use him as their bouncer if Scotty did anything stupid.

"Let's do this," Kellie suggested. "Finish packing up the basics, grab breakfast, and figure out what comes next."

"When's the last time you ate?" Eli asked Marlee as gently as he could. He may not be able to swing a hotel room, but he did have the skill set required to whip up a decent meal. "You know what? Never mind. Don't answer that. I'll make breakfast."

"Awesome." Kellie held out her knuckles for a fist bump.

He met it.

Becca started taping together boxes. "It'll be just like when we were kids."

His gut twinged at the thought. Not that he'd minded helping his parents out when he was a teenager—he was the oldest and, in their family, that meant it came with the territory—but his mom had gotten sick, and his dad had worked crazy hours, and that meant Eli had taken care of his four little sisters and, by default, their friends. The stress of that year still raised his blood pressure, and he'd sworn he would never repeat it. Would never put himself in another situation where he was solely responsible for anyone's well-being.

"Marlee, you should help Eli." Becca was already headed upstairs with Sadie. "And by help, I mean you should do nothing and let us all take care of you."

"I'm not going to let you guys do it all." Marlee started to stand.

Eli caught her hand and pulled her back to the couch. "We've got our orders."

"I'd like pancakes." Kellie followed Becca up the stairs. "Pancakes are my favorite."

Eli headed to the kitchen and pulled open the Sub-Zero refrigerator that blended in with her maple cabinets. He drooled only a little at the brands and the luxury of Marlee's appliances. The La Cornue range just begged to be fired up. Petted. Appreciated for the work of art it was. As a professional, a kitchen like this practically made his fingers itch to bake something.

But he wasn't there to eye-fuck her appliances. He stuck his head in the door of the fridge and paused. One jar of pickles. Two tablespoons of ketchup left in a plastic squeeze bottle. A couple of Styrofoam takeout boxes.

This was like the biggest middle finger to a brilliant appliance that he'd ever seen.

"We usually order in, it's just easier," Marlee said from behind him.

He glanced over his shoulder to where she peered into the refrigerator, her palm resting against his upper back.

He denied his body's desire to lean into her hand. To dive into the perpetual kindness in her eyes, the soft look she got when her gaze focused on his, the way her little touches didn't bother him—when they would have from anyone else.

His attention turned back to the pickles and away from

her continual touch. This would absolutely not work. Channel Ten News had called him a genius in the kitchen. A master of turning nothing into something. One of the national cooking shows had even approached him about doing one of their segments that relied on a chef being able to turn a pot of coffee, whipping cream, and a pork loin into a three-course meal.

He could not, however, turn a jar of pickles—he reached for it and turned it over in his palm—nix that, a jar of *expired* pickles, into a breakfast worthy of Kellie's fist bump.

"We're going out to find ingredients." He stood, closed the door, and set the jar on the countertop next to the stainless-steel sink. "Then, as part of your getting over Scotty, I'm going to teach you to cook."

"I'm already over Scotty," Marlee insisted, but the light didn't quite reach her eyes.

He didn't buy it. He gave her a look that, he hoped, broadcasted just that.

"There's a King Soopers just around the corner." Marlee moved to let Lothario back into the house. "We can hit that for supplies. And I *am* over Scotty." Her voice cracked a little at the end. She cleared her throat.

He leveled a you're-full-of-it stare at her.

"Fine. It's a work in progress." She tilted her head to the side, daring him to question her any further.

He wouldn't, because unlike her ex, he wasn't a dick about things.

Lothario trotted beside her to the front door. "Are you driving or am I?"

"I'll drive." He already had the keys to his Jeep Cherokee in his hand.

"Perfect." She turned the door handle and pulled it open. Lothario began to follow her outside.

Eli scratched at his ear in confusion. "Mar, you're you, and I know you can convince people to look away from most anything"—it was part of that talent she held that drew people to her—"but even *you* can't bring a dog into the grocery store."

He wasn't besties with the health inspector, but he knew the rules—no pets.

Marlee rolled her eyes. "Lothario goes where I go." She pulled a red vest from her purse and Velcro'd it around the mutt. "He's my medical alert dog."

Eli had seen a lot of things. He'd never in his life seen a medical alert vest on a chihuahua. He shook the dust bunnies that seemed to settle in his ears.

She wasn't serious. No way was she serious.

"A medical alert dog?" he questioned.

"Well, he's not just pretty." She smiled down at the pup. "Although, he is definitely a pretty doggie."

Lothario puffed up at the compliment.

"Are you just making this up?" he asked. Marlee was one of those people who could convince a man to pay an extra ten dollars for a bottle of water when he wasn't even thirsty.

"Of course not. I have asthma, he lets me know if I'm about to have an attack." She made kissy faces at Lothario. "Don't you?"

Eli wasn't buying it. She was screwing with him. "Does it work?"

"Yeah, he does his job really well." Marlee clipped a leash onto Lothario's collar and stood. "He's trained to tell me if I start wheezing."

Eli wasn't mistaken. She was definitely screwing with him. "You don't notice if you're wheezing?"

"Not when I'm asleep."

Then Scotty didn't notice she was wheezing? The guy was losing punches left and right on his fiancé card.

One thing though. Eli held up an index finger. "So you can train the dog to alert you when you can't breathe, but you can't get him to stop defiling shoes?"

"It's only your shoes," Marlee said like it wasn't a big deal. "He also likes Scotty's shirts." She took a deep breath. "And pretty much anything that moves. Especially bicycles… Hence the leg. That's a touchy subject, though, so we don't talk about it around him."

Of course, because Lothario was a super smart wheezing-detection device. One wouldn't want to offend him.

"A bicycle? And it was moving?" Eli raised his eyebrows in her direction. His own dick retreated into his boxers at the idea.

Not that he hadn't noticed the cast on the little dude's leg. He'd just assumed it had come from getting caught on the wrong side of a pair of Sketchers. Not the rubber on a bicycle tire.

"But he won't do that when his vest is on. He knows he's working now," Marlee assured, setting Lothario beside her. He stood at attention as if illustrating her point.

Eli, and his shoes, didn't buy the innocent act of the chihuahua.

"Why don't you leave his vest on all the time then?" That's what Eli would do—out of respect for his shoes, sweaters, and non-motorized transportation, if nothing else.

"He deserves a break sometimes." Marlee opened the door and headed outside. "No one wants to work all the time. You understand that."

Of course, he did. Eli could use a break, too, come to think of it. "He'll only tell you if you're wheezing when he's wearing the shirt thing?"

"That'd be ridiculous. He'll always tell me, but he knows he has to behave like a professional when he's in uniform."

"How much does one of these dogs cost?" Eli asked, pulling the door shut behind them.

She lifted a shoulder. "Not much, around sixty."

Sixty? The gears in Eli's mind cranked.

He stared at her blankly. "Sixty thousand?"

Yeah, definitely, the ridiculous part of the dog was that he only stopped defiling things when he wore his vest—not the fact she'd dropped enough on him to buy a new car.

"Training is expensive." There was that *duh* voice again. "Are we grabbing stuff for breakfast or what?"

Definitely grabbing stuff for breakfast. And apparently, taking along the dog.

Enjoyed the sample?
Take It Off the Menu is available now!

Take It Off the Menu
Copyright © 2019 Christina Hovland
All rights reserved.

www.ingramcontent.com/pod-product-compliance
Lightning Source LLC
Chambersburg PA
CBHW031954120726
47898CB00002BA/443